I0552131

Jezábel and the Assassin

Louise Furley

Jezábel and the Assassin

ISBN- 978-1-7363452-4-5 (Paperback)
ISBN- 978-1-7363452-3-8 (eBook)

Cover design by Pixel Mischief Design

The characters and events portrayed in this book are fictitious. Any similarity to real persons, living or dead, is coincidental and not intended by the author.

Halo Valley

Isle of Orainn

Anastasia

The Kissing Number

The Poser

Wrath of Wolf

Jezábel
and
the
Assassin

As always, to my greatest supporter, Bob.

Chapter One

Outside, the night was black and still and quiet as death, just like him, *ná což však,* the Silent Death.

Inside the secured mansion, Premier General Frantz Vanoir, the man responsible for ordering the slaughter of hundreds of indigenous people, tribes of the miniscule, profoundly poor country of Bohatého, relaxed in opulent comfort.

The massacred people were guilty of nothing other than their tiny village happened to be in the easier path he desired for his troops to pass through the mountains.

It was more expedient, and cheaper, to just eliminate the natives rather than relocating them elsewhere.

Thinking less of the tribe than ants he would grind beneath his exorbitant Thorogood Tactical boots, the omnipotent general had ordered their complete extermination. Every single man, woman, child, baby, and any animals that inhabited the path.

His majordomo lit his expensive cigar for him, poured him a Courvoisier in a goblet made of Venetian crystal, then left to retrieve the young teen snatched from her home earlier.

General Vanoir waited completely at peace, fully aware he was as safe as the gold in Fort Knox. Soldiers patrolled the mansion's perimeter and a security detail guarded the dwelling inside.

The compound was surrounded on three sides by water, any vessel approaching would be seen a mile away. The only road leading through the forest to the mansion was heavily guarded a half mile out, and thickly wooded to prevent a vehicle assault.

The forest was so densely saturated with trees not even a bicycle could get through. Yes, he was as safe and snug as a bug in a lux Persian rug.

Vanoir took the time to savor the anticipation of his pending assault of the girl.

Sucking deeply on the cigar, his dark eyes devoid of any moral kindness watched the smoke spiral and dissipate. His hand settled on his already hard cock over the perfectly tailored slacks.

Picturing the girl splayed naked on the table, bound, waiting for him, sobbing and screaming in terror, he squeezed his erection. The obscene anticipation deepened lines of cruelty etched around the sixty-year-old general's foul eyes and perverted smile.

***

Three hundred yards behind the mansion, Járon Rameau, *ná což však,* slithered out of the water and up the bank like a fish with feet.

Dark clouds muted the moon's cool silver light. Under the cover of a pitch-black sky, Járon crawled on his belly to the closest grove of trees. Removing his dive tank, scuba gear and dry-suit, he ditched them in the bushes.

His fins were designed to hold and keep dry the industrial padded socks. So hard and thick, the socks were almost like boots without the weight.

Attired completely in black, the only things wet on him were his hands and face, and the hair at his temples that was as black as his clothes.

General Vanoir thought he was safe from attack by water as a boat could be seen and heard long before it could reach shore. But Járon was an expert diver and an iron-man swimmer. He left his boat anchored miles out and easily swam in undetected.

Invisible in the copse of trees, Járon tossed his pack over his back and smiled grimly at Vanoir's misjudged security of his grounds.

He moved to stand casually beside the bark of a broad, rough tree trunk and observed the guards performing their pattern of patrol. It never changed. Another flaw.

Járon had been to Stwan Peninsula several times to observe the guards' regiment, and he had studied blueprints of the mansion.

If Járon were Vanoir, he would execute whoever was head of his security. It was a joke, designed to keep out only the most bumbling of villains intent on assassinating Vanoir.

When the patrol detail left an open space in their pattern, Járon crept out and darted through the trees until he was 250 feet away.

Again using a tree trunk as cover, he removed a software-defined radio, encrypted to intercept and replay communications. He activated the UP N245 to jam the house alarms.

By sending radio noise to prevent the signal from getting through from the sensors to the control panel, he was jamming the intra-home communications, suppressing alarms to both the occupants and the monitoring systems.

The guards were returning on their round.

Járon dashed to the thicket of trees closest to the house, and climbed up a tree as silent and easily as a monkey.

Trees placed so close together to prevent vehicles from getting near to the mansion had interlaced branches making a perfect climbing net.

Invisible up in the foliage, Járon crept along thick branches, sometimes swinging or jumping from one to the next until he was close enough to the ledge near the head housekeeper's room.

Járon was well aware through his diligent recon, that right now the help was all sequestered in the far wing of the mansion, while Vanoir met with his subordinate staff and prepared for his violent assault of the native girl.

Using a tool from his pack, he cut a hole in the glass window, and reached in to unlatch it.

Climbing inside, he moved through the dark room to the door. Opening it carefully, he peered out, then exited the room.

He moved stealthily along the carpeted hall to the back staircase and sprinted down the stairs. Quite capable and prepared to single-handedly take out an army of men, it was fortunate that he did not encounter anyone lest possible noise alerted Vanoir, allowing him to flee before Járon could get to him.

Járon kept moving quietly until he found the hidden door the blueprints had so foolishly indicated.

Slipping into the secret passageway designed for Vanoir's escape if ever needed, Járon followed the screams.

The guards had brought the young girl and by the sounds of it, were stripping her and binding her to the special table.

Járon had learned through loose talk from drunken guards at the village pub that Vanoir liked to have his victims bound on a cushioned table so he could play with them. For hours.

The general used torture gadgets on their defenseless bodies before raping them in every possible tormenting way, with his penis as well as other horrendous objects.

Just inside the hidden panel to the chamber, Járon waited until he heard the guards leave. The girl still screamed and cried in terror as Járon slid the panel open and stepped out.

Vanoir was standing beside the nude teen manacled to the table. Holding a vicious looking implement in his hand, he was speaking calmly to the hysterical girl who was straining at her restraints, twisting and jerking her body to get free.

Her face was sodden with frantic tears so profuse her hair and the sheet under her head were damp.

With a deviant smile, the general said, "Now, now, sweetheart, you should count yourself lucky having been specially chosen as a worthy receptacle to be used by the Imperial, Premier General Frantz Vanoir."

His slightly flaccid face, a haughty picture of grandiose deservedness, he drew the razor-edged side of the implement slowly down the front of the girl.

The soldiers that brought her left, his majordomo stood just inside the door.

Not breaking the tender skin yet, the blade lightly incised over the pulse pounding in her neck. A red streak trailed as he drew it down through the valley between her young breasts, and down her quaking belly to the budding sex between her thin legs.

So frozen with terror, the girl stopped screaming, but her thin chest hitched rapid fire up and down.

"Ah, that's better, darling, enough of that caterwauling, it won't do you any good, now will it?"

Holding the point of the blade at her sex, Vanoir brushed back a lock of grey hair that feathered over his brow. Thin cruel lips drew back and up in a callous, lusty smile. Greedy vile eyes relished the helpless feast spread before him.

He set the apparatus down on a table. The tool had various features. Besides the blade implement, it had a cudgel, pincers, a rod with spikes and a few other things meant for inducing agonizing torture.

Vanoir removed his outer suit coat and laid it neatly over a chair. Unbuttoning the cuffs of his starched sleeves, he rolled them up.

He picked the hideous tool back up, and set the knife-edge against the teen's throat. Enjoying watching her panicked gulps twitching the blade up and down, he pinched then savagely twisted her tiny nipple with the coarse pads of his thick fingertips.

His older, age-spotted skin was an ugly contrast against the smooth youthful breast. Shuddering goose bumps rose through her sweaty flesh from his deliberately painful tweak.

He said, "You will soon experience this..." he gazed fondly at the tool in his hand. "Device, inside you, deep inside the delicate channel of your blossoming womanhood, sweetheart."

Sniggering like a depraved dingo at her already hoarse, pitiful screams and futilely struggling body, he moved his hand down between her thighs to grasp her tender, untouched flesh, his finger poised to penetrate her virgin's hole.

"My plan was to just come behind you and slit your ugly throat, Vanoir." The words uttered in a lethal whisper a few feet behind Vanoir, Járon's heavily accented voice was cool and dark as a bottomless crevasse.

Járon grunted a mirthless laugh. "I mean, that is all I am paid to do." His harshly sculpted mouth curving with caustic sarcasm, he said, "But I find I want to watch the awareness of your death as it appears in your rabid eyes. That will be my tip."

"What the fuck-" Vanoir swung around with the gruesome tool raised to strike. His malevolent eyes tapered in curious anger at the male that stood calmly as if he was watching nothing more interesting than a sailboat drifting lazily on the horizon.

Vanoir's grey brows lowered over unafraid brown irises studying the quite tall, thickly broad-shouldered man dressed in all black.

Although taking in the coal-black hair tousled and damp, powerful chest revealed in the tight shirt, biceps twice the size of Vanoir's, the general wasn't afraid. After all, he held a weapon, the intruder did not.

Then Vanoir's gaze rose to the obsidian orbs hooded with cold contempt, and he did, in fact, see his death reflected in the merciless depths.

"Who are you? What the fuck are you doing in my house, rather," the general's eyes darted back and forth. "How the hell did you get in here? The alarms, my guards-"

"Are all less than useless, Premier General," Járon snorted. The sharpness of his angled cheekbones tightened in derision.

"If you were going to live, I would have suggested you dispose of every inept one of them, alas," he sighed, "you are not going to live." His gaze flipped briefly to the young girl strapped naked to the gurney.

Eyes wide as petrified saucers, skin ashen and clammy with sweat and tears, the small body shook with her mindless fright.

Tears rushing down her young face, she looked from Vanoir to Járon with equal fear that they would both be taking her, one after the other, maybe at the same time.

Vanoir was a sick, feral demon, but the stranger was huge and even scarier looking with his hard face and empty eyes, her body vibrated in an overload of terror.

"Huh. Fuck 'em. I've faced off with a lot tougher than you, boy, prepare to die in horrific agony," the general announced as he slashed out with his weapon.

Járon effortlessly jerked his chest in to avoid getting cut.

When the general struck out again and again with the device, slashing it back and forth rapidly advancing on Járon, Járon ducked and dodged with a smirk lifting the corners of his callous face.

Then, as if tiring of the game, Járon spun like a top, kicked the weapon out of Vanoir's hand and twirled again and slammed his heel into the general's head.

Stunned, mouth flopping open, Vanoir crumpled dazed to the floor. There was a gasp at the door as the majordomo fled.

Grabbing up the ugly tool Vanoir had wielded, Járon crouched down beside Vanoir, and set it against his neck like he'd done to the girl.

Now the terror wrung from the general. Drool leaked from the corner of his mouth, blood poured from a cut to his temple inflicted by Járon's foot.

Anxiously trying to gain time, his voice weak and raspy, Vanoir asked again, "Who are you?"

A slow, unpleasant smile turned up one side of Járon's harsh mouth, and in that instant, the general knew who had come for him.

The quiver of his own sure demise in his voice, Vanoir murmured, "*Ná což však,* the Silent Death."

"*Da,*" Járon said, and leaning back to avoid arterial blood spray, he lashed the sharp weapon across Vanoir's throat, almost severing his head from his neck.

Wiping his prints from the tool on the general's shirt, Járon dropped it, stood up and picked up the jacket Vanoir had neatly laid on the chair. He moved to the gurney.

"No, please," the girl whimpered hoarsely, face flushed with tears and wretched fear.

The men had danced their deadly ballet around the gurney, she had seen everything. Now, the maniac had killed the general and he was taking aim at her. Her best hope was that he would kill her quickly, without the torture the general had planned.

Járon draped the jacket over her. Then he unfastened the manacles and lifted her off the gurney, setting her on her shaking feet.

He wrapped the jacket securely around her and gripped her arm.

"Come," he said coolly, and drew her with him even as she struggled to get her thin arm free of his huge tethered grip.

He brought her through the room and down a long corridor. She whimpered and sniffled as he pulled her with him. Young and small, she couldn't fight him any more than the burly general had.

9

When they stepped into the main gallery, armed soldiers suddenly swarmed them.

Járon tucked the girl into an alcove and leaped into the center of the charging guards.

Spinning like a whirlwind, he pulled two daggers from the back of his belt and slashed, stabbed, punched and kicked, slaughtering his way through the assembly of soldiers, until the last one came at him.

His daggers were embedded in two deceased men, so Járon dodged the remaining soldier, grabbed his head as he passed by and snapped it. Breaking his neck, he opened his hands to let the corpse fall to the ground.

Járon hurried and grabbed his daggers then got the girl and dragged her out of the mansion and out into the crisp, dark night.

He pulled her down the tree-bordered drive under the black crown of starless night. Fighting off several more bellowing, attacking soldiers, he left their bodies strewn behind them like litter.

About to enter the forest, Járon realized the girl was in her bare feet. He quickly tossed her over his shoulder and made for the woods.

Finally, after striding quickly for almost a mile through the dense forest, they reached a truck parked well down the road out of range of the patrol guards. Not that there were any left.

Beside the truck was a motorcycle. Járon had brought the bike in earlier with the man in the truck then they had gone back out to get the boat.

He never would have made it on the bike coming in from the extraordinarily thick forest, but now without the patrolling guards, it would be effortless to take off down the road. He carefully set the girl on her feet and grasped her hand.

A door opened on the truck and a man hopped out.

"Papa!" the girl screeched. Tugging her hand from Járon's, she ran to her father who came for her with open arms.

Father and daughter hugged with grateful sobs.

When the father turned to Járon, all he saw was swirling dust, and the echo of the motorcycle roaring over the hill.

Chapter Two

The four men sat hunched and huddled at a table in the back of the dingy bar.

One of the men tossed back a double shot of golden liquid. Dragging the back of his hand across his mouth he said, "All I'm saying Járon, is you shouldn't have done it on your own. We are here, your *bráthairs,* your brothers; we always have each other's backs. Stop playing the lone fucking wolf and work with us."

His thick, unusual accent drew curious looks from people sitting nearby.

Slugging down his own bourbon, Járon grunted. "It was time sensitive, Khol, and you guys were still in Tyre."

"J," his brother, Victoro started, "we could have left Egypt earlier-"

"Enough!" Járon slammed his glass down on the varnished wooden table. "Tis done, over. I do not want to hear about it anymore, stop whining like little schoolgirls for fuck's sake." He raised a hand to the bartender to bring another round.

His third brother, Remington, switched to their own language to block nosy ears. "You just like the kill, bro, too much I fear." A dark brow arched over a chocolate brown eye, the four brothers had the same ebony eyes under identical heavy ridged brows.

But, Járons's were so dark and hard, as if anything alive had been squeezed out of them, leaving only glittering onyx to reflect the dangerous man that he is.

All had sharply angled cheeks and stony jaws, but Járon's face seemed to have been carved with an ice pick, making him look like one scary motherfucker. Which, of course he was.

"We all suffered, Járon," Victoro said, his voice barren of emotion. "As such young children, they inhumanely molded us into fearsome fighters, vicious warriors. You," his face stoic, but his gaze commiserating on his brother, "bore even more savage beatings than the rest of us."

Where the three brothers had a faint bit of warmth and humor in their shadowed orbs, Járon's were empty, pure black wells of hate and vengeance.

Unfortunately, he had no one to assuage, wreak his vengeance on anymore. So he accepted the most dangerous, deadly, suicide missions. Killing strangers for pay, and to exorcize the eternal feelings of guilt and embittered sorrow.

The oldest brother at 29, Khol leaned closer to Járon and said, "You can kill all you want, *má bráthair,* my brother, but you can't bring them back. We were all too young to have prevented our parents' grotesquely violent deaths.

"The guilt you wear as a mantle is ill-used. You, we, none of us could have done anything to stop their murders. You battle against ghosts, those responsible have long been dead. We can only kill them once, bro."

Victoro added, "The régime that allowed them to steal children to brutally and heartlessly sculpt into soulless soldiers is gone. We saw to that. Kapitan Clarice Monnesset died in the fire that her husband set trying to trap us. She has paid for murdering our mother when máma fought to take us back home."

Khol said, "You are still tormented that we could do nothing to take the régime apart, kill Kolonel Thad Monnesset and the others until we were old enough, tough enough, in our teens to seek out our revenge and stop their abduction and brutality of other children."

Khol's voice softened, "Be grateful you had the honor of taking out the Kolonel yourself, although sadly, not your first kill at 13," his smile slightly droll.

Keeping his hand flush to the table, Khol resisted the urge, he knew better than to try to touch and comfort his damaged brother.

He went on, "And, it wasn't any of our fault that we were abducted at such young ages, barely toddlers. Forced into the assassin military institute we were beaten, whipped, and brutalized more severely if we tried to stop them from hurting any of us brothers.

"You received the brunt of it because you refused to bow down, always goading them to hit you again to distract them, to take the heat off us. Even bloody and crushed to the floor, you would not-"

"Did I miss the part where you obtained your psychiatrist's degree?" Járon slew him a sardonic glare. "Keep your fucking diagnosis to yourself. Enough of the warm fuzzy memories, I'm ready to move on the Porth mission."

"*Na, má bráthair,* you forget our *bráithreachas,* our brotherhood," Victoro scolded Járon who was the second youngest.

"You are not an orphan," Victoro reminded him. "We work as a team. We all suffered our own captivity. Khol in the fighters' cells, me, imprisoned and tortured by the Stealers, and Remi," he glanced at their youngest brother. "He has the scars to show what he endured before we rescued him."

Around the pub, surreptitious glances shot continuously to the four, huge bruisers, brothers at arms, clearly trained *gaiscíoch,* warriors. There was enough muscle at the table to pull a tank.

All dark haired and tall, experts in everything from martial arts, sword fighting, boxing, mountain climbing, gymnastics, made the fearless, indomitable Rameau brothers popular covert hires for the toughest, most impossible jobs.

His jaw working was a clue that Járon's patience was at end. "Fine," he groused. "I will get the goats and set up a house, rent the farmland."

At his brothers' nods, he went on, "Khol, you and Remi do the recon on Anastas Porth. Get blueprints of the house his son lives in, all of their schedules, full perimeter specs, maps of the area. I want a full workup on his security team."

Glancing at his brothers who continued nodding in affirmation at him, he said, "Also the auditorium, full prints inside and out."

He said to Victoro, "Vic, you tail Maximillion Mandrake, and do a workup on his team. Have Marcos gather the electronics, tracers, phones, weapons etc. He knows what to get."

His three brothers stared at him with wry smiles.

"What?" Járon asked.

His sigh rough and affectionate, Khol said, "You. Always the ruthless robot, the perfect killing machine. Faster than lightening, you get the job done and are gone before the cooling corpses are leaching worms."

15

"Nice, bro, seriously?" Remington the youngest, grimaced at him. He said to Járon, "All right. We start tomorrow."

The brothers stayed in the tight huddle discussing aspects of the pending mission, drinking, and smoking Gurkha Black Dragon cigars.

Chapter Three

Three months later

Demolishing a quick breakfast of toast and peanut butter, Járon chugged coffee so strong and bitter he considered using it to fuel his truck.

He gathered the files, blueprints, maps, and piles of papers he'd been studying nonstop, and shoved them into a briefcase then locked it in the desk in the small office.

In case of an absconded animal, he grabbed a coil of rope, slung it over his shoulder and headed out the door.

First thing he did was check the high fence around the roomy pens to make sure they were sound and secure to keep the goats in and predators out. He didn't need an escaped farm animal roaming around as free food for the next step higher up on the food chain.

Several of the goats woke and jumbled over to him.

He offered the early risers carrots that they greedily accepted and chomped away on.

Járon had cleared the plants that were toxic to the small beasts, and brought in shrubs and small trees for them to nibble on the leaves.

He picked up a bucket of pellets and cereal grains of corn, oats, barley, milo and wheat, and poured the mixture into feeding bowls for the goats.

Next, he examined the hay in the enclosed bedding pens; it still looked fresh and dry. He had allowed for a lot of open space for the ruminants to get exercise to avoid boredom and getting into mischief.

A frown pulled his harsh features down as he checked on the food supply. The last thing he wanted to have to do was go back into town and get more.

If he heard, "Hey there cowboy, I'd ride you anytime," one more fucking time he'd shoot his own head off with his Sig.

There didn't seem to be a shortage of men in the town, but the women flocked around him like pigeons picking at a french fry in a McDonald's parking lot.

He could have had his choice of horny young women, but their damned aggressiveness was a turnoff. He was old fashioned, he liked to do the choosing.

Besides, last thing he needed was a female latching onto him, trying to force him into a relationship. When he needed a relief fuck, he sought out whores in the next town over. In, out, fast and rough, with the modicum of touching.

Right now, he was on a job and needed to keep a low profile.

When he was satisfied the animals were healthy, fed, and comfortable, Járon stopped inside for his shotgun then went to the stalls.

His Arabian, Damion, a shiny russet with white socks, gave him several welcoming snorts. The long horse head bobbed up and down waiting for his carrot and Járon's strong hand to stroke down the front of his nose.

"Good boy," Járon praised the horse with sturdy pats to his flanks.

After chomping down a carrot, his hooves clomping in rhythm, Damion's tail swished as Járon led him out of his gated stall.

Once saddled and armed, Járon rode off to check the border fences.

The property he'd rented was over 800 acres. Under the cover of running a goat farm for spider's silk, he needed extreme privacy so he could monitor the Porths, and know when someone was in Járon's own proximity.

Riding along the east perimeter bordered by steel and barbed wire fencing, Járon noticed part of the fence had a huge separation in it.

Dismounting, he held the horse's reins as trod to the damaged fence. He examined the hole. It appeared to be the result of a lightning strike. The edges of the broken steel were singed and the grass beneath it charred.

He also noticed that the grass around the fence was mushed down, and he saw a trail leading further into the interior of his rented land.

"Sonofabitch," he blew a string of curses. Some fuckcr was traipsing across his fields and trespassing into his woods. Poachers, no doubt.

Mounting the horse, he followed the tracks through the thicket of leafy forest.

Under canopies of colorful leaves in full autumn bloom, Járon followed the trail through the grove of trees. Dried leaves crunched under the horse's hooves, red and yellow leaves kicked up in confetti hail behind him.

Both man and steed's ears pricked.

Járon could hear the clump-clump of a different set of hooves' muffled strikes on the hard-packed earth under the grass.

Leaving his shotgun on the horse, he dismounted and removed the coil of rope.

Staying concealed, Járon silently darted from trunk to trunk, until he spotted the trespasser.

The chestnut colors of an Estonian horse wavered between trees and shrubbery.

Járon crept through the brush until he got a good sight of the horse without the rider being able to see him.

Then, what he saw, stalled him. His eyes narrowed in suspicion.

A woman was hunched over the horse, bobbing gently with the steed's slow steps. A stream of long curly hair, tawny golden red like the color of a vixen fox spread over her, hiding her face. So brilliant and kaleidoscopic, the tresses put the autumn colors to shame.

The way she stayed curled over the mount, shifting and swaying, it appeared she was barely conscious, if at all.

Assuming it was a ruse to trick him into being complacent and coming close to her so she could get the drop on him, Járon swung the rope down, tied it in a loop, and hurled it.

The lasso arced high before dropping down over the woman's torso, over her arms. She didn't so much as twitch.

Nerves of steel, Járon gave her credit.

He yanked the rope, tightening it, so she would be unable to free her arms, and he ran to her.

As he reached the Estonian, he jerked the rope, roughly pulling the woman from the horse. She slid right off into his arms.

He caught her easily. She was small and slender. Her neck arched, head fell back, the long hair swept over his arm. Járon stared down at the petite female in his grasp.

The rope still tied around her, she seemed indeed to be unconscious. Her eyes were closed, but the lids cracked a hair letting out a glimmer of light. The small plump lips parted, she was as pale and smooth as ivory.

Járon knelt. Still holding her in his arms, he rested her against his knee on the grass and checked her for wounds.

There were bruises and cuts on her arms and legs. He lifted a slim hand, then frowned. There were red rings around her wrists, she'd been restrained.

He brushed her hair from her face, his fingers lingered in the locks, they were amazingly…silky. Suppressing the urge to feel more of them, he cradled her small head with his large hand and studied her face.

Ignoring the delicate beauty of the heart-shape, and the up-turned nose, long lashes curled on her rounded cheeks, what caught his attention were the faded bruises on both sides of her face, as if she'd been struck.

The very young woman, she could even still be in her teens, had been mishandled, maybe abused, but he saw nothing to indicate what had knocked her out.

What the hell was an injured woman doing on his sequestered property?

Standing up with her in his arms, his boots lightly clomping over the grassy dirt, she didn't stir as he carried her to the Estonian.

Taking the reins, he led her horse back to the hole in the fence, brought it through the hole, then slapped it hard on the rump. The horse took off like a bat out of hell charging recklessly across the meadow.

Járon carried the woman to Damion. He slung her over his shoulder, then mounted and drew her down to sit with her side against his chest.

Wrapping his arms around her to secure her to him, he headed back to the farm.

She never stirred the entire way. Dead weight like a soft rag doll in his arms, Járon was certain she was not faking her unconsciousness.

After dismounting, he went to gather her into his arms and he almost dropped her. She didn't even blink much less throw out her arms to save herself.

He carried her into his house, laid her on the over-large couch, left and returned with a length of chain.

Removing the rope he had lassoed around her, he shackled her one wrist to the sofa then stood back and stared at the girl.

He pondered, was she an assassin like himself, sent to kill him? Or an undercover officer? A spy?

Dropping to his knee beside the couch, he checked her pulse, it was shallow but present. He felt around her head to see if she had a concussion. There were definite contusions but nothing big enough to be serious.

But, his lids tapered over cold eyes, there was something about her…

Leaving her to sleep, Járon trod to the study and retrieved the paperwork his brothers had provided for the mission. Bringing the files to the living room, he reviewed the information regarding Maximillion Mandrake.

Járon had recalled reading notes about rumors of glimpses of a beautiful woman who had recently been staying at Mandrake's compound.

She was described as petite, delicate, with a cock-pounding beauty. Járon looked over the woman's vulnerable figure. He took in the lush breasts pressing against the dirty, torn blouse; the creamy full flesh was half exposed in the ripped material.

Forcing his attention away from her tits, he looked further down at the belted tiny waist, then lower to the soft flare of the curve of her hips, then to the slender shapely legs in torn slacks.

He glanced down at the notes. The gossipers had commented on Mandrake's new girlfriend's remarkable hair. They said it was flowing curls not red, not blonde, indescribable as a flaxen flame. Her eyes, he looked at the closed lids, were supposedly a unique crystal shade of blue.

Gossips said she was young, less than half of her lover's forty years, young enough to be his daughter. Absent was the woman's name.

Putting the paperwork up, Járon left the living room of the rented, rustic farmhouse containing four bedrooms, a study, and two baths.

The house came partially furnished. The master bedroom was completely furnished, but the three other bedrooms were bare. All of the cupboards, linen and kitchen, were stocked.

To Járon, the thin girl looked like the tea type. Dainty and feminine. He ambled into the kitchen. The farmhouse was quiet except for his tinkering making a pot of tea and a ham sandwich.

He brought a teacup on a saucer and the sandwich to the living room. Entering the room, he could sense she was awake. He strode around to the front of the couch.

Emitting faint moans, she was struggling to sit up, then shoving the long hair out of her eyes she tugged madly at the restraint around her wrist.

Setting the teacup and plate on the coffee table, Járon said calmly, "Stop fighting it. You will only harm yourself further, you cannot break the chain."

The woman threw herself against the back of the couch cushions in fright at his presence. Eyes wild and terrified, shaking stammers hitched from her throat constricted with fear, "Who- who are you? Why am I ch- chained?"

The more she took in the heavily muscled, tall man with hard carved features tightened in a grim expression, and cold, hostile dark eyes, the more she quailed, trying to move further away from him. Her eyes darted frantically around the room looking for other occupants.

Crossing his arms, his biceps like boulders, he stared with dispassion at her. "The question should not be who am I, but who are you? You were trespassing on *my* property, not the other way around."

Cowering from the big man with the harsh face and strange accent, she perused his unruly black hair, broad shoulders, chest thick with slabs of iron muscles that tapered to a flat abdomen and lean hips.

Her gaze flit to the enormous biceps bulging as his arms folded over the big chest. When her gaze reached the black voids of his eyes, she flinched. Her pale face lost any color it had. The plump lips closed, she said nothing.

His voice as hard as his face, the annoyance clear that she hadn't answered him, he grated, "I asked you, who are you?"

Clamping her mouth shut, her huge eyes lowered to the floor.

But Járon had caught the color of them. Dazzling blue was noted in the recon, topaz was what came to his mind. He stared at her so hard and so long, the gleaming blue eyes rose to his.

She shook her hand rattling the chain. "Why am I chained like an animal? I insist you release me immediately." Although she fought to sound angry and imperious, the tremor in her words betrayed her fear.

His roughly pared lips pressed in a callous line. "As far as I am concerned, woman, you *are* an animal. From what I can discern, you are Maximillion Mandrake's lover. Mating with that slime makes you a fucking *kurva*, a whoring Jezábel."

Járon regarded her under hooded lids, observing her stricken face scrunch, and blanch even more at his filthy words. Whether her reaction was fear of Mandrake or fear that Járon knew who she was, he couldn't tell.

He said, "I can only assume Mandrake sent you here to either kill me or spy on me. Therefore, there is *na* reason I should not just dispose of you."

It took her a minute to understand his heavy accent, then her lashes flapped up, brows flew to her hairline. Her hand splayed over her heart. With panicked tremors, her voice hushed, she whispered, "You- you are going to…ki- kill me?"

"Why not?" His black brow winged icy with lack of emotion. "You were undoubtedly sent here to dispatch me, why shouldn't I take you out first? I could snap your skinny neck like a twig. No messy blood to clean up, and I can bury you out there so deeply your bones would never be found."

Her mouth dropped, skin turned to ash. "But- but no, I don't even know who you are, why would I wish harm to you?" She jumped to her shaking feet, but was unable to go further than the length of chain let her.

He commanded tersely, "Sit down." His impassive gaze rolled with chilled indifference over her.

She gripped the chain with her free hand and tugged at it.

Taking a step to her, he put his big hand over the top of her chest and shoved her.

Falling back onto the couch, her ripped blouse tore further revealing more of her breasts. When she saw his gaze drop to her chest and stay there, red bloomed, staining her cheeks.

Her lips quivered closed. She did the best she could to cover herself with her arms, and sank back into the cushions.

"Huh," his grunt an insult. "Do not worry, Jezábel, I have *na* desire to see your used tits, or fuck Mandrake's sloppy seconds. God knows what kind of filthy diseases you carry," his lip curled in a disgusted sneer.

"Eat that sandwich, for now you will stay prisoner here until I decide what to do with you. You are scrawny as shit, I don't want a feeble sick female on my hands."

He swiveled on his heel and strode out of the house, the screen door banged shut behind him.

Járon repaired the broken fence and hunted around looking for evidence of anyone else on his property but only found the tracks the woman's horse had made.

He returned to the house, locked up his shotgun and dumped his Stetson on a hook by the door. He had to admit his curiosity of his young captive was stirring him to move more quickly.

His boots thumping across the hardwood kitchen floor left behind faint bits of soil as he made his way back to the living room.

She was much as how he had left her. Sitting up, legs crossed tailor-style, the hand that was chained rested on the arm of the sofa.

The woman was as shockingly beautiful as the reports had indicated. It was going to take all of Járon's formidable skills to shield out her looks.

Huh, he grunted. What, was he a pubescent schoolboy that he couldn't control his libido over a pretty face?

He'd had to work with and against beautiful women in his career, these thoughts had never even entered his brain before.

Annoyed that any of this even crossed his mind, he stomped louder as if the action and the sound could erase his musings.

Chapter Four

Keyleigh's body stiffened as soon as she heard the door slam. Her heart hammered against her ribcage at the sight of the big, angry looking man.

Gosh, she thought, he was huge, all rocky muscles, and foreign looking. He sounded like a Russian gangster or something.

Scars on his harsh face did not mar that he was good-looking in a fiercely hard, violent way. And the way he looked at her, she shivered, like she was a disgusting insect he wanted to crush beneath his heel.

As he approached, she scrambled back, trying to burrow into the safety of the cushions.

He frowned at the barely touched sandwich. "I told you to eat, bitch. I won't be taking care of an ill female." His glance flicked to the tea, it was gone. A person could be too anxious to eat, but they required fluids.

Keyleigh winced at his aggressive hard voice and the hostility that radiated from those glittering dark eyes.

His shoulders bunched- thinking he was going to strike her- she gasped and turned away from him, covering her face with a hand.

The man stared at her cold and tough, his eyes narrowed at her reflex of self-protection, but he didn't move. He ground out, "I'm going to clean up. I expect that sandwich to be gone by the time I come back. You eat it and you can take a shower."

His gaze flickered contemptuously over her like she disgusted him.

Then, he trudged off leaving her still frozen in fear pressed against the cushions.

Keyleigh pulled her knees up and wrapped her quivering arms around them. She wondered who he was and how had he captured her.

The last thing she remembered was climbing out the window, almost breaking her legs when she dropped to the ground. Counting her blessings when she'd found the saddled horse at the nearby ranch and no one around.

She had thought she was home free, except she hadn't much experience with horses and she couldn't control or guide it, it ran at will.

The time that followed, she only recalled flashes of sleeping on the ground, in barns, eating berries, tumbling down hills she hadn't seen in time.

Somehow she had managed to keep the horse with her. She had no idea how long she'd been on the run until she woke up chained to the big, mean looking man's couch.

The sandwich on the table teased her. She glared at it. Her stomach was too tied up in knots to eat. But, she looked down at her stained and torn clothes, she would sure love a shower.

A corner of her lip pulled in ruefully. The front of her blouse was torn, her breasts were partially exposed, color flushed her cheeks.

The stranger had stared fixated at her chest for so long she feared he was going to assault her, until he sneered his revulsion of her. He used a foreign word first, and his accent was thick, but she clearly heard him say 'whore.' And he called her a Jezebel.

Her lips pursed, how dare he, call her nasty names and look down his strong nose at her. She winced. Her arms, skin, she hurt all over. Cuts and bruises, her entire body ached, maybe a shower would help the pain.

She ate as much of the sandwich as she could force down, then waited for him to return. Listening to hammering, and then water running through the old pipes, she looked around.

The house had big roomy rooms from what she could tell. The building was old, the furnishing not lush but comfortable and adequate.

The couch she was on was over-large. A recliner and a few other mismatched pieces of furniture with some scuffed up tables on a wood floor covered with scattered rugs, made up the living room.

A bowed picture window let in light and overlooked the green grounds at the front of the house. She had no idea where she was. Not what town, not even what country.

She hadn't noticed the water shut off, suddenly, she jumped. He was standing in the hall doorway with a towel around his neck partially covering his bare chest.

He wore faded jeans, the top button was open, he was barefoot, his wet black hair hung messily down his forehead and dripped in those cold, hard eyes. The dark eyes lowered to the sandwich on the plate. She'd managed to shove down most of half of it.

"You are bleeding on my couch." He strode to her, noticing her shrink from his approach.

Picking up the chain, he pulled out a set of keys and unlocked the clasp. Removing the chain from her wrist, he set it on the end table beside the sofa.

She rubbed her freed wrist and warily watched to see what he was going to do next.

"You can take a shower now. Wait," he suddenly trod from the room but returned right away with some clothes.

"That shit you have on is ruined. Here, I hate women wearing my clothes, but unless you want to sit on the couch naked, they will have to do for now." He handed them to her.

She stared blankly at them.

His brows drew down. "*Get up*," he almost shouted.

She struggled to her unnerved legs, unsure if they would hold her up. He shoved the clothes at her, she had to take them or they would fall.

"Um, Mr. uh," uncertainty wrinkled her smooth fair face as she trailed off.

"Not that you don't already know, but I am Járon Rameau. Now *kurva*, get your ass in the bathroom and take a shower, or sit your ass back down on the sofa and sit in your own filth. I don't care." The dark mean orbs glowered at her like he really didn't care one way or the other what she did.

Ire spat from her topaz eyes. She demanded, "Stop that, stop calling me a whore, how dare-"

In a flash he clinched his hand around her neck. Pulling her up on her toes, he snarled into her petrified face, "I will call you whatever the fuck I want. You don't tell me your name, doesn't matter, you are *kurva*, whore, to me. That I know."

He held her close enough she could feel the heat radiating off him. The dark shadow of his early evening

31

beard almost scraping her chin, the indomitable glint in his angry eyes seared her.

Frantically, Keyleigh scraped at his hand with her nails in an effort to get free. He squeezed tighter until she stopped fighting him.

Struggling to keep the tears from falling, she glared as mutinously as she could back at him.

A slight curve pulled at the side of his mouth, he released her, set back on her feet.

"Now, Jezábel *kurva*, you see who is in charge here. Go take your shower. Don't think about escaping out the window, I have boarded it shut."

He stared her down until, clutching the clothes to her chest, she strode quickly to where she thought the bathroom was.

Chapter Five

When he heard the door close, Járon wandered over and leaned a hip against the wall, crossed his arms, and a foot over an ankle, and listened. An odd feeling churned in his stomach at the muffled sobs he heard on the other side of the door.

He didn't like it; he hadn't felt his stomach churn since he was a toddler watching his brothers getting brutally and relentlessly beaten as they were trained, molded into ultra-assassins.

He wondered why she held in the tears until she was in the privacy of the bathroom. It would make more sense for her to try to use them on him thinking he would soften towards her. That would be bullshit, as he didn't give a fuck how Mandrake's bitch felt.

Relief eased the churning when he heard the shower turn on. He'd left a wrapped toothbrush and deodorant on the bathroom counter for her. The bathroom like the kitchen was well stocked with supplies.

What the hell was he going to do with her? He couldn't let her go, whether she was sent to get cozy with him, to get close and spy on him, or kill him, releasing her would be a problem.

She had no forms of contact on her, no phone, no tracers sewn into her clothes, no jewelry, he'd checked while she was unconscious. So, if Mandrake sent her to seduce him, or kill him, right now, she would have no way of telling Mandrake what was happening.

Na, the only choice he had at the moment was to keep her until he figured out what she was up to.

Thoughts of her seducing him filtered through his brain as he waited for her to come out.

Images conjured in his mind of those plump cherry lips pressed on his with a sultry smile, her lush naked breasts wedged against his chest, her small hand cinched around his cock - damn, he shook his head.

Last thing he desired was that *kurva's* body under his, or on top, or bent over on her hands and knees with that fine ass raised up in front of him.

It was peculiar though, if Mandrake had sent her to seduce him, why was she half-starved, barely conscious when he found her, bruised and cut, hurt, and in shredded clothes?

The water shut off.

He listened to the rustling sounds of her dressing, brushing her teeth, then it was quiet for a bit.

Never having watched a woman do her toiletry before, he had no idea what feminine kinds of things she could be doing in there.

He pictured her nude body leaning over, tits like ripe fruit dangling, her foot on the rim of the tub as she dried her legs- strange noises squeaked and scraped, her grunts and wounded moans slid under the door.

"What the fuck-" he tried the knob, it was locked.

34

"Woman! Open the fucking door right now or I'll take it down!" He pounded his fist several times so hard the wood shook. But she didn't unlock it.

"I said open the door right now!" Nothing.

He cursed, "Motherfucker." Then yelled, "Get back, the door is coming down-" he lifted his boot and slammed it into the door. It flew open crashing into the wall taking half the molding with it, wood splinters shot into the room.

She was standing on the rim of the tub trying to pry off the planks he'd hammered over the window to prevent her from escaping. Her fingers were bleeding, tears streamed down her face as she frantically tugged and hit and yanked at the unforgiving wood.

Muttering, "Damned bitch," furious, Járon stomped over and grabbed her by the hair jerking her off the edge of the tub. She fell off the rim with a squeal.

Járon threw his arm around her waist, snagging her in midair, and carried her out of the bathroom, down the hall to the living room and threw her onto the couch so hard she bounced.

Her wet hair slapped over her head covering her face, she scrambled at it, anxiously shoving it off her face. Her eyes wide with terror at the enraged Járon who stormed out of the room and then right back in.

He stomped over to her.

Expecting a thrashing, she turned from him with a whimper.

He sat down on the couch beside her, the cushion denting with his weight. Ignoring her efforts to shuffle away from him, he opened the first aid kit then grabbed one of her arms, jerking it to him.

Through her tears, she stared in shock at the damage she'd done to her hands, her fingers. Her arms were already bruised and gouged, but her hands were bleeding from her efforts to get the boards off the window. She tried to yank her arm out of his grasp.

He released her to grip both her upper arms and drew her in his face like he had before. Anger darkened his tanned skin, blacked out his eyes, and toughened his full lips.

Shaking her, he spouted, "This is your only warning. You try to escape again and you will be punished. I do not joke. You will cooperate with me. I don't want blood on my couch, or watch you die from infection before I can find out exactly who you are and why you are here. Now, you will sit still while I repair the destruction you did to yourself."

He shook her hard until satisfied when he saw the fright of him brilliant in her big blue, tear-filled eyes. His gaze fell to her lips, they were parted with her rapid breaths, then she pulled them in as if trying to still their trembling.

Becoming aware of his hard grip on her arms, he was probably only damaging her further with his brute strength, he let her go and grasped her wrist and set it on his leg. Reaching into the kit, he took out antibiotic, swabs, and bandages.

Járon could feel her quivering under his touch. It was a strange experience to have this small woman so afraid of him her body shook, her teeth chattered with the intensity of it.

He was used to striking fear in the most lethally dangerous of men, but not women. They threw themselves at him declaring something about his roughness, his size, his violent aggression, whatever, turned them on. It gave him a weird feeling having this girl petrified of him. As she should be.

"M- mister." She swallowed hard and said, "Please, let me go. I'm not here to- to do anything to you, I just want to go home. Please. You can't just- just hold me prisoner."

Without looking at her, his voice quizzical, he replied, "*Yah*? And where is home?" He dabbed at the blood with a wet washcloth then dried it with a towel.

"Please," she cried not answering his question. "Let me go. I will leave your property and you will never see me again. *Oh!*" she winced when he poured isopropyl alcohol on her open wounds.

"Not until I know who you are and why you were sent here."

Closing her eyes, she responded, "I wasn't sent here. I," her lips pinched against the pain. "The horse must have wandered onto your property by accident. I was not...conscious, I think. We didn't mean anything by it."

"Uh huh." He slid the antibiotic around with the tip of his broad finger. "Whose horse was it? He wasn't yours, you obviously don't know how to ride, the stirrups were way too low, and the bridle was hooked up incorrectly."

"Just let me go, please," her plea rolled out in a tired sigh.

When he failed to answer her plea, forgoing struggling, she watched him nurse her wounds in silence.

He was twice her size with muscles of an ox. The arm he'd wrapped around her waist lifting her off the tub was like a band of steel, there was no way she could get away from him.

He kept his eyes livid with fury at her attempted escape on his work. As if he could care less who she was, that she could be an injured dog he was tending to for all he cared.

When he finished, her fingers were covered with bandages and there were bandages up and down her arms, and over her neck.

He reached for her shirt, actually his t-shirt that was big enough to be a dress on her, to lift it to see if she had wounds to her torso. With a slight yelp, she wrapped her arms around her body. "No, please don't, I- I am okay...there."

Járon hesitated. His gaze went from her shaking hands hugging, protecting her body, to her eyes still shimmering with tears, begging him to stop.

With an irritated growl, he said, "I told you, Jezábel, I have zero desire to see your nasty tits. I don't need to see Mandrake's handprints all over them." He reached for the hem of the shirt again, but her arms tightened.

"No, please," the plea broke in her voice. "I am not hurt under my, uh, your shirt."

"Humph," he grunted giving in, "fine." Nodding at the sweat pants she wore, he said, "Take the pants off."

Her eyes popped. "Excuse me? I will not!"

Clasping his hands together, he bent, and rested his forearms on his legs. Shoulders hunched, he tilted his head up at her with a scant amused smile. He almost laughed out loud at her shy self-conscious act.

"Again, *kurva*, little whore, you think I have any interest in dipping my dick into Maximillion Mandrake's well used hole?"

Fury overrode her terror of him; she threw her hand out and slapped him- then cried out at the sting on her palm as it connected with his hard face.

Her expression shocked at her own audacity to strike the monster that held her captive, again she quickly turned her head expecting him to beat her.

Járon hadn't even blinked when her small hand connected with his face. He didn't move, just sat and smirked at her.

"I could have stopped you, little *kurva*, but I wanted a lesson for you. Show you that you cannot hurt me, you will only hurt yourself. Now," his glaring gaze shifted down to the pants, he ordered, "drop the drawers."

She held her stinging palm to her chest and scowled at him. "I have only simple cuts and bruises on my legs."

Pulling her knees up, she hugged them to her chest, her shoulders bunched around her ears. She had rolled up the too long pants to her ankles.

"*Na*, you lie little one, I saw the damage done to your pants. You have serious gouges." Losing his patience, he sighed and reached for the top of the sweat pants.

"No!" She held her hands out to stop him. She had nothing on under the pants. "I will uh, push them up from the bottom, all right?"

His mouth twisted side-to-side as he watched her, then shrugged. "Go on. I don't understand such false modesty in a whore, with that young and sensuous face you're likely, a prostitute. Or, with that body," he scanned her figure with a contemptuous look. "One of his dancers? A stripper no doubt."

"Oh! You-" she reached out to slap him again, this time he caught her wrist.

"Ah, the *kurva* does not easily learn her lessons." Járon pulled her to him, stopping bare inches apart. So close, he felt the minty wisp of her panicked breath on his mouth, and he could smell her faint fragrance.

She had used his soap and shampoo yet she smelled differently than him, feminine, fresh. He leaned in to sniff more, she tried to pull back from him. But he held her taut, their mouths close, as if lovers about to kiss. She was rigid and trembling, he could feel his cock harden.

He released her with a slight, irritated shove. "Go, push them up, I am tired of this game."

39

Without a word, her hands shaking, she pushed up one pant leg then the other. She didn't look down as he ministered to her wounds; she had seen them in the shower. Yes, she had lied, they were deep, a few jagged, all painful.

Seeing her wince when he spread the antibiotic on a cut, he asked, "How did you do this? How did this happen?" He held her hands turning them, pointedly looking at the rings around her wrists.

At her silence, his head down, he peered up at her.

Paling, she pulled her lips in tight and turned her head without answering him.

He didn't pursue the questions; she obviously had things to keep hidden from him. Like her name, and how she got the horse she didn't know how to ride, where is she from, how did she get to his property, how did she find him and his property, why is she there, to kill him or spy on him- yeah, there were a lot of things she didn't give the answers to.

Finishing, Járon closed up the kit while she rolled the pant legs back down.

She quailed when he grasped her arm, tugged her over to the end of the couch and clasped the chain around her wrist. Her face creased in pain.

He had clamped the cuff right over the restraint wounds she already had, the irony was not lost on him.

Perplexed, his gaze traveled her lovely face, what reason could someone have for restraining this beautiful, delicate girl?

Yes, he was keeping her bound, but he had unique reasons. He couldn't let her sneak up on him and harm him, and he couldn't let her go until he had all the answers to his questions.

He got up and left the room.

When he returned, he had a cloth in his hand and a glass of water. Sitting back down, ignoring her cringe from him, he leaned across her and stuffed the cloth around her wrist, inside the cuff.

She pressed hard back against the cushions trying to avoid his thick torso brushing against her.

His huge shoulder was near her chest, so close she could feel his heat, the slight brush of his sleeve against her arm, see the muscles flex in his biceps as he moved, his thigh pressed against hers.

"Here, take these for the pain, I don't want to be kept awake tonight listening to your sniveling." He handed her some aspirin and the glass of water. She took them without comment.

Hours later, after the sun had long set, Járon brought her a slice of leftover pizza and a soda.

Then he shrugged into a jacket and went out to make sure the goats were penned up securely for the night and they had fresh water.

When everything was closed up outside, before he went back into the house, he unclipped his cell and pushed Khol's speed-dial number.

"*Yah,* bro?" Khol answered.

Járon gave him a brief rundown on the girl, then said, "I'll see you guys tomorrow night for the meet. *Da?*"

"*Da.* I will call our *bráthairs* and tell them."

"Oh, listen, the bitch has no clothes, can you borrow some stuff from Jennie?"

Khol's chuckle came through the line. "Oh *yah?* You got her naked and handcuffed to the couch? Shit bro, you have all the luck! If she's who you think she is, the word is she's beyond gorgeous, right?"

"Just bring me some fucking clothes, asshole, she's wearing my shit right now." He clicked the phone off and snapped it back in its holder and went into the house.

First thing he did was check on her. God knows the trouble she'd already given him. Fucking trying to pry nailed boards out of the wall with those dainty little fingers, how stupid.

He leaned over the back of the sofa to check out how she was doing. Considering the wounds she'd incurred, she had to be in considerable pain. He'd made sure she had swallowed the aspirin.

She was curled up, sound asleep. Between whatever had occurred to her out there, and the aspirin, she was out for the count.

His gaze travelled her exposed arm the chain clasped, and her neck and face. Some sonofabitch had done a number on her. It was likely she was there to murder Járon, nonetheless, he couldn't stop the sudden inexplicable urge that struck him to desire a few moments alone with the asshole.

She moaned slightly as she turned a little. Her lashes fluttered as her eyes crunched faintly in pain. The aspirin had helped her sleep, but she could still feel the pain of her wounds. And not just the ones she'd sustained today.

Maybe he could use more than just a few moments with the perp.

Who beats on a tiny defenseless woman? When Járon discovers who, he'll see how the asshole likes getting his own beatdown.

Járon went to the closet and picked up a sheet and blanket and grabbed a spare pillow. She didn't wake as he slipped the pillow under her head and laid the sheet and blanket over her. Then he stood back and stared down at her.

There were four bedrooms in the house, but he needed to keep her where he could keep a close eye on her.

Besides, the whore was there to harm him; she didn't deserve the comfort of a bed. Three of the rooms were unfurnished anyway.

The golden tawny curls tumbled down the side of the couch like a shiny shawl. Her hand was curled up tucked under her chin; she looked like an innocent sleeping child.

Huh, he snorted, conniving Jezábel was more like it.

Chapter Six

Dawn was breaking, soft light streamed in through the kitchen window. Járon made some sandwiches and went into the living room with them.

He was surprised to see her kneeling on the cushions and watching him, her forearms folded on the back of the couch, her chin resting on them.

"What is that noise?" she asked, turning around as he set the plate of ham and cheese sandwiches and two glasses of water on the coffee table.

After her solid sleep, she looked much refreshed, eyes bright, some of her fear of him waned. After all, she was there vulnerable all night and he hadn't raped or beaten or killed her.

Picking up a sandwich, gesturing to the plate, he grunted, "Eat." He stood a few feet from her and took such a big bite of his sandwich half of the half was gone.

He motioned to the window with his head while chewing, mumbled, "Chickens."

She turned to face him and sat down, crossed her legs and reached for a sandwich. Tearing off a tiny piece of bread she slipped it in her mouth. "You have chickens? Is this a farm?"

Chewing slowly, he regarded her thoughtfully deciding how much to tell her. Answering, "*Da*," he nodded, "goats, some chickens and a few horses."

Nibbling at her sandwich, she set the sandwich back on the plate and asked with interest, "Goats? What are they for? Do you milk them?"

He shrugged and replied, "Spider silk."

Seeing her bewilderment, he smiled briefly, then explained, "Biotechnologies produce synthetic spider silk from transgenetic goats with their milk. The goats carry a gene that tells them to make the same protein that spiders make.

"This gene is harvested in the goat milk and made into fabric that can be sewn into Kevlar vests, strong enough to stop a bullet, but flexible, washable."

"You're kidding, you're making that up. I've never heard of such a thing." She studied his face for a mocking smirk.

Her look of disbelief tugged a grin at the side of his mouth. He hadn't shaved this morning, he scratched at the dark scruff that covered his square jaw and explained, "I quote, 'Until World War II, Spider silk was used in crosshairs for gun sights, microscopes, among other things.

"The ancient Greeks closed bleeding wounds with cobwebs. Bullets shot by cowboys in the old west did not penetrate silk scarves or handkerchiefs.'"

He stuffed the rest of his sandwich in; it made a lump in the side of his mouth as he chewed. He gestured with his head to her own food, indicating for her to eat.

When she picked up her sandwich, he continued, "Scientists observed spiders themselves and their weaving process then mimicked the process in order to fabricate bulletproof material. Spider silk had been used by Polynesians and Australians centuries ago to build fishing lines. It can even be used to make tendons, ligaments for humans."

Eyes wide, she exclaimed, "Wow, that's really strange, fascinating actually," she chewed delicately. "How do they turn, what is it, their wool? Into silk?"

"*Na*, I told you, tis their milk. I collect it and take it to a biostechtic lab. They spin it into a fiber and then sell it. This specific fiber goes to the government for military purposes."

Taking a sip of water, she set the glass down and asked, "Can I see them? The goats?"

Dragging the back of his hand over his mouth, he paused, studied her for her earnestness.

Her eyes glowed with curiosity and interest, she licked the tips of her fingers, he should have given her a napkin.

He grunted, he wasn't used to hosting females. The women he was used to were there to be quickly used and even more quickly left.

Járon and his brothers hadn't a mother to teach them how to treat the fairer sex. The four young boys had been forced to watch her be torturously, grotesquely taken from him, by another woman.

That was one of the reasons, and there are more, that Járon does not trust, or particularly like, women. Sure, his body desired them, to fuck; otherwise, he saw no other need for them.

If he wasn't immune to her soft looks, he would be a tongue-dragging fool for her allure. His gaze swept down her figure and then up.

She appeared so interested, Járon considered showing her the farm. She had no weapon and as slight as she was, she posed no physical danger to him. What trouble could the small bitch be to take her with him?

It'd be better to have her with him to keep an eye on, than on her own here at the house. He forked his fingers through his ebony hair and shrugged.

"All right. I have to let the goats out and feed the chickens. I will bring you. But," he bent over her and gripped her arm, squeezed hard. He threatened, "You try to run, I will easily catch you and you will be painfully sorry. Are we clear?"

Long light lashes drew down over her cheeks, she blinked at his harshness, but nodded.

Járon unchained her. He said, "Use the bathroom, I will wait."

Rubbing her wrist, she got up quickly before he changed his mind and hurried to the bathroom holding the sweats up so they wouldn't drop to the floor.

His parting words of, "Don't fucking touch the boards again-" ringing in her ears. He had set the broken door partially over the open archway for semi-privacy.

When she came out, he gave her a jacket to wear.

"Tis a cool morning," he said, and handed her a small length of rope. "You need a belt or you will be tripping all day." He headed to the door, she hurried after him wrapping the rope around the sweat pants.

The sun was still rising, yet it was already brilliant. The crisp of the dawn was edging into warm, the sky clear blue above.

She held her hand over her eyes to stop the glare. Contentedly murmuring, "Mmm," her head tilted up with a slight smile. "It smells so new and fresh, grassy, even the breeze smells so clean out here in the country."

Lowering her head, she scanned her surroundings and acknowledged, "The meadows are beautiful, Jah...*rone*," she said his name shyly, pronouncing it differently than he did with his accent. "The grass and last of the wildflowers still there are sparkling from the dew."

He narrowed his eyes at her, then looked past her to the pastures. Seeing them as if for the first time with a different view, he grunted but said nothing. The land had been rented for a cover, what did he care about the rolling ribbons of greenery and sprigs of flowers?

He took her first to the chicken pens. When they went inside the hens hopped around them, cackling and cawing.

She giggled at them, then bent to pick up a tiny fuzzy chick that hopped with tiny peeps.

"*Na-*" he said quickly catching her arm. "Do not touch the babies. The mothers will chase after you and peck you to death."

He bit back a smile when she jerked her hand back. Taking a rake, he scraped back some of the straw scattered on the wood floor and saw that the feed buckets were full.

Then he grabbed a few handfuls of feed and tossed them. A flurry of wings and squawks chased after the feed.

While the chicks and hens were occupied, he put his hand under a few of the remaining hens perched on nests and brought out some eggs. Slipping them into his pockets, he checked the other nests the hungry mothers had briefly left to feed.

The girl stood silently watching him. She carefully stroked one of the prettiest hens. The fat hen was beautiful with green and orange tail feathers.

Járon stepped outside the coop and waited for her to follow him.

They strolled over to the goat pens. A handful of goats trotted over to them.

"Here," he said. Pulling a couple of carrots out of his jacket pocket he gave one to her. "The goats won't hurt you, but watch their teeth, they can get close when gobbling the carrots."

She looked at him surprised, then accepted the carrot and held her hand through the fence.

One of the goats came right to her, the others stood back shyly at her unfamiliar presence.

"That is Jocky," Járon's baritone contained faint humor. "So named because he is always jostling everyone else out of his way. See how he bullies to get your carrot?"

She laughed at the beige and white goat's antics, watching him chomping up the carrot. "They have no horns, just little stubs?"

"*Yah*, they are dehorned at a young age to protect us and them."

"Can I touch him?"

Stuffing his hands in his pockets, Járon nodded. "*Da*, he is a slut for attention."

She canted her eyes at him for his odd description, then reached through the fence and ran her hand over the fur between his ears.

"Oh, he is soft." She stroked him, others came over for attention.

When she went to pet another one, Jocky nudged the other aside making her laugh.

"Oh, you are a bad boy, aren't you?" she teased and stroked his ears. "Don't they eat the fence? I heard goats eat everything and anything."

Nodding, Járon shoved back a lock of black hair that tumbled over his heavy-ridged brow. "*Da*, but these are special reinforced fences particularly made for goats. However," he sighed, "they do nibble through occasionally and make a run for it. Then I have to go find the escapees and repair the fence."

"Hmm," she hummed, petting two goats at once. A whinny raised her head. "Is that a horse?"

"*Da.*"

"Can I see him?"

Járon watched her under hooded lids.

Gleeful, relaxed, the long, golden tawny curls pulled back in a ponytail making her look barely sixteen, cheeks rosy from the cooler weather, her eyes gleamed with vitality.

How could any man resist- he almost said yes, then remembered he had caught her on a horse. She was no kind of rider, he had seen that at a glance, but still, he wouldn't put an easy escape in her hands. "*Na,*" he said flatly.

"But-"

His voice sharp, harsh, "I said *na*. Enough, *kurva*, time to go back."

A tiny gasp slipped out at his anger, his meanness at calling her a whore. The hurt immediately reflected in her big blues, the laughing lips curved down then pushed out into an unconscious pout.

Shoving aside the pinprick of guilt, Járon grabbed her arm roughly and snapped, "Let's go." He strode quickly forcing her to almost run to keep up with his long irritated strides.

"Járon," she huffed. "I don't understand, what did I do? Whatever it was, I- I'm sorry, please don't be mad." The sunshine had left her face. The confusion and hurt that shuffled out with her words only made him move faster, and angrier.

He silently dragged her back to the house, opened the door and practically shoved her inside.

"Járon, please-"

He grabbed the jacket she wore and roughly jerked it off her and tossed it on a hook. Then he snatched her arm again pulling her to the living room and pushed her to sit on the couch and stalked off to his office.

Yanking out his laptop, just as he sat down Járon remembered he hadn't cuffed her.

He left the study and went back to the living room and cursed. Fuck if she wasn't gone.

"Goddammit, I'll beat her fucking ass." He raced outside and saw her immediately; she was crouched down on the ground.

He ran to her, grabbed her arm and jerked her to her feet. "Sonofabitch, don't you ever learn? I'm going to whip your ass so-"

"Járon, the bird, please." The cry in her voice made him look down. "I saw him through the window."

A bird lay in the grass. Its wings fluttered but it didn't fly off, it must be injured.

"Stand back, I will kill it." He held his hand out to push her away so she wouldn't have to watch him put it out of its misery.

"No! Járon, please, don't kill it, let me help him, please!" She knelt and went to scoop the bird up, but with an irritated huff, Járon crouched and nudged her away.

"*Na*, I will get it, he might bite you, he's hurt and scared, my skin is tough as nails." He carefully slid the bird in his hands and they went back inside.

He got a bowl and handed her a towel. "Make a little nest for him, if he dies at least he won't be lunch for something else."

She said softly, "Thank you, Jàron," and touched his arm, then she bunched up the towel and pressed it in the bowl. Jàron set the bird inside.

Her thanks bothered him, her touch on his arm made him feel weird, he lashed out, "Tis nothing. I would take care of any little stray animal. I tended to your wounds didn't I?"

At her pained, surprised expression, he grabbed her arm and brought her to the living room and pushed her to sit down on the sofa.

Without a word, he clamped the chain on her wrist and then left, avoiding looking at her dejected and bewildered face.

He stomped off to his office, slammed the door, threw himself into the chair at the desk and glared at his laptop.

An image of her hurt and bewildered expression floated in front of him. He felt a twist in his stomach, it pissed him off. What did he care if her feelings were hurt? Whores don't have feelings.

Raking his furious fingers through his hair, he pushed aside the image, done with worrying about how he had treated her. He reminded himself; she wasn't there for a friendly visit and a tea party for fuck's sake, she was there to either spy on or kill him.

He turned on his computer.

In the living room, Keyleigh sat stunned, murmuring under her breath, "What did I do?" She couldn't understand it. They were having a pleasant time outside with the goats; he actually seemed to be enjoying himself.

His hard face had softened the faintest bit, the stiff square jaw not quite so clenched; there was even a spot of light in his grim dark eyes. Then, she mentioned the horse and that was it. He'd turned into an ogre.

"Well," she fumed, snatching up a magazine off the coffee table, "screw him and his attitude. What a jerk." In the time they were outside with the animals she'd actually forgotten he was holding her prisoner. He'd actually even been fun for a little while.

She'd best remember her perilous situation, especially how she got to be there in the first place.

An hour passed, he didn't come out of his office, her eyes were getting heavy from reading his boring sports and science magazines. Her back settled heavy against the cushion-

The door burst open and three huge, burly, fierce looking men tromped in and stopped in a semi-circle in front of the sofa and gawked at her.

Keyleigh sprung to her knees on the cushion and screamed-

Less than a second and Járon leaped over the couch, landing in front of her with his Combat Sig raised in protective offense. Light did not glint off the nitrate slide and barrel, or the flat, dark earth color.

With an annoyed growl, he lowered the 10 mag pistol with a spat curse. "You motherfuckers ever hear of knocking? And you know to come in the goddamned side door."

The three men stood grinning like idiots at Járon, their gazes flit from him to Keyleigh to him again and back to her.

Járon moved closer to the couch to block their view of her.

She climbed to her feet, her one arm down held back by the long chain. In her fright, she pressed her chest against his broad back and her fingers curved over his shoulder digging into it. She peered over his shoulder at the men.

Color seeped up Járon's neck at the pressure of her firm full breasts pressing against his back, her frantic breathy huffs in his ear.

"Tis all right, *neníta*, these are my asshole brothers."

Her body still stiff in fright pressed on his back, her fingers didn't lesson their clutch of his shoulder.

One of the men bowed his head slightly to Keyleigh then said to Járon, "We came in the front, *bráthair,* because we knew you would stash her once you were aware we were here, and we wanted to get a gander at your prisoner- uh, guest." He smiled pleasantly at Keyleigh, trying to get a look at her, but Járon kept her shielded with his body.

A mischievous twinkle in his eye, the man grinned roguishly and told her, "I am Remington, Remi, the youngest. Since our rude, blockheaded brother is not going to introduce us, this is Khol, our oldest brother," he nodded to the man beside him, and this is "Victoro, second oldest."

All three men stared with rapt curiosity at her.

She stayed behind Járon and blinked at them over his shoulder.

"*Yah*," Victoro spoke in a language she did not understand, "tis true, she is a frighteningly gorgeous female. Have you fucked her yet?"

Járon scowled at his brother, and growled, "Shut up." He replied in their language, "I do not shit where I work. You think I want Mandrake's used *kurva*?" He spat to the side in disgust, his body intensely aware of the woman's torso still pressed against it.

He could feel his manhood reacting to her feminine contact, and it pissed the fuck out of him. Yet he made no effort to move her, or move from her.

54

But she understood the word *kurva*, whore. She leaned back from him, her head lowered, she sat down, pulled up her knees, wrapped her arms around them and set her forehead on them so they couldn't see her ashamed blushing face, and she couldn't see the expected repulsion of her on theirs.

"Tis clear you are not fucking her, J, at least with her consent," Victoro said darkly. "She may have sought your protection, but she is clearly terrified of you, and right now is looking upon you with distaste and distrust."

With a sneer, Járon growled, "What do I care about a *kurva's* trust or silly feelings?"

"Fuck, Járon, what the hell is the matter with you? You insult her. She recognizes the word, *kurva*, you must have called her that a lot," Khol chastised his younger brother, which only brought a darker scowl to Járon's already angry face.

"I call her what she is, *bráthair*. She was sent to either spy on me or kill me, she is nothing but whore shit. Let us go into the kitchen, we don't need her hearing our conversation." He resisted looking back at her curled up in despair, chained to his sofa.

"Ah," Victoro said with a smirk, "but you came to her rescue quick enough, throwing yourself in front of her with guns blazing. One tiny scream from the little girl and you-"

"Fuck off, Vic," Járon snarled at him and stomped off towards the kitchen.

His brothers, each with pursed lips, regarded the woman's hunched shoulders, the fiery tawny veil covering her, and followed Járon out of the room.

In the living room, Keyleigh swallowed her tears of embarrassment and misery. What a horrible man he was. As soon as she saw all four men together she could see the resemblance.

They were all well over average height, each built like a bulldozer, hard faces like murderous gangsters, she still got a Russian feeling from them. But the accent, the words they spoke were not Russian, they were a mix of something.

She had a neighbor who was Russian and Keyleigh had learned a little, she recognized that wasn't what they were.

Each man had black hair and dark eyes, but Járon's inscrutable eyes were darkest; uncompromising, pitiless pits of hate.

She settled back with his stupid sports magazine and read the entire time the men met in the kitchen.

After quite some time, she heard the side door bang closed and she knew they had left. She wasn't even worth his notice to introduce her to his brothers, or to theirs to say goodbye to her. She was treated as scum for no reason.

Waves of scathing hatred for Járon Rameau rolled through her, lancing pain and despair into her heart. She hadn't done one thing to deserve his despicable treatment of her, or for him to hold her prisoner.

She could hear the deep rumble of their conversation outside the door. They stood in the driveway then she heard a car door open but not close by.

Keyleigh was so angry at Járon's offensive behavior to her, she tugged and twisted her wrist in the cuff, not caring that she was leaving skin and blood in the steel clamp.

But, her painful work paid off, she was able to pull her hand free. Jumping up from the couch, without hesitation, she ran to the back door. Not taking the time to grab a jacket or shoes, she flung the door open and ran.

A blast of chilly air struck her in the face, the temperature had drastically dropped, but she didn't care, she just kept running.

Across the tall grass of the meadow, ignoring the wet grass and stones under her socking feet, she headed for the barn, she could use it as cover until she reached the woods.

Once she was in the forest he would not be able to find her-

"Oof!"

Járon snagged her hard around the waist causing her to fly up in the air, her limbs swinging.

When her feet hit the ground, he wrapped his fist in her hair. Without a word, he pushed her in front of him and about dragged her back to the house.

Pulling at his hands she cried, "Let go of me, you have no right-"

Forcing her to move, he kept her in front of him or she would have fallen not able to keep up with his enraged pace.

Keyleigh didn't utter another sound, only gulping to keep the tears back, her scalp stung with his fist yanking her hair. She allowed him to push her without struggling, it would be to no avail for her to fight.

Trying so hard to keep her back from touching his powerful chest, or hearing his furious rough breaths, she stumbled. His grip still tight in her hair, he wound iron fingers around her arm keeping her upright and moving.

At the house, he opened the door and dragged her by her hair inside, across the room, and shoved her to the couch.

Falling hard, she cried out when he came after her. She put her hands up in defense; he grabbed one and snapped the cuff back on, so tight it pinched her skin. Her teeth were chattering like a damned woodpecker from the chill.

Letting her hand drop, he tossed a blanket at her then turned and stalked off down the hall.

Wrapped up snug in the blanket, Keyleigh sat without moving, trembling, trying to prepare for the beating he was surely going to give her.

But he didn't come out again, for hours.

In his office, Járon slumped on his chair, set his elbows on the desk and dropped his head into his hands. He was livid with the bitch for running, no shoes, no coat, stupid little twat, it was all he could do to keep himself from striking sense into her.

Yet, she was so small and delicate, one hit and he could kill her. *Yah*, maybe he should anyway, get the worry of her out of his house, one punch, or just snap her neck.

He pictured his big hard hands around her slender fair neck, those huge topaz eyes staring up at him, so childlike, so scared, so pretty.

"Ahh, fuck!" he shouted, pounding his fist on the desk. He needed to stay away from her until he was able to calm himself.

Jerking his laptop open, he sank back in his chair with a huff and stared at the screen waiting for it to power on.

Hours later, as the sun was setting, Járon's footsteps barely audible with his socks on the rug came down the hall. He passed the living room and went into the kitchen without looking at her.

After preparing the same ham sandwiches he'd been making, he brought a plate and a soda to her and plunked them down on the coffee table without a word.

She didn't look at him either.

Out of the corner of his eye, he saw that her face was stained with tears. Her cheeks and the tip of her tiny nose were red. She'd been weeping.

Her head down, she whispered, "May I use the bathroom? And, I'd like to check on the bird. Please don't make him suffer for my, uh, misdeeds."

He stood staring down at the top of her shiny head. Even in his blind rage he had still been able to feel the softness of her hair wrapped around his fist.

Bending over, he unlocked the clamp. His eyes struck at the red welts and skin scraped raw, mostly from her escape, some from how hard he'd clamped the cuff around her wrist in his anger.

Moving back to let her stand up, he said, "I gave the bird some water and seeds. He is fine."

Her eyes widened in surprise at his caring actions when he had been initially prepared to kill the bird. Then, warily, keeping her distance, she got up and moved gingerly to the bathroom, expecting him to attack her any second.

As she reached the bathroom, she saw he had at some point repaired the broken door. She must have been dog-tired to have slept through the hammering.

To her back, he said with chilled menace, "You try to escape again, little *kurva*, I will beat you. That is a promise."

She closed the door, his dark growling threat in her ear. She didn't doubt for a second that he meant it.

When she emerged, he was waiting on the sofa with the first aid kit.

In jeans, socks, and a long-sleeved shirt rolled up to his elbows, his head was lowered but his eyes tilted up watching her approach.

Her guarded gaze on his brawny forearms covered with dark hair, she sat down without remark and allowed him to douse her wrist with alcohol, the sting and burn made her cry out. Wheezing gasps squeezed from her panting chest with the pain.

He paused, waited until the pain eased. Gently holding her small wrist in his iron grip, he said coldly, "You will remember this pain next time you try that foolish escape again, eh?"

Ignoring her hateful scowl, he administered the antibiotic over her wounds, and wrapped gauze around her entire wrist. When he was done, he clamped the cuff over the thick bandings and got up abruptly, taking the kit with him

Chapter Seven

The forty-something man slammed his glass down on the antique table disregarding the liquor that sloshed out, spilling onto the exquisite lace cloth and splattering his suit.

Setting his palms on the table, broad shoulders hunched, he glared at his pompous reflection in the mirror.

In it, he saw a long, aquiline face with the ancient Castilian features, a sharp chin, full lips carved with greed and power in a perpetual sneer.

Dark hair lacquered and combed straight back, cut neatly straight an inch above his collar slivered with only a few splinters of grey at the temples. The furious dark brown eyes flashed their sociopathic wrath back at him.

"Warren!" he roared, teeth bared, canines glinting in the glass.

The door to his den opened. A hulk with a light brown buzz cut in a bulky sweater and black slacks sloughed his girth with a noisy grunt into the room. The lack of intelligence in the marble brown eyes and on his thick doughy face, indicated his use was purely for muscle enforcement.

In a gravelly dull voice, he muttered, "Boss?" As he spoke, his doughy face morphed. The pockmarks that littered his skin meshed together, making him one homely, albeit dangerous looking brute.

Clearly a hired thug, Warren appeared acutely out of place in the ornate den of highly polished mahogany and rich furnishings, his biker boots clomping over the 16th century Turkish rug.

Without taking his rancid eyes off his reflection, the pompous man's voice, a perfected cultured tone with undercurrents of suppressed debasement, carped, "Have they found her yet?"

Although a foot taller than the arrogant man, the hulk blinked back a frisson of fear. Shaking his heavy head, he replied with a guttural throat clearing, "Uh…" After another unseemly throat clearing noise, he finished with a nervous, "Ah, no sir."

Skimming his palms over his smooth hair, the boss clenched them into tight fists.

Teeth grit, raven-winged brows enraged slashed over his profane eyes. Snatching up his glass, he snarled, "Fucking find her!"

Warren hopped out, shutting the door just in time as the glass smashed into it.

Chapter Eight

The morning after Keyleigh's escape attempt, Járon told her she could take a shower, and handed her a stack of women's clothing.

When she cocked a surprised brow at them, he said gruffly, "*Ma bráthairs,* ah, my brothers borrowed them."

When she came out of the shower, Keyleigh felt better not having to wear *his* clothes. Although he had given her clean shirts to wear, she imagined she could still smell him on them.

His unique masculine scent, it felt like he himself completely enveloped her when she had his clothes on, strangling her, suffocating her with his hard, mean, presence.

Of course that had to be her imagination. The clothes were clean, if any scent lingered it would be from the detergent.

At least he had washed her underwear for her. Although her cheeks flamed knowing he had handled her panties and bra. Still, his brothers hadn't provided lingerie so she was grateful hers weren't torn up like the rest of her clothes had been.

Leaving the bathroom, she glanced around, but didn't see him. What should she do? Go back to the sofa?

Hearing noise coming from the kitchen, she cautiously made her way there.

When she reached the threshold, she paused.

Járon was at the stove, he turned his head slightly. His gaze rolled over the blouse and snug jeans, but didn't reach her eyes.

He grunted, "Sit at the table." Black hair combed back damp from his shower, he was barefoot in jeans.

Thinking, *he has an amazing butt for such an ogre,* Keyleigh stared at him unsure, then at the table.

It was set for two. Cream, sugar, syrup, cutlery, mugs steaming with fresh coffee, butter, and napkins were neatly laid out. She didn't move.

Without looking at her, he gruffed, "I said sit."

She padded to the table, pulled out a chair, the back of it carved with a design of swirls and lines, and sat down on a blue plaid cushion tied to the seat.

The matching blue plaid curtains were pulled back to let the morning sun sift in.

The kitchen was a big country kitchen with a table for informal eating in the center of it, large enough to seat six. The appliances were old, the milky white of the stove and refrigerator was chipped and worn, but everything worked fine.

In a minute, he came over with a plate filled with funky looking pancakes, lumpy and unevenly cooked, along with still pink sausages and burnt toast. He set the plate in front of her.

Before she could react, he plunked down the first aid kit and without speaking or looking at her, re-bandaged her wrist, then he got his own plate and sat down.

She stared down at the plate of funny looking food.

He grunted, "Eat," and lifted his mug. His solid bicep flexed in the dark blue T as he tipped the mug up and drank. Wiping his mouth with the back of his hand, he picked up a knife and fork, and glowered at her indicating again for her to eat.

Keyleigh picked up her fork, cut a piece of pancake, put it in her mouth, and tried to hide the grimace of the awful taste of it.

Under thick lashes, she watched him pour butter and syrup on his cakes, cut a big piece, and make a face as he chewed and swallowed. He tried a bite of sausage, still half-raw, it tasted just as bad.

His gaze flit from her plate to her, he commanded, "Eat the fucking food, *kurva*."

"Humph," she snorted, pushing the plate away. "You call that food?" Red infused her cheeks as soon as the words had popped out. Oh dear, would he throw his mug at her? She prepared to duck and run.

Instead, a dry lopsided smile turned up one side of his mouth. "You think you can do better?"

"Huh," she snorted again. "A goat could do better. Maybe we should bring Jocky in and give him a spatula-"

"Enough, I get it. Fine, you cook us something." Járon got up, grabbed their plates, padded to the trashcan and scraped the food into it.

He turned to her when she hadn't moved. "I said, you cook. Can you do eggs?"

"Huh," she grunted getting her feet. "You might as well toss out the mud, I mean the coffee too." She made her way to the refrigerator.

He hesitated, then set the plates on the counter and picked up their mugs, poured the coffee down the drain, and took the pot and poured its contents down the drain too.

Then he went and sat back at the table. Elbows on the table, he propped his chin on his folded hands and kept his steady gaze on her.

Picking up a rubber band off the counter, Keyleigh tied her hair back, opened the fridge door and took out bacon and eggs and set them on the counter.

First, she tended to the injured bird in its bowl on the counter, speaking softly to it, petting it gently while humming. Járon had already fed it and given it water. The bird made tiny peeping sounds but didn't seem afraid of her nurturing attentions.

After starting the coffee, Keyleigh pulled two pieces of bread from the bag, then skewed a look at his brawny body. Reaching back into the bag, she took out a handful of bread and set four of them in the toaster.

Under the cover of his lashes, Járon watched her care for the bird, cooing at it like it was a baby, then she turned back to the cooking.

Seeing her busy at her task, fucking humming with contentment, Járon got up and left for his office to retrieve his computer.

He brought it back to the kitchen and was met with the intoxicating smell of bacon sizzling and hot buttered toast.

The aroma of percolating coffee filtering in, he sat back down at the table and worked on his laptop while she cooked.

It didn't take long before she set plates of perfect fried eggs, the center yellows glistening, crunchy hash browns, bacon crisp yet tender, perfectly cooked buttered toast dolloped with honey and sprinkled with a dusting of cinnamon, and rich coffee.

Járon's eyes rolled with delight when he sipped the hot brew. "Ahh," he drank more, groaned, "now that's coffee."

He wolfed his food down so fast he didn't look up again until he was mopping up the last of the yolk with his fifth piece of toast. Licking his fingers, he glanced up at her.

Keyleigh sat poised with a piece of toast with butter and strawberry jam on it, an amused expression on her face.

Licking his last finger he said, "What?"

"Hmm, nothing. I've just never seen a man eat like that before, so…voracious."

Járon sat back with a sated sigh, a palm on his belly. His gaze scrolled down her and back up. "I have many voracious appetites, small Jezábel."

Her brows pulled down. "I wish you would stop calling me those offensive names, Mr. Rameau."

His own brow lifted at her haughty use of his formal name. "You have not disclosed your true name to me, not that I really care to know it."

He got up abruptly, picked up his computer and strode from the room.

Sitting there aghast at his rudeness, she muttered, "You're welcome, creep."

With a glum sigh, Keyleigh gathered up the dishes and washed them.

Just as she finished drying and putting the last dish away, Járon wandered back in. His surprise at seeing the kitchen all clean and tidied up was apparent on his harsh face.

He walked up to her, gripped her arm, rudely saying nothing as he took her back to the sofa and cuffed her.

As he opened the door, a draft of cool air rushed in, the curtains on the windows rustled. She asked quickly, "Can I not see the goats and chickens again?"

His hand reaching for the jacket on the hook paused, then he grabbed the jacket, dropped the cowboy hat on his head, stepped outside and shut the door.

Several days passed. For breakfast, Keyleigh cooked eggs, or pancakes that were so rich and light they could pass for cake. Succulent burgers and spicy fries with a hot mustard dipping sauce that Járon couldn't get enough of for lunch, and some sort of savory casseroles for dinner.

In the evenings, he would sit at the kitchen table, work on his computer and watch her cook.

She clearly enjoyed it; humming and dancing around as she easily flit from the fridge to the oven and back.

He got a longer length of chain and chained her in the kitchen so he could leave her to bake bread and desserts while he tended to the animals. When he did this, her face fell with bleak gloom.

"Kind of medieval huh," she said with glum sarcasm. "Like a wife in olden days, barefoot and pregnant, chained to the kitchen?"

His head down as he buttoned his jacket, his dusky eyes flicked up to her, and then down, he said brusquely, "Whores don't get married, they are merely pin cushions for men's pricks." Slapping on his hat, he left the house.

The door closed to her humiliation and sting of tears.

Chapter Nine

A few hours later he came in and ate a hurried lunch, one of the goats had gotten out and he had to rush to find it before a predator did.

Not acknowledging Keyleigh cleaning up at the sink, his mind on the missing goat and the meeting he was having on Thursday with his brothers, Járon was distracted.

Thirty minutes later, the errant goat strung around his shoulders, he brought it to its pen and then set about to repair the fence.

The goats hopped and skipped around him, it brought to his mind the day he had brought the girl to see them.

She had giggled and petted them, delighting in their antics. Her little squeals when Jocky bit the carrot up to her fingers brought a rare smile to his lips.

Those topaz eyes sparkling with gaiety, innocence, her dazzling smile so pretty outshone the last of the wildflowers that wafted in the meadow. He felt a tightening in his pants.

He'd been colder and crueler to her since his brothers had suddenly appeared scaring the bejesus out of her.

That day, hearing her pealing screams, he thought she was being murdered. His mind filled with terrible visions of her being cut to pieces, he had raced to her, weapon out ready to kill to protect her.

Only to find the mirthful grins of his brothers gawking at her, and laughing at him.

Then right after, she had made a run for it, proving she couldn't be trusted. Of course, in a similar situation, he would have done the same thing himself.

His gut crimped at the memory. If Remi hadn't seen her through the window racing across towards the woods, she could have gotten seriously hurt before he realized she was missing and had gone after her.

She couldn't have hid from him for long though, he was an expert tracker and her prints were clear as day smashing down the damp grass. Still, she could have gone a distance and toppled off an unseen cliff, or fallen into a ravine and broken her stupid neck.

Twisting a piece of wire with pliers, he thought, maybe he could take her out to see the goats, his horses, after all, she cooked every day for him without comment or complaint.

And, there was no match for her cooking. She was the best cook he'd ever had the pleasure of enjoying the fruits of her labor. And her baking? Cakes, cookies, homemade bread, maybe in her real life she had been a chef somewhere in a fancy restaurant.

He shook his head. No, she was way too young to have started her way too far in the restaurant business.

The air had turned so cold his breath gusted in a vapor. Pulling his collar up around his ears, he strode to the house wondering what delicious food she had prepared for dinner.

Opening the door, his ears instantly tweaked, his step stilled. The house felt...empty. Too quiet.

Járon ran to the kitchen, it was empty. He raced to the living room, bathroom, the bedrooms, the fucking house was empty, she was gone.

He had forgotten to chain the bitch after they ate lunch.

"Motherfucker," he snarled with fury "I will kill the cunt when I get my hands on her-"

Roaring with rage, he strode out the door searching for a sign of where she had fled.

He started opposite to where the goat pens were as it was likely she would have run in the complete opposite direction to where he was. The road in was too open and long for her to chance.

It took some time before he picked up where the grass was slightly flattened. Of course, she'd gone straight for the woods.

Snow flurries from an early onset winter drifted down, he needed to find her trail before the snow filled in her prints. The biting wind smacked his face, rifled through his hair, making a racket as it swept through the trees and swirled the powdery snow.

He moved quickly, following the smashed grass, then the small prints in the chalky snow on the ground. His heart clenched, if he didn't find her before nightfall she would not survive.

Savage animals still stalked the forest for food. She had no protection against the elements, no way to stay warm, she could not possibly find her way through the miles of woods and get safely out.

If she tried for the road, he could quickly and easily find her. It was open space, and miles to a main road, buffeted by thick scrubby forest, and just as dangerous as the fucking woods. She would be in clear, broad view of a carnivorous bear searching to fatten up before complete hibernation.

The tips of his ears were red from the chill, steam misted from his mouth and nose, snow salted his dark hair. He pushed branches aside as he trampled the dusting of snow.

Járon traipsed for an hour until he saw her bright hair flutter through the mostly leafless trees.

She was almost upon a cliff.

Just as he thought, she had gone in circles and now was about to plummet to her death.

"Woman!" he called out.

She froze, turned slowly. The big blue eyes alive with terror at the wrath that grizzled his forbidding face.

Járon moved steadily toward her, fierce and snarling like an enraged bull, boots snapping twigs as they pounded towards her. His big hands in tight fists, wide shoulders hunched, steam poured from his mouth as he powered to her.

She inched back as he got closer. Her heels hovered over the crest of the cliff.

"Come here, now!" he barked at her. Approaching her, his skin dark with anger, jaw clenched, the unmitigated compulsion to hurt her blazed from the infuriated, cinder blackened eyes.

"No," her voice shook with her fear and she was chilled to the bone.

Her hands up as if to hold him off, she cried, "Stay away from me! You have no right to hold me pri- prisoner," she clamped her chattering teeth together. The wind snapped and spiraled her hair like a fan behind her.

He stalked closer. "I will do what the fuck I want. I warned you, *kurva*, what I would do if you ran again. Now, move away from that edge and get over here."

It took everything she had not to cower from the huge, steel-bodied, enraged man that kept coming at her.

"No! Stay away from me!" Backing up, her hands still up to ward him off- but then there was nothing beneath her foot, her arms flailed at the open air-

"Damned bitch-" Járon vaulted forward, throwing his hand out he snagged the front of her blouse-

She was already starting to tumble over the edge with a scream- He jerked her back so hard she smashed into him and they both fell backwards.

He landed on his back; she slammed on him belly to belly about knocking the air out of them both.

But before he could blink, she rolled off him and started to run, he grabbed her ankle and jerked her down and rolled on top of her.

"You stupid whore, have you no brains? Is it preferable to die out here an icicle or torn apart by a wild beast before he devours you rather than be inside warm and fed with me?"

His panting breaths from the exertion huffed in her face, blowing wisps of hair back. His hand curled around her throat.

Furiously he snarled, "Or, you preferred the quick death of plunging a thousand feet to break apart on rocks?"

"Get- get off of me you big oaf!" She tried to hit at him, but her blows didn't faze the big man.

On his forearms, his weight immobilized her, one of his legs lay between hers.

His enraged eyes narrowed at her scared, angry orbs, his mouth was so close to hers their breaths misted together. Járon could feel her frantic heart beating against his ribs, her body shivering under his, her soft breasts pressed against the weight of his chest.

Every part of her was soft against every part of him that was hard, and everything was hard, and getting harder. She would soon feel his burgeoning erection.

He rolled and got to his feet pulling her up with him. Without a word, he shrugged his jacket off, dropped it on her, then bent with his broad shoulder at her waist and lifted her over his shoulder.

"No! Rameau! Let me down!" Her muffled screams joined her fists pounding his back. It didn't slow him down.

He strode hard and fast through the forest and back to the house.

Snatching the door open, he stepped inside, kicked it closed behind him, and marched into the living room.

He dropped down onto a chair and let her slide to her feet in front of him, to stand between his spread legs. She turned to get away from him but he grasped her arm jerking her back.

"Hey-" she protested.

When he tore the jacket off her, she saw the glint in his eye, and realized she was in deep trouble. "Please, Rameau, don't hurt me-"

"I gave you plenty of chances, plenty of warnings, you will see I mean what I say." Járon roughly grabbed the front of her borrowed jeans, and yanked at her rope belt.

Shocked, she cried out, "Stop! What are you doing? Stop it-" She scrambled at his hands but he jerked her rope belt apart and let it fall to the ground then he tore open the button on her jeans and yanked the zipper down.

Her face white with panic, she punched at him, shrieking, "Stop!"

But the man was built like a tank and just as strong. He swung her around, lifted her and set her face down over his lap.

"Like a child running out in front of a car," the furious bruiser muttered, "risking your stupid life like that in the fucking raw wilderness." He wrenched the back of her pants and panties down exposing her bare butt.

"Rameau!" she screamed, kicking her feet, she hit at his legs. When his palm smacked down on her butt, it stung so sudden and sharp, it took her breath away.

His hand on her back to hold her down, Járon spanked her bottom again and again, she screamed until she was hoarse.

Gasps caught in her throat, sobs hitched in her chest, until she stopped screaming, and he stopped hitting her.

His palm stayed flat on her bottom; he stared at the quivering rounded flesh under his hand. It was soft and firm, and bright red from his smacks.

The urge to squeeze, caress it, bite its plumpness, grip the roundness with his big hands, dig his hard fingers in the tender crease was overpowering.

A buzz filled his head with the hardening of his cock, he could think of nothing but if he spread her legs he would be able to see her woman's sex. He could touch it with his thick fingers, he bet it was as pretty as the rest of her-

When he stopped moving and kept his hand on her bottom, his fingers clenching and unclenching as he fought the irresistible urges that threatened to consume him, his fingertips edging towards her womanhood, she struggled and started screaming again.

Her wails filtered into his ears and banged at his brain to drag him out of his haze of lust and get a grip.

The inner struggle to halt his seething craving of taking her right now, her obviously being unwilling, was staggeringly daunting, almost painful.

His inhale giant deep, and exhale grudgingly rugged, when had he ever lost such control of himself over a woman, or want to fuck her so badly his body vibrated with the need, the desire, the hunger?

Járon could have any woman he wanted, he sure as hell didn't need to force one, especially one he held captive and helpless. It'd be like a despicable cop raping a prisoner trapped in her jail cell.

Dammit, clinching her around the waist, he lifted her to face out from him and jerked her pants up.

Breathing heavily, he growled, "Get on the couch."

She hesitated only a second then trod to the sofa, fixed her pants then gingerly sat down. Turning toward the cushions, she pulled her legs up, and pushed her mortified face into a back cushion to still her hitching gasps of humiliation.

Járon watched her for a minute, then wearily rose to his feet and went over to her. He bent and grabbed her ankle, yanked off her shoe, then the other tossing them aside.

She kept her face buried in the cushion.

He took her arm, drew it back, and clamped the cuff on it.

Her body shook with the chill from outdoors that had burrowed into her bones, and the pain and humiliation of what he'd just done to her.

He could hear her trying to muffle her sobs into the cushion, but her shoulders shook with the weight of them.

Járon retrieved several blankets and draped them over her shivering body.

Wood already in the fireplace, he opened the flue and quickly strew tinder under the wood. Then he struck a long-stemmed match and held it to the tinder until a strong hot fire roared, quickly warming the room.

Then he went into the kitchen thinking, this was not something he was going to share with his brothers. They would be appalled.

His brothers were some of the most ruthless government hired assassins in the world, but they would never lay a hand on a woman. Especially a defenseless woman, not even half his size.

He had been so fueled with rage, so pissed that she ran from him, and his heart had stalled when he saw her about to tumble over the cliff to her death.

That she had left him, the adrenalin of possessive ire thundered through his mind mixed with horror as she flailed over the perilous edge.

Fear mingling with anger railed through his body, igniting such tremendous emotion he struck out at her before he could stop himself.

But, he reconciled, he had warned her, he had to take drastic measures to prevent her from leaving. He couldn't let her go, and he sure as hell wasn't going to let her die out there.

In the kitchen, Járon trod over and leaned forward toward a wall and set his forehead and forearms on it letting out a heavy exhale.

Rolling around to rest his back against the wall, he scrubbed his fingers down his eyes, down his mouth, rubbed the scrub on his jaw. He was here to complete a mission, not spank a beautiful spy he was holding prisoner.

Unbidden, the picture of her body squirming on his lap, her pink bottom wriggling from the smack of his hand came to his still fired-up brain. He had felt himself irresistibly drawn to shove her onto the floor, rip the jeans the rest of the way off, and drive into her.

Her screams had brought him back to his senses, thank God. Otherwise, he was so out of his mind, so out of control with anger and fear, and raging lust at that moment, he would have fucked her bareback, without a condom, as it hadn't entered his mind, and it would have been rape.

Try to explain that one to his brothers. He couldn't tell them, they would fight him to take her away from him, to protect her from him.

"*Fuck,*" he cursed, dragging his sleeve over his sweating forehead. He needed to keep his dick in his pants, and his mind and hands off her.

Shit, he didn't even know the name of the woman he held captive, assaulted, desired so intensely, the like he'd never before experienced. And just by a hair of getting a grip on his will power, he had not raped.

The beautiful sweet spy was worming her way under his skin. He needed to build a wall up between them, quick, a thick wall.

Járon hung around in the kitchen and fed the bird to give them both time to collect themselves.

He cleared his throat as he came into the room to let her know he was there.

Staying facing away from him, she dashed at her wet eyes with the heels of her palms.

He set a cup of tea on the table. Said, quietly, "You will drink this tea. Now. Too stupid not to know better than to run blindly out into a treacherous forest in freezing winter, fuck. I don't want to have to nurse a sick woman with pneumonia. You are already too thin to withstand an illness." Járon felt stupid himself rambling on awkwardly.

She didn't move.

Letting out a sigh, he said coldly, "You wish for a repeat of earlier?"

78

Turning towards him, eyes bright and blurry with tears, cheeks red, mouth trembling, she glared at him.

Járon stood impassively with his boots planted hard on the floor, arms crossed over his strapping chest, biceps bulging, he glared back at her.

His voice rough and emotionless, he said, "I won't tell you again. You don't do as I say, I will fucking punish you. Again."

He prayed she obeyed him, he didn't know if he could withstand another spanking. *Yah*, he knew he was being a bullying bastard, but he didn't want her to get sick because she was stubborn, and humiliated.

Her eyes welled with fresh tears at her untenable position, lowering her lids over them, she picked up the teacup.

He watched her under his own hooded lids and the fringe of black lashes.

Keeping her head lowered, clutching the blanket around her for warmth, and as a useless shield against him, she sipped at the tea until he finally moved away and the side door squeaked open and closed.

Járon trudged back outside to check on the animals, the temperature was rapidly dropping.

Seeing that they were tucked safe in their pens stuffed with hay for added warmth, he went back to the house.

Mouth hard pressed, he combed his fingers through his hair brushing the snow off it. Never sure what to expect, he entered the living room.

She was sitting quietly, calmly reading one of his science magazines. Her head stayed down, she asked politely, "Would you mind making me some more tea?"

Surprised, she had never asked him for a single thing since he'd taken her. "*Da*, of course," he bent to retrieve her teacup, but she snapped it up and swung it at his head.

With a barked laugh he ducked and wrapped his hand around the teacup and her hand.

"Seriously, woman? A fucking teacup? You were going to brain my hard noggin with a tiny fucking piece of fragile china?"

Furious at his mocking her, she pulled at her hand, snapped, "Let go of me!" But he kept his fingers wrapped around it.

"Listen sweetheart, I'm going to give you a couple of tips." He leaned over to get closer in her face, to intimidate her, and, to inhale her scent.

"Number one," he said with smug arrogance, "you choose a weapon sturdy enough to knock a man out. Like," he glanced around. "Not that lamp, tis only thin ceramic, not hard enough, maybe," he spotted a liquor bottle he'd left on a table.

"The bottle, if it was full might work. Number two," their eyes connected, he smiled inside at her defiant chin rising up.

"You wait until I have unchained you. What if you struck me, knocked me out, and I fell away from you? You could not get the key out of my pocket to unlock the cuff, and you are too small and weak to drag my body to where you could reach it. And," his lip nicked up at the corner, "when I came to with a headache, I would be really pissed, and you would be trapped. Right?"

At his taunting, she got mad and wrenched at her hand, "Let go of me," she repeated louder.

Leaning over further, his breath on her face, so close she could count every dark hair of stubble on his jaw, so close she could see her reflection in his eyes like black mirrors.

He said, "It amuses me to anger you. Tis like poking at a kitten with my finger and watching it swipe a tiny claw at me."

Her mouth opened in fury and Járon slapped his over it.

Pulling her closer by her hand, he ground against her lips, assaulting her pride and purity with his fire and rage, lust and dark hate, until she whimpered at his tongue thrusting down her throat.

He suddenly jerked back.

Releasing her like she'd burned him, Járon stormed off

Chapter Ten

They came to an uneasy truce the next few days.

Due to his incongruent behavior, she eyed Járon with wary bewilderment.

He had told her she disgusted him, he had meted out corporal punishment, spanking her, and then so baffling kissed her.

She cooked, but always in his presence.

After the first day of utter silence, furious on her side, vexed on his, out of boredom, she occasionally asked him questions about the farm, the goats, some of the things she read about in his science magazines.

Járon was quickly getting used to hanging in the kitchen while she cooked and hummed, played with the healing bird, while he did research on his laptop, and discussed scientific information that was new to her.

He found her to be engagingly curious, highly intelligent, grasping new concepts quickly and asking perceptive questions.

She was sweet and witty. He found himself truly smiling with a good feeling, a rare experience for him, as his acidic smiles were usually more cynical than pleasant.

Járon was finding it harder and harder to look at her, so young, pretty, kind, and remember she was the whore of the man who had sent her to spy on him, the very man Járon had come to take down.

He chained her when he tended the farm animals or went into town. He was never gone long, not wanting to leave her alone and vulnerable, trapped, unable to get away if danger struck.

He'd worried about her so much, he found it hard to concentrate on his shopping. There could be a fire, he mused, intruders, even though he'd fixed the fence, he hadn't set it up to be electrified. Didn't need one of the escaped farm animals to get fried.

Recalling she had gotten onto his land through a fence that had been struck by lightning, he pictured flames licking out from every window, the girl chained to the couch screaming for him, and he wasn't-

"Oh, there you are," a woman gushed, stopping in his path, blocking him from leaving with his purchases.

She drawled in a low throaty purr, "Hey cowboy, you've been like a hermit out at that ranch of yours, with no woman to warm your bed." Moving closer, she brazenly stroked his arm, snuggling against him.

Jolted from his musings, Járon vacantly nodded politely and took a step to move around her.

"Honey," she cooed, moving again to block him, "that's a job I would be more than happy to fill. What do you say? I can come," she giggled coquettishly, "no pun intended, ah, over."

Rubbing on his body, she angled her head up to him with bold enticement and giggled. "Or maybe I did mean it." Sliding her tongue around wide glossy lips she offered, "I can go with you right now, how about it?"

Keeping his head straight, Járon lowered his eyes to the blonde pawing his arm, bosom rubbing all over his bicep.

She looked about late twenties, built like a Renoir painting, big tits and hips. Her dress tight, low-cut, she shook her ample wares in his face.

"Ah, Miss…"

"Shannon, handsome, Shannon O'Shea. So, I'm ready and available to go with you right now-"

"Ah, *na*, I'm busy." His annoyed features hardened at her shamelessly swarming all over him. "And I'm not interested-"

"Here," she said, not taking no for an answer, a card appeared in her hand. Tucking it in his pants pocket, she patted his chest. "Call me. Anytime. Day, or," she flapped her lashes in coy invitation at him, "night. I can't wait to hear that deep sexy accent whispering filthy dirty things in my ear."

Before Járon could respond, she set her lips on his and kissed him wet and lusty. Then she patted his backside, and stepped back. Wriggling her fingers at him, she sashayed her big rounded hips, sloshing them side-to-side out the door.

A sour taste in his mouth, Járon wiped his hand over his lips with a curl of distaste. He chided himself, she did nothing less than what he had done the woman at his house, forced his kiss on her without allowing her the choice to say no.

And, he had touched her- spanked her intimately without her permission.

"Fuck it," he cursed. Grasping his packages, he hurried out to his truck and drove quickly back to the farm.

Inside, Keyleigh sat by the window. Járon had moved the sofa so she could look out instead of staring at nothing all day.

She had noticed knitting needles in the linen closet when he retrieved clean sheets for their beds, and asked if she could have them.

He had joked about her stabbing him with one of the wooden needles, but brought them to her and gave her some of the goat silk she requested, to see if she could knit it into something.

Járon came in the front door, Shannon's perfumed taste still tainting his mouth. Stomping his feet to clear the snow, he brushed flakes off his dark hair and observed his captive.

Her head was down as she knit, the weaker winter sun streamed through the dusty panes lighting the tawny fire of her tresses.

The old farmhouse had oil heating, but he had made a fire in the fireplace before he left. The warm flickering light issued a soft glow in the room, the flames a rival for the highlights in her hair.

She smiled up at him when he came in.

A flutter of…something peculiar ruffled in his stomach. He felt a flash of being in a Rockwell painting. A warm, cozy, homey scene with a beautiful woman on his sofa waiting for him to come home. A shiver rolled across his shoulders.

Normally that kind of thought would leave a worse taste in his mouth than that floozy blonde's abrasive kiss, but now…

85

"You're back," she said redundantly. Then, realizing she had smiled at her abuser, she firmed her lips, bowed her head and turned her attention back to her knitting.

"*Da*. I think I got everything on your list, and uh, I got some chocolates you might like." He took the bags to the kitchen and put the groceries away.

In a few minutes, he came back out padding across the rug in his socks, and set a bowl of candy on the coffee table within her easy reach.

"How is that silk to work with?" he asked, perching on the arm at the other end of the couch. The burgundy sweater he wore with jeans stretched across his thick broad shoulders, emphasizing his powerful chest. The black hair curled over the back of the woven collar.

One shoulder shrugged, she replied, "Hmm, it's not too bad. Different than wool, takes a bit getting used to." Her nose wrinkled. Bottom lip pushing up, she said, "You smell like perfume. Strong perfume."

Járon's side-glance at her with a shrug belied the unfamiliar tingle he felt at what almost sounded like a jealous wife. His mouth pulled in, it bugged him that the feeling didn't irritate him like it should. In fact, he had to bite back a grin.

"I, ah, ran into an…old friend." Not that he had to explain himself to her.

"Humph," the small sound indicated she didn't believe him. The frown stiffened on her face. "You must have hit her hard," she put her attention back to her knitting.

"So, ah, listen, uh," he still didn't know her name and didn't want to call her 'whore' and break the peace between them. He said, "I have a barter for you?"

Her blue eyes slanted up to him with mild suspicion, "Oh?"

86

"*Da. Ma bráthairs,* ah, I mean my brothers, are coming tomorrow for a…meeting. How about you cook for us, serve us, and tomorrow in the morning I will take you to see the goats and chickens?"

"Really?" Her face brightened. "And your horses? Can I see them too?"

Picturing her on a steed racing away from him, bright hair flowing behind her as she disappeared into the forest, his lips pursed in a frown. He shook his head slightly. "*Na.* Just the goats and chicks."

Disappointed, her smile dimmed. She had grown fond of the horse she'd fled on. When Járon had told her how he had sent the horse back across the meadow she had hoped that the steed would be found safely by its owners.

It's not like she had anything else to do, so she agreed. "Um, okay, I will cook for you. I can't wait to go outside in the fresh air and see the animals."

"Cook, and serve," he grunted. If she served them, he could keep his eyes on her without having to keep her restrained.

His brothers would taunt him endlessly if she was shackled to his couch or chained in the kitchen, and he didn't need to add more to her embarrassment by being manacled in his living room in front of other people. Not, he affirmed to himself, that he cared a whit about how she felt.

He couldn't have her sit with them either, because he couldn't have her hearing their conversation. Even if they spoke in his language, he had no idea if she knew his language and was keeping that information from him so she could spy.

Shit, his brow scrunched over his eyes as they darkened, lips crimped. The more he knew her, the less he believed she could be capable of such subversion.

But still, she was in his woods, she refused to tell him her name or how she got there, and she fully matched the description of Maximillion Mandrake's girl. *His* girl, Járon reminded himself rubbing at the muscles tightening in his belly.

You would think though, he pondered, that she and Mandrake would have previously come up with a fake name and story of why she was there. None of it made any sense.

Her forehead creased. She had gone from a whore to a servant. "Fine," she agreed.

"Good," he said shortly and got up. He un-cuffed her and took her knitting from her setting it on the table and said, "I am hungry now."

She blinked at him, he was the hardest man to decipher she had ever met. One minute he was almost kind, almost gentle, the next, he was a crude, abusive jerk.

"Oh. You want me to start dinner now." Under her breath, she mumbled, "*Caveman.*" Resisting the urge to roll her eyes at him, she stood up gracefully and sauntered through the room to the kitchen.

Járon followed her like a puppy after a bone.

While she prepared smothered chops and braised greens, Járon sat at the table in front of his computer. But he barely glanced at it. Watching her browning the chops, he asked, "Do you have siblings?"

"What?" Her head half-turned to see his eyes, onyx lasers at her back.

"Your brothers and sisters, have you any? Tell me about your…early life, I am…curious. It would have been vastly different than mine."

Sautéing an onion, she glanced at him again, but he seemed sincerely interested. "Um, well, I have a brother, Danny, he's older. My father was an ambassador in Alger la

Blanche. It was actually, rather dangerous there, so we were kept...inside.

"We were home-schooled, seldom left the...guarded estate. I had little contact with, um, regular people, until I just started...my university studies."

She added the greens to the onions. Tossing in chopped garlic and a sprinkling of spices, she poured chicken stock over everything, gave it a few stirs then set a lid tilted over the pot. Next she started on pealing the potatoes to make ranch mashed potatoes.

"Hmmm." His elbows on the table, Járon set his chin on his fists and asked, "How did you meet Maximillion Mandrake?"

Stiffening, she set a wooden spoon on a plate on the oven top. She turned, and leaned back against the counter.

"I would tell you, but you would never believe me. You have it stuffed into that, as you said, hard noggin, that I am involved with him, and judging by the frigid flint in your distrusting eyes, you would not believe a word I said."

"Huh," he exhaled, peeved at her words, and his ambivalence in believing anything she said. "You don't have to explain to me how you are Mandrake's whore. How does it feel to fuck a killer?"

Leaning back in his chair, an arm resting on the back of the chair next to him, his legs spread like men do, he appeared relaxed and calm. But, he regarded her under hooded lids; he was again poking the kitten. She had no idea how searing gorgeous she was when she was angry, and how hard it made him.

Stepping towards him, her hands rolled into fists, eyes spitting blue fire, she ground out, "I don't know, I'll ask your girlfriends," and snapped back to her cooking, gulping back the furious shame she felt at his insults.

"Women," Járon said, shaking his head at her being upset. The blue eyes were suddenly damp, he'd wanted to provoke her anger, not make her cry. "You are such a sensitive lot, you have always confused me. I don't understand your gender."

She turned around, the tears shimmering. "Because you don't try to understand. You don't care enough to try."

He stared blankly at her, then nodded thoughtfully. "That is correct. You did not deny knowing Mandrake, that tells me everything I thought, is true. Are you done yet with dinner?"

Clenching her teeth, she stuck a fork in a chop and lifted it to a platter.

When it was all ready, she set the food on the table then happened to look out the window.

A gasp sputtered out and she ran to the door, flung it open and ran outside.

"Get back here-" his shout would do no good, she was already gone. Through grit teeth he snarled, "I'm going to splinter her fucking hide."

Járon charged outside after her, she knows she can't outrun him, why does she try?

He didn't have to go far. She was only a few yards away kneeling on the ground. It was dark and chilly; a cutting wind whipped their hair.

"Goddammit woman, I am going to smack your ass so hard you won't be able to sit for a week! Fleeing again without even a damned jacket what the fuck do you think-"

She was kneeling over a fawn that lay in the cold grass. "Járon, we have to help him, he's hurt, please?"

Járon looked down at her pleading, big blue eyes, and the injured fawn's sad doe eyes, and sighed.

He carried it inside while she made a bed for it out of her ruined clothes and some towels.

As promised, the next day, he told her to make some sandwiches and then took her outside.

She trailed him while he fed the animals, repaired part of the fence, and contrary to his saying no yesterday, he lifted her onto his horse, then mounted behind her and they strolled around the pastures.

One hand draped around her to keep her from falling, Járon let his nose drift in her hair and inhaled her fresh scent. The longer they rode, the further his arm rolled over the front of her, his hand set on her hip, holding her against him.

Her bottom bounced gently against his cock making it hard as concrete, he used his hard learned control to compartmentalize the flaming desire, and enjoyed the ride.

The day was cold but the sun was warm, her hair drifted in the breeze wafting back, brushing his chest and flowing around his arm.

They conversed quietly about nothing, the nature around them, watching the ducks waddle around by the pond not yet iced over.

She gushed at the deer that watched them briefly before dashing off, wondering if they were her injured fawn's family.

He helped her down to pick some pussy willows.

Walking with the horse, they stopped by the water. Finding a comfortable spot where there were big rocks, they used them for chairs and ate the sandwiches she'd put in a sack with chips and sodas.

Keyleigh took a bite and asked, "Is it just you and your brothers? Do you have other siblings?" She chewed slowly as she observed his body stiffen.

It didn't seem he was going to answer then he said, "*Na*. Tis only us four, our parents were killed." A shadow fell over his eyes, he stared blankly out over the small lake they sat beside. "It was a long time ago," the dark eyes went vacant.

She tried to change the subject. She'd heard a bit of the brothers talking that day they popped in. "Um, so, your job, are you like a…what do you call it, men who hire out to- to," her lips pulled in, her question would likely only make him angry.

"Mercenary?" he said, nodding. "You might say my brothers and I are…somewhat like that. Only, now, we work for the government, not private parties."

He tossed a handful of chips into his mouth, glanced at her then away; the warmth earlier in his dark eyes had cooled. Why was she asking about this? She would know what he did, Mandrake would have told her.

Or, maybe not. She was so young, gullible, maybe Mandrake just told her what to do without any explanation. And being in love, she would have done what her much older lover told her to do without question. Járon's stomach soured.

"Oh." But she was curious. "Do you-"

"Tis covert ops, I cannot discuss it. Are you ready to go?"

They bagged up their trash, Járon tucked the sack in the side saddlebag then put his hands around her waist and lifted her up to sit on the steed.

He swung up behind her and made a clicking sound. The horse instantly started moving.

They rode in silence. Járon felt a stone lay in the pit of his stomach. The afternoon had been so, light, pleasant. He was actually enjoying himself for the first time in longer than he could remember. And, with a woman no less, one he wasn't even fucking.

He knew he had shut down when his job was brought up. She was an involvement in his mission, and what that was, he still didn't know. But it reminded him again, that she belonged to the man he was after.

Suddenly a snow white fox darted in front of the horse. Startled, the steed tossed his front hooves up, pawing the air, he danced back on his hind legs with a shrill whinny.

Thrown back against Járon, Keyleigh squealed.

His arm tight around her, Járon spoke gently, softly but loud enough to be heard. "Damion," he murmured words in his own language, holding the reins firmly but not tight.

The horse calmed almost immediately. "Shh," Járon crooned, patting Damion's neck.

"Já- rone," she gasped, clutching the saddle horn with one hand, her other on Járon's thigh. She leaned forward, away from him and panted, "Is- he okay?"

His voice as gentle as when he calmed the horse, Járon said with a smile, "*Da*, little one, he is fine, just startled. Everything is fine."

He made a tsking sound with his tongue and Damion started moving again.

With a will of its own, Járon's hand raised and slid under her hair, he lifted the heavy locks and caressed her neck and then shoulder.

She stiffened, but didn't protest when he stroked his hand over her shoulder and down her arm.

He couldn't tell if the shiver that trickled through her body was fear of him, nerves from the horse, or arousal at his touch.

Disregarding the burning that heated his loins, Járon brushed his hand across the front of her to pull her back comfortably against his chest. He kept his arm wrapped around her, keeping her snug against him the rest of the way back.

Chapter Eleven

By the time they returned, it was late afternoon, his brothers would arrive in an hour or so.

Keyleigh took a shower first so she could start dinner.

She was in the kitchen and coating a roast with seasoned flour when she heard Járon shut off the water.

The roast was in the oven and she was rubbing oil on the potatoes when he came into the kitchen.

"Thank you," he said quietly. Buttoning his shirt, he combed his thick fingers through his wet hair.

Sprinkling salt over the potatoes, puzzled, she asked, "For what?"

"For not running." Boots braced on the floor, he tucked his fingertips in his front pockets and slightly cocked his head at her, looking down over his angular jaw.

The fluorescent kitchen lights glanced off his sharp cheekbones and shone over the handsomely carved lips for once not set in a harsh grimace.

Closing the oven door on the roast and potatoes, she started tossing the salad and said with a shrug, "We had a deal. I would of course stick to it."

"Hmm." He left at the knock at the back door. "Sure, for once they knock," he muttered, to go answer it.

Keyleigh could hear the deep rumble of their voices as Járon fixed them drinks in the living room.

They spoke in hushed tones. Járon and his brothers were a quiet, serious, tough lot. She tiptoed to the door to hear their conversation.

In the living room, "*Bráthair,*" Victoro was talking, the ice clinked in his glass as he took a sip. "Why don't you simply take her to the local law enforcement and get rid of her?"

"*Na.*" Járon shook his head taking a swig of his own drink. "Mandrake would only send another one of his whores, or assassins to get to me. Better to know your enemy."

His circumspect gaze on his brother, Khol said, "Seriously, J, how the fuck would the guy even know about you, know you were here to stop him? We are too…covert, he can't possibly have known about us."

Hunched over, Járon rested his forearms on his thighs and held his glass with both hands. He shrugged, took a big sip and replied, "Then how do you explain her presence here?" He nodded towards the kitchen.

Remi asked with a grin, "What's up with the menagerie?"

The men had been in the house earlier while Járon and Keyleigh were out, then left when they saw the house was empty, sort of.

With another negligent shrug, Járon told them, "The whore has something about injured animals, insists on bringing them in and trying to help them."

Khol cleared his throat. A slight irritation grated in his deep voice as he rebuked his brother, "Why do you insist on calling her a whore? To me she looks very young. Innocence freaking radiates out of those amazing eyes, bro. She scarcely looks used hard and put away wet."

"Hah," Járon snorted. "She is likely a prostitute recently taken in by Mandrake to be used. To fuck, and because of that innocent beautiful face, he sent her out to spy, thinking I would be enamored by her beauty and spill my guts about our plans."

Keyleigh sunk back into the kitchen almost collapsing against the wall. How could he say those things? They had made peace, the shared afternoon was a delight, and all the time he was faking to keep her compliant, and under his will, the bastard.

Humph, she'd show him what a real whore looks like. While they drank, she snuck down the hall and changed her clothes.

After half an hour, she poked her head around the corner of the wall and said sweetly, "Dinner is ready, gentlemen." Under her breath she muttered, "And I use the term 'gentlemen' *very* loosely."

A man who would spank a helpless woman, drag her about by her hair, and call her vile names was certainly no gentleman.

In the living room, Járon stood up and announced, "Okay, *ma bráthairs,* you are in for a treat, the *kurva* can really cook."

He led the way to the dining room they seldom used. Normally they sat at the kitchen table in the big roomy kitchen.

"Hey, this is nice," Remi complimented with pleasure as they entered the dining area and went to sit at the beautifully laid out table.

Keyleigh had set it with flair and style, placed the pussy willows she'd picked in vases on the linen tablecloth she'd dug up with the crystal glasses, and china plates.

"Smells fucking amazing in here, bro." Victoro sniffed, suddenly very hungry, he looked towards the kitchen with anticipation.

Seating himself, Khol said to Járon with more rebuke, "You ever find out her name, or do you still call her *kurva* to her face?"

Shaking his head, Járon sipped his drink. "*Na*, what's the difference, whore works perfectly fine, she-" He stopped mid-word as Keyleigh came in carrying a platter of mouthwatering roast.

All four brothers stared at her with hanging mouths and cartoon- popping eyes, and they weren't gawking at the food.

She had changed into tiny shorts with kitten heels one of the brothers had supplied for her, and a tight blouse with the top few buttons undone revealing the top swells of her plump breasts.

A miniscule apron was tied like a sexy handkerchief over the front of her shorts.

Setting the platter on the table she said, "Here you go, fellas, I'll be right back," the little kitten heels clicked behind her as she sashayed back to the kitchen moving with femininity oozing from her swaying hips.

Tossing her hair over her shoulder, she drew a hand with coy allure down the long locks and disappeared into the kitchen.

His eyes on her bouncing butt cheeks, and the apron ties flipping over them with each strut, Khol moaned, "Fuck me."

"Mercy mama," Victoro groaned beside him.

"*Shut up*," Járon hissed at Remi before he could open his mouth.

Remi grinned back with jeering impudence. "I have a feeling the little miss heard you talking and did not like what she heard." He laughed at the red creeping up Járon's neck and the tips of his ears, his jaw working.

"*Da*, showing you what a whore actually looks like, she is shrewd, *ma bráthair,*" Victoro taunted. "You'd better watch your back, bro, you know, a scorned woman's wrath and all that shit."

"*Da*," Remi agreed with a sly grin, "a canny one that, she will have you wrapped around her little finger before you can blink, bro. You'd better set her free while you still have your nuts."

"Fuck you, fuck you all, just eat, don't fucking look at her," Járon growled, his brothers snickered.

Keyleigh strolled back in with bowls of spiced corn and baked potatoes.

Their eyes stayed glued to her, peering down her blouse when she bent over to place the bowls on the table, and staring at her ass when she went back to the kitchen to get rolls and gravy, and returned again with a chocolate cake and a bottle of wine.

Bypassing Járon, she brought the wine to Khol. Handing it to him along with a corkscrew opener, she said, "I apologize, I've never opened one before, and uh, this is the second bottle I tried, the other one, well," a hand tucked with abashed appeal behind her back.

She cocked her head, and twirled a piece of hair around her finger as she explained, "The cork sort of broke off, and I couldn't get it out."

Her gaze flit to Járon, who sat stone-faced. "Sorry, Mr. Rameau, sometime, when I'm home and have cash, I will mail you money for it. You need to tell me how much it cost."

Járon muttered, "Forget about it," and glared at Khol who had taken the bottle from her and managed to stroke her arm while doing so.

Khol easily drew out the cork and handed the bottle back to her. He said, "It would be a joy to watch you pour, sweetheart. By the way, what is your name?"

She bent and poured his glass, his eyes dipped down her cleavage. Across the table, a low growl rumbled.

Khol ignored Járon's warning and set his hand on the small of her back.

"Mmm," she murmured, stood straight and moved to Remi. "Keyleigh. My name is Keyleigh."

"You spell it Kee-Lee?" Khol asked, sipping his wine.

Shaking her head she spelled it as she poured Remi's then Victoro's, leaving Járon for last, making him have to watch his brothers ogle her, and caress her back, her arm, whenever she was near.

He sat back, arms rigid with his fingers digging into the table, jaw crunching. Brows so low his dark eyes were barely visible.

"Well, then," her pretty smile showed a row of pearlies with one slightly crooked tooth that only made her look younger, sexier, and even more appealing. She said cheerfully, "Enjoy, I will tend to the dishes while you eat."

"Sure, thanks Keyleigh honey," Remi called out as she left the room.

"*Da*, don't be a stranger, honey, come back anytime you want," Victoro echoed him.

"Thanks sweetheart, check back with us, often!" Khol yelled.

When she reached the sanctity of the kitchen, Keyleigh let out her held breath and buckled against the sink.

She couldn't believe she did that. Dressed like a hooker and pranced around half naked in front of Járon's brothers.

Recalling Járon's clenched jaw, wrath and promise of retribution billowed like black thunder in his eyes.

Stomach twisting, her bottom hurt already and he hadn't even touched her yet.

"Oh Lord, what have I done?" Well," she sighed, turned on the water and picked up the dish-wash soap. Pouring it into the sink, she muttered, "It's too late now to go back and undo, the bell has been rung."

The backdrop of their deep voices, speaking low, quietly, and in a foreign language, told Keyleigh this time they would not make the mistake of letting her overhear their conversation.

As she washed the pots and pans, she prayed his evening with his brothers would calm Járon from any threat of reprisal. Besides, what would he care what she wears? She could be stark naked and he'd still scowl at her.

However, the glare he had arrowed at her bode not well for her behind.

When she heard them move to the living room and smelled the aroma of their Black Dragon cigars, she rushed into the dining area, picked up all the plates, glasses,

101

silverware, and hurried back to the kitchen to wash them, and put up the leftovers.

The sooner done, the sooner she could change out of-the side door closed. She could no longer hear their voices.

Only a few glasses left to wash, she hurried, then… her skin prickled, she could feel him.

His energy, his wrath, flowing through the room like a fog burning off the night's ocean, swirling around her feet, her ankles, climbing up her body.

The little hairs on the back of her neck rose one-by-one, she didn't dare turn around.

"Turn around, *Key*-leigh," his snarl of her name was a mock.

When she didn't move, he said very quietly, "I said, turn around."

She did slowly, nervously, her hands behind her, clinging to the sink.

"You try to make a fool of me, *Key*-leigh?" The anger in his eyes glittered with predatory viciousness. He prowled towards her with light grace for such a big muscular man.

Keyleigh worked at not backing away from the fearsomely angry man. She tried to look levelly at him, but the furious fire streaking from his eyes was so fierce she had to lower hers.

He stopped a few feet from her; she could feel the danger, the heat from his gaze, his body, searing her, terrifying her.

"Look at me, *Key*-leigh."

"Stop messing with my name," she snapped, nervous of his anger, and furious at the way he had spoken about her to his brothers.

In a blink, he was in front of her, clutching her chin, holding her head up to his. His growl a guttural warning of an animal about to rip her to pieces, he snarled, "Don't you ever, *Key*-leigh, fucking tell me what to do."

Eyelids so low with threat, bare blackness gleamed under their slits. His voice sounded like a dark pit of proprietary fury, "And don't you ever wear shit like that again," he jerked her chin up.

Gripping her jaw, he said harshly, "If you do, next time you will be serving us with a blistered red bottom you got me?"

"Let go of me you- you monster! There will not be a next time. I am not your servant, your- your whore." She shook her chin free of his grasp and took a step back. "I will do as I please, you are not my owner, you can't tell me what to-"

He grabbed her so fast her head spun.

Gripping the front of her blouse in his fist he pulled her close, his snarl raw with the discomfited way he'd felt watching his brothers ogle her, touch her, and infuriated now at her defiance.

"I *will* tell you what to do and you *will* do it without argument, do you hear me, *Key*-leigh?" His fist wrapped in her blouse, he shook her.

"No," she grated brazenly, turning her head because his gritted teeth and incensed eyes were so close to her face.

His big fist under her chin, knuckles digging into her chest. She declared, "I will not. I insist you let go of me, right now. I am done doing what you-"

With a savage growl, he grasped her blouse with both hands and ripped it apart. Yanking it back down her shoulders to her elbows, he swung her around with her slim back to his broad chest, and seized her breasts over her black lacy bra.

"*Yah*? You defy me, little whore?" His hard hands painfully gripping her breasts, lowering his head, his mouth fell to where her neck met her shoulder. He opened his lips, bit then sucked fiercely on her flesh.

"No, stop, Rameau, stop!" Keyleigh struggled futilely in his arms of iron.

He pulled her tight against his chest, cupping her full breasts, his long, thick fingers roughly kneading them. Sucking harder on her neck, ruffled growls trundling deep inside him hummed against her throat.

Black hair brushing her jaw, Járon hissed huskily against her skin wet from his mouth, "You want to show anyone your beautiful tits, *Key*-leigh my little *kurva*, it will be to me."

"Stop calling me a whore, dammit," she cried, fighting to get from his embrace. But, he continued clutching her breasts with his big tough hands, and sucking on her skin, licking his way up to her mouth.

He released a breast to grip her hair. Pulling a handful of her locks, he bent her head back muttering, "If it walks like a duck and dresses like a duck," his mouth came down hard on hers in his anger and possessive jealousy.

He took her lips harshly, with an edge of violence. When she opened her mouth to protest he plunged his tongue in and chased after hers.

Keeping her back pinned against his chest, his punishing kiss fusing their mouths, Járon pushed at the bra cups trying to push them down to free her breasts so he could feel her bare skin against his coarse palms.

His hands cold on her warm flesh, his thumbs grazed over her nipples. Feeling them harden to tight little buds, he groaned into her mouth.

Moving his mouth to lick her neck, in a frenzy of firing lust he returned to suck at her lips, then kissed his way to behind her ear.

Járon's heavy breaths, growling groans, and crushing hands broadcasted he was rapidly becoming aroused to the point of no return.

"Please," she begged. Feeling the length of his hard erection pressing vehemently against her backside, Keyleigh pulled at his burly forearms. She could feel his arousal rising like fevered mercury in a boiling thermometer, the ferocity in his torrid touch burning off the charts.

She cried, "Stop, please, Rameau!" So strong, powerfully masculine, his aggressive assault terrified her, yet, her nether lady parts felt…enflamed.

Deaf with lust that filled them to buzzing heights, her pleas bounced off his ears. Her soft, hot little body squirmed in his arms. Tits full and lush in his hands, Járon caressed them, feeling their suppleness squeezing through his long hard fingers, her nipples rigid peaks, they were crying out to be licked and suckled.

He pushed her forward. Making her face flat pressed against the wall, he forced her hands up over her head. He untied the tiny apron, snatched it off and threw it with disgust, then reached around her and grabbed at her belt.

"Rameau, please," her stunned squawks muffled against the wall.

Járon held her secure with his chest, his mouth seeking her neck. Biting into it, he tore at the button on her shorts. Sucking like mad, he sounded like a voracious animal snacking on her flesh, his breathing abraded rapid and laborious on her skin.

"Please, Járon," she sobbed, "don't take me in anger."

Flipping her around with her back against the wall, struggling to get her pants open, Járon was blinded with lust that mushroomed and burnt through his body, driving him virtually insane with the need to possess her.

He snarled in an inebriated red haze of fury, "Tis the only way I can take you, Keyleigh," he rasped, "because you are not mine."

He brought his hands back up to ravage her breasts, his unyielding groans louder, stronger. Then he lowered one hand to shove her shorts down while his mouth sought hers again to plunder and devour.

Her whimpers feathered in his mouth, as his lips, teeth, tongue razed her mouth inside and out. He crushed her breast in his racing, out of control grip while still tearing at her pants to get them off her.

She twisted and pushed to get away, he jerked her back against the wall to take his violent onslaught.

Then, he felt rather than heard her sob into his mouth. Becoming aware of her frantic resistance, Járon struggled to clear the brain fog of his inflamed desire; he could hear the desperation in her cries for release.

In slow motion, he forced himself to unclench his hands from her body, move his mouth from her lips, and step away from her. His hands shook with the effort it took to let her go as he panted like a wild beast on the chase.

Grabbing the sides of her blouse with shaking hands, she pulled the material back up over her shoulders and around to cover herself.

Her head lowered, Keyleigh stared at the floor, not daring to incite him further. She was at his mercy and she knew it. He could rape her, beat her, murder her, and no one would know.

He was a big, strong, infuriated man that killed for a living, and clearly he had no mercy. Her arms strung in futile protectiveness around her trembling body, long hair draped over her face, covering her shamed eyes and red-roughened lips.

"Ah, Keyleigh," he said her name without a mock. Drawing in long deep breaths to calm himself, he wiped at his eyes, his mouth.

His sigh was thick with the ardor he fought to choke down, and heavy with the effort to keep his hands off her, to not push her to the floor, rip off the damned shorts and thrust inside of her.

Taking a deep breath, exhaling slowly, he shoved his palm up his forehead pushing his hair back, and mumbled, "The, uh, kitchen is pretty well, ah, cleaned up..." His fingers gripping his hips, he lowered his head.

He didn't look directly at her, but he could still see the embarrassed shame spread over her punished face, bruised and still damp from his brutal mouth.

She was so small and dainty, and he had brutalized her with his strength and out of control lust.

Guilt lacing his words, he told her, "Why don't you go and... change, get ready for bed. I'll put the rest of the dishes away."

Keyleigh stood for a moment, unsure. Would he pounce on her the second she moved from the wall?

Raking his shaking palm over his mussed hair, his savage growl so low, almost inaudible, he said, "You may be Mandrake's fuck, and I would not want to touch anything he had his hands on, or his dick in, but, at the moment my cock doesn't care. You need to go, while you can." *While I can still let you-*

"Oh!" She swung and slapped him, then clutched her hand with the sudden pain, and ran from the room.

Járon stood still, didn't lift his head until she left.

He gently touched the side of his cheek where she'd struck him. A small smile creased his face, she was getting better, he actually almost felt that one.

But, the next one could break that delicate little hand. He needed to stop her if she tried again. This time, he let her hit him; he deserved it after assaulting her like he had, then deliberately disparaging her to put distance between them.

He had to make her mad, he needed her to stay away from him, not provoke him. Next time he might not be able to stop himself.

Járon had never in his life touched a woman who did not want to be touched. But, Keyleigh, he smiled at her name, it was cute and sweet like her, then the smile stiffened. He hadn't been able to stop himself from putting his hands on her, ruthlessly groping her.

Fueled by a jealous anger at his brothers leering at her, her having fun with them, smiling, flirting with them, and they were caressing her.

Once he'd broken and touched her, he was gone. Those sweet soft tits, her silky skin under his tongue, the taste of her in his brutal kisses.

Da, he knew he had been too damned rough with her. He'd seen her swollen lips, mottled bitten hickies all over her whisker-burned soft skin. Fuck, he was a savage, a feral primate.

God knows how much he'd hurt her tender breasts with his hard manic grip. He had been so crazed with unhinged desire to feel her, kiss her, fuck her.

Damned she's so hot, he palmed his hard-on straining against his jeans, squeezed it remembering the feel of her body in his hands.

Well, he sighed, he'd had a few firsts with little Keyleigh. His first abduction, at least of a female, his first punishing spanking- that wasn't part of sexual games, his first sexual assault. Hell, he was turning into an even worse bastard than he thought he was.

He put up the rest of the dishes, then went outside to check on the animals.

Seeing them attended to for the night, he smoked a cigar to calm his raging body.

When he returned, he locked the doors and turned out the kitchen lights and went to the living room.

She was asleep, curled up under the blanket, the fiery curls spread over the pillow and down the side of the sofa.

He cuffed her wrist, stuffed the cloth around the inside of the metal then stood watching her.

Guilt rose again. He should put her in his bed; he should be the one to sleep on the couch, he was the man, he was tougher. But, he had to make her know he considered her a danger, an evil.

Looking down at the tiny plump lips that moved slightly with her breaths, the lashes curled over rosy rounded cheeks covered with tear tracks, ah, she could not truly be evil. The tears she shed because of his abuse gave him a sharp pang.

A deep sigh released some tension in his thick shoulders. Before he could prevent it, the thought of her in his bed popped into his mind.

Slender arms reaching for him, topaz eyes beckoning Járon, turning to a deep blue with her steeping desire.

Those sweet lips beguiling, her legs spreading as she told him she wanted him- *fuck*, his erection hardened more, damn. It was a big mistake thinking about her in his bed.

He roamed away from her before he made good on his fantasies.

Turning the lamp off, Járon went to take a long, steamy shower

Chapter Twelve

The next few days Járon stayed outside as much as possible, having as little contact with Keyleigh as he could.

He un-cuffed her to cook and tend to the injured animals. They'd added a squirrel he brought in from the field.

But then he would re-cuff her, avoiding making eye contact, and ate in his office. He had to ensure she didn't try another escape attempt. And his willpower was rapidly dwindling. He wanted her. So badly, in his mind he could palpably taste her in his hungry mouth.

If she tried another escape attempt, in his present primitive-minded mode, he had no idea what he would do with the wrath that would bring. More than the anger of her escaping from her captor, he couldn't stand her running *from him*.

Whenever he was near, Járon saw her stiffen and move away when she could, when she couldn't, she held her arm rigidly while he snapped the cuff on her wrist.

She watched him anxiously, like she expected him to pounce on her any second and rip her clothes off while smacking her around.

It was later afternoon when he came into the living room where she was quietly knitting with the silk.

"Keyleigh," he started.

Cutting him off, she pronounced stiffly, "You will not touch me again. I mean it." Her arms wrapped around her body, useless shields. They both knew, if he chose to take her, there was nothing she could do about it.

His face darkened, black brows slashed down. "Listen, little *kurva*, you deliberately dressed provocatively to tease, incite me and my brothers. The next thing I expected was for you to climb up on the table, lie on your back, spread your legs and offer your cunt for dessert." Fuck, he sounded like a jealous boyfriend.

The white flew from her face then whiplashed with red. Her gasp a sharp inhale, pained and mortified.

"How dare you! You are a pig, a swine, a vile-mouthed crude boor. You are a horrible, despicable man! Not even a man, you are lower than the belly of a snake!" Her fingers absently touched her lips that were still slightly bruised from his assault.

"*Da*, I've been told." His own sharp cheeks were flushed with a sliver of red; his gaze followed her fingers tracing her abused lips.

Keyleigh demanded, "As far as I am concerned, the rest of the time you keep me here, stay away from me, and we do not need to talk. I do not want to hear the filth that comes out of your mouth. I refuse to speak to anyone who uses that kind of language to me."

Crossing her arms, she snapped her head away from him. Facing the window, she stared out as if he was not there.

Járon spoke quietly, "Keyleigh," he stared at the back of her head. She didn't move.

"Listen, ah, I…" he didn't know what to say. Damn women anyway. You can't talk to them like they're men, so what's the point? He stomped out of the room and slammed the door as he left the house.

Járon decided to make a quick trip to town.

As he exited the store, he saw that Shannon woman bearing down on him. Huge breasts rolling and bouncing as she headed straight for him with a sly brassy smile on her wide red lips.

Sure, he could manhandle Keyleigh all day long, but he couldn't stand to have that blonde slut pawing him. *Yah,* hypocrite comes to mind.

Turning his back to her, he tossed his purchases into the truck and sped back to the house.

Hanging his jacket by the door, he sauntered casually into the living room.

"Here," he said with nonchalance to Keyleigh, "I bought these," he set magazines on the table.

She didn't look at them or respond.

"I didn't know what you like so I got you uh, one on cooking or recipes or someshit, a couple of tabloids, and a couple of women's mags. The girl in the shop said you guys like this Cosmo thing. And uh, I found that yeast stuff you said you wanted to make more bread and pizza dough."

Setting a new bowl of chocolates on the table, he stood waiting for her to say something.

Her despising eyes rolled up to him, then she turned to stare back out the window, her knitting lay on her lap.

"Ah, okay then, I need to check on the, ah, goats." He stood awkwardly, hands in his pockets, the block of shoulders hunched, a lock of black hair flopped over one brow.

"So, Key-leigh, tis uh, the winter chill is in the background, but today is fairly warm. You want to come with me to see that the animals are set for the evening?"

She kept her head facing the window, blinked back a fat tear that threatened to escape.

He saw it, his stomach twisted.

Járon sat on the couch beside her pretending he didn't see her edge away from him.

"Keyleigh," his voice soft, "*nenita*, please look at me."

When she didn't, he reached over and took one of her hands, holding onto it when she tried to tug it back. He stroked one of her small fingers, smiled down at it.

Commenting, "Everything on you is so soft, and tiny, so feminine," he stroked another one with a couple of his thick fingers and his thumb from the top knuckle to her fingertip.

Slowly, she turned her head, looked down at him gently caressing each finger. "Rameau," she started then stopped with a frown, wondering what he was up to now.

"Járon, Keyleigh, call me Járon. You were before…"

He had ill-treated her the past weeks. Calling her nasty names, keeping her chained to his sofa, spanking, assaulting her. Járon realized she called him by his last name now to keep a wall up between them, protect what tattered dignity she had left.

Tugging at her hand, Keyleigh said angrily, "Don't be kind to me, *Rameau*, just to turn around and abuse me again. It is…abusive. I've never done anything to deserve being mauled, spoken to, treated the way you have done. Please, leave me alone."

She turned her head from him, again choking back the frustration of tears that welled.

Remorse was a unique feeling for Járon. He didn't like it, but he couldn't make it go away. "Ah, Keyleigh, I…" the words 'I'm sorry' just wouldn't budge out of his mouth.

"You are right," he sighed. "I have no evidence of who you really are, or how you got to be on my land."

He recalled the shape she had been in when he found her. Wounded, bruised, falling unconscious into his arms with his rope lassoed around her. Her body was so thin, on the edge of being direly skinny from lack of food.

Still refusing to look at him, she kept her head turned, lips closed, firm and thinned with her pain of humiliation.

Járon stroked her fingers, holding on lightly to the end of one. He admitted, "I have treated you…very badly. Not knowing who you were or why you were here, and," he cleared his throat.

"I, uh, realized I was, am, attracted to you, obviously," the tips of his ears turned red. "And, I also realized I liked you and didn't want to. And, uh, well, it kills me you belong to another man. So I've been…mean. To you."

He tried for some lightness. With a crooked grin, he said, "I wouldn't mind though if you did what I said, you know, about lying on the table and being dessert, but only for me."

At the flash of her appalled, indignant eyes, Járon said quickly, "Okay, forget I said that. Anyway, do you think, we can uh, start over, maybe? I…have a mission to complete, so I'm sorry," *huh, that one came out easy*. "Because of it, I can't let you go, now, yet. But, I will try from now on, not to be such an asshole bruiser to you."

115

Keyleigh was trying to follow and make sense of every rambling thing he was saying, and judge the genuineness of his words. Her gaze traveled his hard face.

His mouth was not set as viciously harsh as usual. His head was slightly lowered; he looked up almost shyly at her, his eyes not as empty and cold as before. But the names he's called her, she shook her head.

Watching the play of emotions scroll over her face of satin skin and softness, seeing her shutting him down, he grunted. "Khol would have tried to wash my mouth out with soap if he heard what I…" his eyes lowered, "said to you."

With a tight grinned snort, he said, "He would have tried anyway, but I would have kicked his ass."

The dark brooding eyes turned up to her under a veil of black lashes. He tried again, "Anyway, uh, if I don't jump you, and try to curb my fucking language do you think we can try another truce?"

A tiny smile curved her mouth. "Nice start, Rameau."

"Huh?" He looked sheepish. "Oh, *yah*." The corner of his mouth ticked up. "Uh, sorry. I'm just used to hanging with my brothers, and other men that are…coarse, crude, you know, tough bullies like me. But, uh, will you give me a chance, okay, Keyleigh?"

She turned and looked back out the window.

He said with a slight cajole, "How about we go check on those recalcitrant goats? Jocky and Sammy both tried to make a run for it this morning, they chewed through a weak part of the fence. I got there just as they were about to make their big escape."

Staring at the side of her head, he studied each different hued strand of curls. A blend of golds and yellows and fire, all like the finest silk.

She turned slightly with a shy, uncertain smile. Her topaz eyes glimmered with shiny tears. Járon felt his stomach clutch knowing he'd put them there.

With an unsure sigh, she finally said, "O...kay. I would like to get some fresh air, see that mischievous Jocky. Can we bring carrots?"

Her pretty, shy smile and shining eyes tightened the clench in his gullet. He squeezed her hand gently. "Good. *Da*, I'll get the carrots and a jacket for you."

He unlocked the chain, removed the cuff. They both stared silently at the chain before he set it aside.

"Go, use the, um, washroom, I'll meet you at the front door. Okay?"

Keyleigh nodded, still unsure if she could believe his words.

A quick glance at his hard face showed his full lips pulled in with...shame? Brows inverted over his unfathomable dark eyes made him appear, remorseful.

Still...she'd heard him on the phone, he was a stone cold killer, a...he called himself sort of a mercenary? But government hired? What did that truly make him? Could anything he said be truth? She was unsure what he really was.

Deciding it was worth trusting him to get outside and breathe the early winter crispness, she got up. Feeling his gaze at her back she trod to the bathroom.

When she returned, Járon was at the front door waiting.

He said, "Here, this should be sufficient, there's a dusting of snow but the day really is fairly balmy."

After helping her shrug into a jacket, he put on his own. Setting his palm on the small of her back, he ushered her outside, and kept it there as they strolled to the goat pens.

Járon could feel her soft warmth through the jacket on his palm; she could feel the hard heaviness of his hand on her back.

Before they reached the pens, half a dozen goats trampled out to greet them.

Keyleigh broke from Járon and ran laughing to the fence, digging the carrots he'd given her out of her pockets.

Standing back, hands tucked in his pockets, Járon watched her giggle and pet and feed the crazy goats.

He'd heard that goats were ornery, but his small herd was always cheerful and playful.

Keyleigh had a tinkling girlish laugh that made him smile as she teased the animals.

He let her play for a while. Then he said, "Come, let's take a walk in the meadows, you're probably dying for some exercise." He held his hand out.

She looked at it, then shyly took it and they walked hand-in-hand, traipsing through tall, amber winter grass and withered stalks left from the dead wildflowers, the slight wind ruffling their hair.

"Keyleigh," he said then stopped and pulled her collar up around the back of her neck. He kept his hands on her collar, holding her in front of him, his knuckles grazing her jaw.

"Hmm?" She smiled, breathing deeply of the cool air, feeling it chill down her throat to her belly.

Dropping his hands Járon said, "I'd like to teach you to run, properly. I can catch you so easily, and always will, but still, you run like a girl, and-"

She laughed with a burst of giggle. "I am a girl in case you haven't noticed." Her lips pursed at her words, remembering the other night when he assaulted her.

"*Da.*" He nodded. His eyes hooded, he slid a side-glance at her and agreed, "I've noticed." He took her hand again, and squeezed it gently.

"But, you seem to be in perpetual…danger. I want to give you a few…skills to help you protect yourself. I can teach you how to run faster, and maybe give you some self-defense lessons. What do you say?"

Her face puckered with a brief shock of anguish at his words.

Járon could clearly see his words hit home. She was in danger. He needed to talk with her, try to find out what was really going on, why she was in the forest that day. He was starting to think it had nothing to do with him.

"Key-" he broke off, frowned, something was off.

"What?" She caught his sudden change from playful to wary.

His body rigid, head slanted as he listened, sharp eyes scanned the pastures. There was grass trampled that hadn't been when he was out earlier at daybreak.

"We need to go back. Now."

Clutching her hand, he strode so quickly back to the house he almost dragged her with his long fast strides.

When they reached the house, he said, "Get inside, lock the doors, I need to saddle Damion."

"Járon, what is-"

"Just get the fuck inside, quickly," he barked at her. "Lock the damned doors. You don't open them to anyone but me. Do as I say, now!"

She cringed from his sudden harsh anger, but started for the door as he instructed, then something caught her eye.

"Járon," she gasped, and moved towards the rabbit lying trembling on the ground, obviously injured. Keyleigh started to crouch beside it.

119

Járon snagged her arm, jerked her up roughly and pushed her towards the door. "*Na*, fuck, Keyleigh, do as I told you, leave the fucking rabbit and get inside-" He smacked her hard on the ass and shoved her towards the door.

When he saw her hurt expression, but heading for the door nonetheless, he spun and ran off towards the barn to get his horse.

But when he went around the corner, Keyleigh ran back to the rabbit.

She was almost to it when she heard thunder, what sounded like thunder. She turned around.

Five men on horseback were charging straight at her. At first she froze. Maybe they were there to see Járon.

But, their faces, they were dirty and unkempt with scruffy beards, and the leers on their faces told her all she needed to know. She turned and started running.

One of the men pounded up to her, never stopped, just leaned over, grabbed her arm and hauled her up in front of him on his horse and kept going.

She screamed, "Járon! Járon!" as they thundered into the forest

Chapter Thirteen

He was near the barn when he heard her scream.

Járon dashed to the side of the structure and saw the men grab her. In a heartbeat, he pivoted on his heel and ran straight to the barn.

Sensing his distress, Damion's hooves scraped in the air with an urgent snort of impatience, and a spur to action whinny.

Throwing a bridle on him, not wasting time with a saddle, he just jumped on the steed and raced off to find Keyleigh.

Járon directed Damion to gallop in the direction he'd seen the men go, then he easily followed their horses' prints in the white-flaked hardened mud.

They weren't even trying to disguise their trail. Apparently they felt no fear from a single man possibly chasing after them. Their mistake.

The forest was normally dense, but winter had arrived quickly and most of the leaves were gone. Only a sugaring of snow on the ground, it was easy to see and travel fairly quickly through the spindled woods.

The thugs had a head start and were riding fast. Járon kept his horse at breakneck speed lest he somehow lost the hoods at a sudden turnoff.

Only a mile or so and he heard Keyleigh's screams pierce the chilled air. It froze Járon's blood, were they killing her?

He kicked the horse, spurring him to go even faster. Bare branches scraped at man and horse, the wind an icy blade on exposed skin.

Breaking through a clearing he saw them.

Fifty yards away, Keyleigh was flat on her back on the cold hard ground with five men holding her down.

She screamed and one of the fuckers slapped her. She screamed again and he slapped her so hard he stunned her into silence.

Two men staked her arms to the damp grass, another was trying to rip her jeans apart. A fourth man tore at her blouse and the fifth was kneeling between her thrashing legs with a knife, he was just going to cut her jeans right off her.

Járon pounded into the clearing and jumped from his galloping horse, letting the steed keep on moving away from the danger.

The men looked up at him in surprise.

"Get lost asshole, we're busy here," the man leaning over Keyleigh called out.

Járon ran towards them.

"Fuck-" the man barked. "Get the hell out of here dude, whoever you are! You ain't gettin' a share of her, so beat it, mind yer own bizness!"

Járon was a dozen yards from them and kept coming at full speed, black hair flying, boots pounding the hard earth.

"Barry, José," the man between Keyleigh's legs ordered to one of the men holding an arm, and the other that was pawing at her blouse, "take the stupid fucker out," and he turned back to what he was doing.

Gleefully sawing at Keyleigh's pants, his grin lascivious, the man laughed loud and crudely, enjoying her terror.

Járon ran straight at the two men sent to dispatch him.

The first one who reached him was running so fast when Járon bent and threw his shoulder against him and lifted him, his momentum kept him flying over Járon's shoulder until he crashed into a tree.

Slamming to the ground, his head faced at funny angle, his dead eyes stared at nothing.

The second man roared, rushing at him. Járon continuing heading towards Keyleigh, jabbed his knife in the man's throat and didn't slow down.

"Get the fucker, Gary!" the man in charge yelled, his hands paused on her thighs now, the knife clenched in one fist.

The other man holding Keyleigh's arm jumped up and hurtled toward Járon with his gun out and pointed at him.

Seeing the gun, struggling to get up, Keyleigh punched at the man kneeling between her legs and screamed, "Run Járon! He has a gun- run! Get out of here!"

The man with the knife backhanded her, knocking her back on the ground.

Gary fired at Járon, but Járon had combat training. He ran to the side of the man so he couldn't aim properly and turn at the same time.

Swift as a lightning strike, Járon grabbed Gary's arm that held the weapon and smashed it down on his knee. The snap of the bone breaking was audible in the clearing, as was the man's howl.

Throwing him to the ground, Járon stomped on his head with his steel boot, then crouched, broke his neck with one move and started back towards Keyleigh.

The fourth man got up and jumped on a horse and took off for the woods.

Like a runaway train, Járon kept charging.

Terror at seeing the carnage Járon had committed in only seconds, the fifth man raised his knife over Keyleigh and shouted desperately, "Stop or I'll kill her!"

"You kill her, I gut you, motherfucker," Járon spat still moving towards them. His face set in a hard, dark ferocious mask of promised death.

"I mean it asshole!" the panicked guy screamed, holding the knife blade-side down over Keyleigh's chest. "I'll cut out the bitch's heart and throw it at you!"

Keyleigh reached up and grabbed the arm holding the knife. "Run Járon!" she shrieked.

"Bitch," he snarled and hit her. Jerking his arm from her grasp, he brought the knife down-

Járon vaulted over the last few feet of ground- and crashed into the man knocking him off Keyleigh.

Stumbling to his feet, the thug flailed punches at Járon, tried to slash at and stab him.

Járon dodged the knife, grabbed the man's wrist and with no effort, turned his arm as if it was made of butter instead of muscle, and forced the man to stab himself.

The shock jolted his eyes, he stared at Járon without blinking. His mouth hovered open and closed as he tried to speak. He gagged, managed to choke out, "Who the hell are you?"

Járon put his hand on the man's shoulder and shoved him, he was dead before he hit the ground.

Járon scrambled over to Keyleigh.

Her eyes were closed, blood seeped on her face from the vicious slaps.

"*Nenita!*" he exclaimed, kneeling on the damp grass beside her. He brushed her hair from her face. "Are you all right, baby? Keyleigh," he said, stroking her face. "Honey, talk to me."

Her head shook side-to-side slightly, lids fluttered then raised, she threw her arms around his neck. Terror still clawing in her throat, she cried with a rasp, "I'm okay now, Járon, you came for me," and wept against his shirt.

He slid his hands under her and stood up with her in his arms. "Always, baby, always." He carried her to Damion, helped her up, then mounted behind her.

He'd been so afraid for her it had sucked the air right out of his lungs. Járon rolled both his arms around her, holding her tight to his chest.

"You foolish woman, yelling at me to leave. What did you think, that I would chase after you then see those shitheads and run like a coward and leave you to them? Hah," he snorted, and made a clicking sound for the horse to move.

She snuggled back against him, limbs still trembling from the nightmare of being taken and nearly gang-raped, and undoubtedly murdered when they were through.

"There were five of them, and only one of you. You were the foolish one, not me," Keyleigh admonished him.

Her breath hitched with the fright of seeing Járon race head-on towards those men. "I," her voice soft and shaky, she said, "would have understood if you left me, truly. I am nothing to you, nothing for you to risk your life for." She

125

tacked on with a humorless laugh, "It would have gotten me out of your hair."

Jároń's big arms held her tighter as the horse started trotting. "Hush now, woman, don't talk such shit." His timbre deep and soothing, he said, "You're safe, that is all that matters."

He gently kissed the top of her head, snuffling his chin in her soft hair. The scent of her natural fragrance mixed with cool snow and rustic woods helped calm his racing heart.

They were quiet until Keyleigh's body stopped shaking and she shed some of the mindboggling terror of being snatched and attacked by the five thugs.

Then, after sucking in a deep, bone-strengthening breath, Keyleigh told him, "Jároń, one of the men got away."

He nodded. "*Da*, I know. Tis growing dark now. Tomorrow, Khol will come and we will search for him, make sure he's gone for good and dispose of the bodies."

The brothers would also scour the woods for any others lurking. Jároń kept that to himself, he didn't want her going to bed tonight fearing there were more monsters out there that might come after her.

Keyleigh felt the breadth and heat of the beast beneath her. Aware that without the support of Jároń's body, his encasing thighs, she would have tumbled right off the huge horse, she asked, "There's no saddle, how do you ride him without a saddle?"

Jároń nuzzled his nose in her hair and inhaled. "I don't need a saddle, tis just more comfortable for long rides and to pack stuff."

He moved a hand to cup around her neck and jaw, slid her hair back and put his mouth on her neck. He kissed, then licked, lightly sucked on her skin, felt her tremble.

"You sure you're all right, Keyleigh?" he murmured against her neck, "did they hurt you?"

One burly arm just under her breasts holding her close, lips on her flesh, he rubbed his other hand up and down her arm, her thigh, as if he couldn't get enough of touching her even over her clothing.

His lips curved up at the tiny moan that rolled from her throat, the way she slanted her head so he could lick and kiss more of her skin.

"Ahh, I am fine now." She closed her teeth together as if to stifle the moan. Keyleigh was surprised at her own reaction, then she sighed when his mouth continued roaming her flesh.

"They didn't really hurt me too much." Her eyes dipped to her torn jeans. "You were in the…literally… the nick of time."

Hugging her tight, he moved his palm to set on top of the upper part of her chest, feeling her pounding heartbeat. His thumb brushed under her jaw, his fingers gently curled around her throat.

Keyleigh's sigh fell out with a tremor. "I was so scared, Járon, it happened so fast. They- they were going to take turns, they said, all night, raping me, and the- the man said when they were tired, done, they would kill me-"

She broke off with a cry, her body stiffened, recalling her fear.

Five men had abducted her, threw her cruelly to the winter hard ground in the dead of the cold dark woods.

The pain in her wrists and legs as they forced her, staked her to the ground, she could smell the grass wet with frosty dew dampening her skin, her clothes. The stink of unwashed skin, cigarettes and skanky booze assailed her nostrils as they laughed and cursed.

The thugs brutally held her down, not caring if they hurt her. Pulling, stretching her arms over her head, they viciously groped her, while one of the filthy men was cutting off her jeans so he could just- sobs hitched in her chest.

Járon pulled her closer, whispered in her ear, "Shh, tis okay now, my *nenita,*" he pet her hair, stroked her arm. "I will never let anyone hurt you again, baby."

He wasn't going to tell her how terrified he was that he wouldn't find her, or get there in time. The back of his neck heated with shame, he has treated her just as badly as those rampaging bastards.

His hand under her jaw; he turned her head and kissed her, very gently, without the rough aggression of the other night when he'd been shot through with jealousy, and so mindlessly intoxicated with her.

He was just as riotously sexually aroused for her now as he'd been then. But now, he'd almost lost her and he wanted nothing more than to hold her and taste her, convince himself it wasn't a dream, that she really was there with him, safe.

His loins quivered when she responded, yet, oddly, now that he wasn't in a blind raging lust violently raping her mouth he could taste, feel…innocence, in her kiss. How could that be?

She was Mandrake's…no, he was never using that word again. He knew the second those topaz eyes opened to him that very first day she wasn't a whore.

He called her that because he was afraid of his own instant intense reaction to her. Had to keep reminding himself she was not his, and at some point he would have to return her.

But at the moment, he wasn't going to think about her…leaving. Or belonging to another man. Holding her in the crook of his arm, Járon cradled her delicate jaw with his big hand, and took a longer, hungering, nourishing kiss.

This time he didn't go ape-shit on her, instead, he held back part of his lusting strength to make sure she wasn't resisting, no one was going to force themselves on her ever again, including him.

Her body relaxed against his, she greedily accepted his kisses and that urged his intensity to amplify, his skin heated as his manhood swelled.

The forest was still, a cocooned quiet with the light blanket of snow on the ground and skimming along the branches of the bare trees.

Even the wind ceased its howling. It was as if the earth stopped spinning, just for them, just for now.

Soft moans from Keyleigh, dusky growls from Járon, moist resonance of their lips savoring, tongues mating, fingers in each other's hair, hands caressing faces, quiet lovemaking muted in the stark coldness.

Puffs of snow like sparkling diamond dust skipped up under Damion's hooves as they clomped, the only other tranquil sound in the woods. Snow muffled clippity-clops, and his occasional snort and huff.

When they reached the house, it took effort for Járon to tear his lips from Keyleigh's. He slid off Damion, reached up and pulled her down to slide into his arms. He carried her into the house.

"Járon," she giggled, "I can walk."

"*Da*, I know." But he kept going until he set her carefully on the couch. "I have to go to see to Damion, I'll be back. When I return, we will discuss your punishment."

"What?!" Her brows shot up. "Why? What did I do?"

His hands on his hips, one black brow arched at her. "You went back for that rabbit, didn't you, when I told you to get inside and lock the door?"

Her lips shut and pursed, she looked away, didn't deny it.

"Thank you, Keyleigh."

"For what?"

"For not lying to me."

"Hmm. Járon," she said as he turned from her.

"*Da?*"

"Please don't hit me. I've been hit…so much today. Can you please wait until tomorrow." Her hand went to her face that was still red from the man's slaps and Járon's evening whiskers. God, it was miserable being at all these men's violent mercy.

"Baby," Járon growled and went back to her. Bending over, he placed his palms on either side of her shoulders on the sofa.

"The last thing I want to do to you is hurt you. I have no plans to spank you today, sweetheart, but I do have plans for more of this," he leaned in and pulled at her lips with his. Sucked the top, then the bottom, then licked the seam between them with pressure until she opened to him.

When she did, he slipped his tongue in to gently taste her, draw her tongue to tentatively brush his.

Her little tongue shyly made such tiny sexy strokes at his, a shiver rippled through his tightened balls; he thought he would come in his pants.

He broke away and looked at her.

Her lips were still open to the kiss, lids low and heavy, a twinkle of blue peeped deliriously from under them. Her cheeks pink with a slight flush of passion.

"God, you are so beautiful, Keyleigh. Don't move, I'll be back."

While he was gone, Keyleigh decided to take a shower and wash off those horrible men's hands from her body.

She gathered up some clean clothes to change into on her way to the bathroom. A smile eased inside her, Járon had not chained her.

He either trusted her not to leave, or knew she would be a world-class idiot to run right back out taking the chance of those men or others grabbing her. Besides, it was snowing and she didn't have any type of heavy winter clothes to wear.

She hoped he hadn't chained her not because she'd learned a hard lesson today, but because he trusted her. Of course he had no reason to trust her, she'd made numerous attempts to escape from him.

But now, her fingers trailed over her lips as she remembered how he had kissed her while on the way back on the horse.

He had kissed her nicely, yet with intense passion, not with the unrestrained aggressive roughness he had the other night. Not that she minded the roughness, it was actually exciting, but she didn't want him wanting her because he was angry with her.

If he liked her, then it would be a different story. Keyleigh suddenly realized she no longer had any desire to run from him.

She needed to remind herself that he has been vulgar and abusive to her, but, he also tended to her wounds, not just once but ongoing. And, he had fixed food for her.

He'd said it was to keep her alive until he knew why she was there, but he could have tossed plain bread at her without going to the trouble of preparing food for her. His skills in the kitchen were rudimentary at best, nonetheless, he still fed her. That was, she smiled, until he realized that she could cook.

Nowadays, practically before she could remove the freshly baked cookies from the oven he was behind her snatching one, and laughing when she scolded him to wait until they cooled.

Now, Keyleigh recalled the feeling of his big tough hands on her body that day in the kitchen when he was so angry about the way she had dressed. He'd acted like a jealous boyfriend, she'd been so confused.

He had gripped her breasts with such rapacious strength then possessively caressed them, his thumbs stroking her nipples. His teeth and tongue on her neck, then his lips sucking her flesh, the frenzied sound of his carnal breaths in her ear.

A fine shiver rolled up her spine, a tingle undulated and heated between her legs, her nipples peaked into pebbles. His manhood had been hard and thick, pressing against her, belying his statements that he didn't desire her. He had acted like he was having a…jealous tantrum.

But, then his horrid words, the names he'd called her, she sighed. Yet now he genuinely seemed repentant and remorseful for the way he's treated and spoken to her.

He had ensured she didn't just have a pair of pants and shirt to wear, he'd asked his brothers to borrow a bunch of clothes for her.

Then there were the things that popped up here and there. A pasta machine and other implements, or treats she only commented that she liked suddenly appeared.

He brought her magazines, and purchased anything she needed including feminine products, her own brand of shampoo and soap, hairbrush, chapstick, the list goes on and on. He denied her nothing she asked for, or even just briefly mentioned.

Of course, a smile curved raising her cheeks; there was also the little matter of him searching for her that day she'd fled into the woods.

He'd done it because he feared she would perish in the forest, not because he didn't want her to run back to Maximillion Mandrake with tales of Járon's business.

Otherwise, he wouldn't have saved her from falling off the cliff. And then today, he rescued her from the men who abducted her. There was no other reason for him to risk his life for her.

Keyleigh pondered all theses things. And, she came to the conclusion that he had to care at least a little for her to do all the things that he had done.

Hmmm, she wondered when her feelings for him had...changed. It had been before today, she thought, because when he had been ravaging her in the kitchen, she had been as turned on as him.

But, she had been so aware of his disgusted hatred for her, his rage. His indomitable strength was frightening when he was angry. And a person had every right to fear him, she'd seen that first hand earlier today.

Yet, he didn't seem to hate her anymore. He'd kissed her so sweetly, with hot yearning but without forcing her like he had before.

She took a quick shower, braided her wet hair, changed and went into the kitchen to prepare something light for dinner.

Keyleigh came to a sharp halt when she saw him standing there, his expression was strange, a mix of fury, and hurt.

He stood staring at her, his arms were curled up over his jacket he hadn't yet taken off.

"You're here," he stated as if in surprise, his Adam's apple bobbed with a hard swallow.

"Of course," she replied, smiling. Entering the kitchen she opened the fridge and took out a container of her homemade pasta that had dried yesterday.

She had been so surprised when that pasta maker had magically appeared on the kitchen counter a day after she'd mentioned how she wished there was one at the farmhouse.

He had acted so innocent, like he had no knowledge of how it got there.

Right now, he still didn't move, just stood staring at her, his expression inscrutable.

She took out a jar of her home made pasta sauce along with onions and peppers, mushrooms and sausage, several spices, and set them on the counter. Picking up a saucepan, she frowned at him when he still didn't move.

Setting the saucepan on a burner, she asked, "What's the matter, Járon?"

Then he moved slightly, his voice husky low, he said, "I came in and the house was dark, and you weren't in the living room. I came in here to see if you…but you weren't here either. I thought you…left."

To Keyleigh, he looked somewhat distraught. She explained, "I took a shower. I felt dirty, those men, their hands," her shoulders shuddered.

"Did they hurt you? You said they didn't hurt you," his voice edged with a hint of angry concern.

"No, they didn't, not really. Knocked me around some, but really, I'm fine. But, you seem, upset. What's wrong?"

He shook his head. Black hair flopped over his forehead making him look so oddly boyish that the hard killer persona faded for a moment.

"Nothing." Clearing his throat, he said, "After what we shared earlier…uh, then I thought you left." He shook his head again, gave her a smile. "Never mind, you are here, and about to cook us dinner?"

Keyleigh returned an enchanting smile. "Yes." Then she tilted her head at him, he still hadn't moved. "Járon, what-"

He walked towards her and she could see what was in his arms. He'd gone back and retrieved the injured rabbit. It was nestled against the warmth of his chest. Its little furry body shaking with fear.

Keyleigh gasped a small cry, "Oh, Járon, you went and got him, oh thank you!"

She hurried to the closet and got a box, brought it to where the fawn was sleeping and put the box down near him, and then ran to get some towels. She hurried back and made a bed for the bunny.

Járon crouched down and gingerly set the rabbit in the box. "At the rate we're going, we're going to run out of towels," he chuckled.

"I think his leg is broken like the fawn's. I can splint it with a piece of wood. All these suddenly injured animals lately. There might be a fox or coyote out there chasing things. I'll look for it tomorrow."

"The goats?" Her hand at her throat, she said, "Are they going to be safe?"

"*Yah*. I don't think it's a very large predator, the goats can hold their own. You've seen, they are a feisty lot. I'll keep them in the barn with the chicks until I find the perpetrator."

He walked over to Keyleigh and put his hand to the back of her head. Cradling it, he pulled her to him and kissed her, with care and softness.

When he felt his manhood getting interested, he released her with a quick kiss on the end of her nose. "I'm going to shower too, I need to get this blood off-"

His lips bunched at Keyleigh's pale face. He murmured, "I'll be back in a minute.

Chapter Fourteen

They shared a quiet dinner with candles, and Járon poured wine for them. They both were silent, deep in their own introspective thoughts.

Something had changed between them, and they were both wary of it, confused by it, and, entranced with it.

He helped her wash up and then went to splint the rabbit's leg.

Keyleigh saw to the other animals. When done, unsure of what to do, she went and sat on the sofa like she normally did. The chain was on the table beside the couch. She stuck her tongue out at it, and heard a chuckle.

"I saw that, *neníta.*" Járon moved towards the couch.

Keyleigh pulled her legs up and crossed them.

Sitting down, he put his hands on her shoulders, and chastised her, "You should still be punished for disobeying me. You see why tis necessary that you do as I tell you, when I tell you?"

"Huh." She stiffened under his hands. "You were just being bossy the other times you told me I had to follow your orders. Today, well," her head tipped back to look up at him as he moved closer to her.

"Today what?" he prompted, pulling her to him.

"Uh," skeptical of his intentions, Keyleigh tried to inch back from him, but he held her.

At first she looked at him, then lowered her head and said, "Well, today you knew something was wrong, and there might be danger, and I should have done what you told me. If I had, then I wouldn't have been-"

A tiny sob broke from her as she recalled the horrifying experience of five murderous rapists holding her down and cutting her clothes off her.

The rogues were laughing, hacking and huffing all over her with liquor and cigarettes, and the stench of un-bathed bodies rough and unshaven.

So many all over her, smothering her with their big bulks, telling her what they were going to do to her, all night.

A violent shudder rifled through her body, she could still feel their hard hands holding her arms pinned to the cold earth, her back damp from the fresh snowfall. They cruelly, painfully groped and squeezed, viciously pinched, deliberately trying to hurt her.

Járon said, "Keyleigh, don't." Seeing the memory of the assault striking the color from her skin, the racking fright in her eyes, he gently squeezed her shoulders to dispel the memory.

Her eyes closed, she couldn't push away the feelings, the images. The thugs had held her completely immobile; she couldn't even struggle. Every time she screamed, the one man slapped her.

Járon had dispatched the men calmly, quietly, effortlessly. Her eyes sick with the grisly picture rolled nervously up to him. He was so strong, and dangerous, and swiftly deadly.

Her eyes quickly lowered, she tried to shift from him. "I could have gotten us both killed, I'm so sorry, Járon. It was...horrid."

Keyleigh looked so woebegone, Járon couldn't help smiling with compassion. He gently kneaded her shoulders. Obviously she wasn't used to seeing men fighting up close and real, or the resulting bloodbath.

She was freaked out seeing the man who has been holding her prisoner on his sofa kill summarily with his bare hands. She had forgotten that he was employed by a government as a skilled assassin.

"Ah, *nenita,* let it go. Tis done, you couldn't have known there was danger in the yard coming to take you."

Now a shudder rushed up his spine at the picture of the men racing away with her on horseback and her screaming his name. And that brought a small hidden smile to his harsh lips. When she was in trouble, it had been his name she'd shouted.

His heavy hard hands on her shoulders reminded her of how easily he broke a grown man's neck, and forced another to stab himself.

Blanching, fearful of seeing the assassin identity back in his dark eyes, she kept her lids down to avoid eye contact, and squirmed from him.

Her returned fear of him apparent in her rigid body and efforts to move away from him, Járon's tenor gentle, he said softly, "They can't hurt you anymore, Keyleigh. And you have nothing to fear from me. Ever."

His hands moved from her shoulders to cradle her face. Lifting it, he said, "I had to do what I did to save you from them." He lowered his head to see into her eyes.

Holding her jaw in his palms, he brushed his thumb over the hollows under her cheeks. Her eyes still reflected her fright of him, the last thing he wanted right now.

"Baby." He leaned in and whispered against her lips, "I swear I would never hurt you."

A butterfly kiss, a tender flutter on her lips, his deep husky murmur against them. "The spanking I gave you, I had to ensure you didn't do something so foolhardy again as to run blindly into the treacherous forest. I didn't really hurt you, did I?" If he had wanted to hurt her she still would be unable to sit on her butt.

With a brief shake of her head, she replied, "No, it was more the humiliation. I don't want you to ever do that to me again." Her voice firm yet breathy, while she spoke, he licked her lips.

"Ah, sweetheart," he responded, his mouth smiled against hers. "Tell me you didn't feel at least a little…let's say, erotic sensation, during it? The slight sting on your bare ass, lying across my lap, my hand on your supple flesh, because," he cupped her face with both hands watching the pink creep into her round cheeks.

"Because, it turned me on so much it was all I could do to not fondle that fine behind, and fuck your pussy, baby, until you screamed in pleasure begging for more."

His fingers tightened around her face as his dick growled at his jeans snarling to be let out. "I wanted to feel that satin skin, savor your sweet juices, stick my fingers inside your-"

She put her hand over his mouth. "Okay, please, stop." So not used to that kind of brazen, crude talk, her cheeks were burning with discomfiture over his erogenous words. But her panties were growing damp.

The long lashes fluttered down. When they rose back up, a worrisome smile went with them. "But you told me you were going to punish me now, how can you do that without hurting me?"

"Hmm." His mouth touched hers, he replied, "I'll think of something." He tugged on her top lip, licked it, sucked on it, then slanted his head and covered her mouth with his.

When she melted against him, a groan rumbling in his chest, he splayed a hand on her slim back to pull her closer.

The kiss deepened. Keeping their mouths fused, Járon gently pushed Keyleigh until she was on her back. Maneuvering his hips between her legs, he nestled his burgeoning erection right on her woman's cleft.

Keyleigh had never been in this position before, it unnerved her, but it was scintillating. It felt…thrilling. His heavy masculinity covering her body made her feel so, female, so womanly.

Aftershave, the strong soap he used, his own virile male scent was inebriating. His manhood long and hard and pressing erotically on her core, generated simmering tingles and pulses from her sex that radiated out, down her legs making them weak. Her stomach muscles pulled in tighter, and oddly, her breasts felt so full they ached…

She wriggled with the uneasiness of inexperience, her hands went to his biceps and she pushed at him.

Járon didn't move his erection, but he braced on one elbow and cupped her face. "I won't hurt you, Keyleigh, I promise. You have to know how badly I want you. You want me to stop you're going to have to say it out loud."

"I-" she didn't know how badly he could want her; she had nothing to compare it to. What he didn't know was that she had zero experience with men.

"What? Talk to me, baby." He caressed her face, kissed her, then lowered his hand to gently cuddle her breast. His thick fingers kneaded her plump flesh, his erection hardened and grew even more, indenting into her rapidly heating sex.

She wondered how much bigger and harder it could possibly get.

Unbuttoning her blouse, Járon murmured, "Keyleigh, talk to me." Sliding his hand into her open blouse, he drew his fingertips lightly over the swells of her breasts, then between them.

His fingers trickled over a nipple, he smiled when her little body shivered beneath him. Squeezing her breast up, forcing it out of the bra, his mouth came down on her exposed nipple.

Under him, Keyleigh whimpered, squirmed, a soft, reticent moan strummed through her throat.

That she wasn't telling him what was troubling her, bothered him, but she was no longer resisting his caresses, and that excited his heart. As well as other things.

His hand cold on her warm, firm plump flesh raised goose bumps up her arms and over her breasts, his mouth wet and vital, biting her puckering nipple gently. He flicked his tongue back and forth over it before sucking it into his mouth.

His mouth full of her flesh he mumbled, "Sweetest little nipples in the world, baby." Encouraged by her trembling and the passionate mewls, he sucked her taut nipple and kneaded both breasts with more vehemence.

Then reaching between them, he unbuckled her belt, unbuttoned, unzipped her pants and pushed them open. Splaying his hand on her belly, feeling it quiver under his tough palm, he moved his hand lower beneath her silk panties.

Fingers reaching down, Járon's moan deepened to a needy growl when his fingers reached the soft folds of her sex. "You're wet baby, so wet, for me." Stroking her slit, when he moved to touch her entrance, she became rigid.

A man had never touched her there before, so intimately. The searing feelings he elicited in her made her apprehensive.

Feeling her lock up, Járon froze. With a fierce exhale in his passion-heavy breath, he shifted off her and pulled her up to sit.

Surprised, Keyleigh blinked, lips parted, a deep blush filled her face.

"Tis Mandrake, isn't it?" he said harshly, dragging a hand through his hair. "You have feelings for him, and you can't, I mean, I understand your loyalty, I just," he trailed off, wiped the back of his hand over his mouth.

He looked at her, but then dropped his eyes, not able to bear seeing her rejection. Lowering his eyes wasn't a great idea. Her blouse was open, breast half out of the bra, a glistening pink nipple called to him, to lathe it, suckle it.

Damn, he shook his head and veered his gaze away. "I, uh, guess we should go." Járon scrubbed his hands down his face.

"No, wait, Járon, listen-" Keyleigh fixed her bra.

Shaking his head, he said, "*Na*, it was wrong of me to even touch you, kiss you, attempt to seduce you. Which I was doing deliberately mind you, when I was fully aware that you belong to another man. When this...mission is over, I have to return you to him, and I...don't fucking want to."

Of course if all goes according to plan, Mandrake will be behind bars. How will she feel towards Járon when he locks up her lover?

His head flopped down, face lowered into his hands, he couldn't abide looking at her.

"Járon, listen to me, dammit." She grabbed the hair on either side of his head and lifted it then got in his face. "I need to tell you about...Mr. Mandrake."

Now her voice disappeared, the fear of what could happen if anyone knew the truth constricted her throat, she could hardly swallow.

"*Mr.* Mandrake?" He snorted with anger, jealousy, frustration. "That's a funny way to call your lover."

Buttoning her blouse, Keyleigh pulled her legs up to sit cross-legged and face him. "Járon, if I tell you something, I need for you to...promise you won't tell anyone who I am, or that I am here."

"I don't understand." Voice stiff with umbrage, he glanced at her then cast his gaze away. Every time he looked at her the overwhelming urge to push her back down and tear her clothes off consumed him.

The misgivings of telling him what happened clinging to her small voice, very quietly she murmured, "I'm in danger."

Now he regarded her. She looked so...afraid. He knew he shouldn't touch her, it was like starting a wildfire again in him, but he grasped her shoulders.

"Tell me, Keyleigh, just fucking spit it out, tell me everything. You've got to know by now that you can trust me. You are very well aware I had no reason to keep you alive when I first found you on my property."

His lip tugged in sardonically at her gasp. "Or at the very least take you to the police since I would never harm a woman. But I did neither. Although I suspected you could be a threat to our mission, I still kept you here, safe, with me.

I could have let those sick fuckers that abducted you, keep you, but," he nudged her shoulders to make her look at him.

When she did, he said, "I would give my life for you, Keyleigh. I would have fought them to my last breath."

A grave inhalation expanding his chest, he said tersely, "Now, tell me, *nenita,* trust me." Járon had to watch his strength, not grip her shoulders so slight under his big hands too tightly in his angst. So intense was his desire for her to open up to him.

Keyleigh shifted away from him and he dropped his hands. She lifted her long curls and shoved them back over her shoulders, then fixed her pants, not seeing his lips thin as she closed herself back up from him.

"I," she paused. Taking a deep breath, she started again, "I told you before, that my father is Ambassador to Alger la Blanche. I was at a fundraising party with my brother. The political powers liked to have family present at these things, made everyone seem more warm and fuzzy.

"Our parents had to be at a different event so we were there without them. Anyway, I had completed just two semesters of college when I was at this party. Mr. Mandrake was there apparently briefly. I never saw him, but he saw me. I didn't make it home that night."

"*Da*, sweetheart," Járon said bitterly. "You don't have to tell me how quickly a man can become smitten with you. So you went home with him, and," he dragged an angry hand through his hair again, face darkened, "fell in love. I just don't understand why you were in the woods injured and starved."

"Stop and listen to me, Járon," she said, then leaned in and kissed him.

He scowled. "Keyleigh, seriously, I'm hanging by a thread here. I should get away from you, get the hell out of the house, but," he sighed, staring at her lips. "I just can't make myself leave you. Stupid, huh? So much for being the big tough guy."

When she started to speak he said, "Just don't freaking kiss me again, you belong to another man, that's not fair to him or me."

The topaz eyes rolled, she blared, "Would you shut up and let me talk!"

Facing her, he leaned his back against the back of the sofa cushions and mimed locking his lips.

"Fine. Now. What happened was, I was kidnapped from the party, and-"

"What?" He shot forward. "What the hell-"

"Járon, please." She waited for him to settle back with a frustrated grunt before speaking.

"Mr. Mandrake, apparently took a shine to me, and that he's a total stranger and like twenty or so years older than me, he must have correctly assumed if he asked me nicely I wouldn't have gone with him. So," she had to swallow down the nauseating fear thinking about it.

"Mr. Mandrake was flying out to somewhere, his country I think, that night, so he had his men take me. When I came out of the ladies room, they grabbed me, put uh, a cloth with chloroform I think over my mouth. The next thing I knew, I woke up tied in a bed. For some reason, you men like to bind me."

His head dipped abashed that he had treated her the same as Mandrake had. Except he hadn't restrained her in his bed. But now the image floated through his mind of her naked, spread eagle, wrists and ankles-

"So," she continued, her sigh grim. "During my more lucid moments, I remember a woman helping me occasionally to go to the bathroom, shower, and gave me water, but no food. She had muttered something about if I'm starving I'll be less likely, too weak to try to escape. She kept me drugged."

Brows down in a scowl of remembrance, her hand went to her face. "Someone must have…hit me. I don't remember it, there were bruises, red marks on my face. Maybe I tried a time or two to run and was," her eyes angled up to him, "punished for it."

"Baby," he groaned. Taking her hand, he couldn't believe what she was telling him.

"Anyway, they were keeping me on ice until Mr. Mandrake returned. Supposedly his plan was to do whatever it was he was here for, then take me and flee back to his own country. They told me that he could hide me away, no one from home would ever know where I was, they couldn't come and get me."

"Damn, Keyleigh." Járon took a gentle hold of her hand. "I can't believe the fucking balls of that man."

"Yeah," Keyleigh agreed.

"Apparently those that were holding you blabbed to people about the gorgeous young thing in Mandrake's life. There was a description of you, but no name. Everyone, I," he looked sheepish, "assumed you were his new squeeze. That's why I thought he'd sent you to spy on me."

The side of her mouth nicked up dryly. "Nice. Anyway," her head cocked with a sly grin, she said, "one night they hadn't tied me tight enough, you would know about that," she smiled at his guilty expression.

"Much of the drug had worn off and it was a bit before they would come to administer more. I managed to get loose and climbed out a window. The outside of the house was made of bricks, thankfully fairly uneven bricks because I was on the second floor.

"I did the old tie a sheet to the bed trick, and climbed out the window, but there were only two sheets and they only went so far. I used some of the bricks to get down further, but then, lost my grip and fell. I was hurt, but I managed to get to my feet and run to the woods."

"*Da*, you like doing that you little minx." His smile lopsided, he pet her hand while she spoke. The smile hardened with angry sadness. "I hate that you were so hurt, my small *nenita*. And I only added to it."

Her smile soft at the marked grief on his harsh face, she said softly, "You took care of me, Járon, fixed my wounds and fed me. Well, gave me ham sandwiches until I was able to cook for us."

At his grin, she said, "Anyway, I ran and ran, eventually I came across a small ranch and there were horses saddled. It looked like a bunch of people were going for a ride but weren't gathered there yet, and the man saddling the horses left to go to the barn.

"I swear I don't know how I did it, but I climbed a fence near a horse and was able to get on, then I just hung on for dear life because the horse was not happy I did that. He took off.

"I think he was a he, anyway, time went odd after that. I was so hungry, delirious half the time, I ate berries and stuff, and slept in barns. Between my injuries and being starved half to death I was barely conscious."

"But, Keyleigh, why didn't you just get help at the barn where the horses were? They could have called the police, your family."

"Yeah, don't think I didn't consider it. But, not only was I not sure who I could trust, I mean they could have been friends of Mr. Mandrake or something. But more so, after I had been captured, one of his men came to talk to me.

"Before he gave me drugs to keep me unconscious, he told me why they had taken me, and that if I told anyone or tried to get help they would kill my family. He rattled off my brother's address and my parents', I," she swallowed her tears in a bundle of renewed fear for her family.

"Someone told my brother a lie that I met someone from school the night of the party and left with them so he wouldn't raise a ruckus when he couldn't find me later. So you see, I couldn't tell anyone. And if you do," she leaned forward, eyes wide pleading.

"Please, Járon, please don't tell anyone. He will come for me and he will hurt my family. Please, promise me-"

"Keyleigh, your parents must know by now you are missing, they will be searching for you, surely tis safe to go home now-"

"No." She shook her head fervently. "I mean yes, they will be worried to death. But, they won't have any idea it was Mr. Mandrake that took me, and his threat will hold that if I go home, tell them about his actions, he will have them murdered. Please, promise me you won't tell *anyone*!"

Chapter Fifteen

Járon slid his big hand under her delicate chin. "Ah, *na* worries there, my precious. The mission my brothers and I are on is to protect a diplomat from another country that is coming here to visit his son and also he hopes, to be elected Prime Dictator of his country.

"Their plan was to do the counting of the votes while the diplomat was here during the election, and where he'd be relatively safer than he would be in his own country at this time." He stroked his hand down her arm to set it on her thigh.

"Uh huh," Keyleigh nodded. "But what has that to do with Mr. Mandrake?"

"The reason Mandrake is here in the first place and rented a house, is because he plans to assassinate the diplomat while he doesn't have his full entourage of security with him.

Her lashes flew up over wide eyes.

Járon explained, "Tis all political. Anastas Porth is Mandrake's rival for the election for Prime Dictator of their country. The politics is none of my concern, but, as I said, my job is to prevent Mandrake from murdering Porth, and my orders were clear, killing Mandrake would be 100% approved. There would be no diplomatic immunity as he would be considered a terrorist.

"Plus he would be attempting to assassinate the candidate to be elected the head of his own country, and they would not abide that. His country came to our government with their fears and theories and asked for assistance.

"So far they only have underground rumors of the attempt at murder. But, the people that have initiated the idea of the scheme are credible witnesses."

Her forehead wrinkled in concentration, Keyleigh asked, "But why would they suspect Mr. Mandrake of anything so insidious in the first place? Aren't these politicians relatively squeaky clean to have gotten so far where they have in the election?"

He nodded in agreement. "*Yah*, generally. However, we're talking about a country that is not America. And, Mandrake has a shady past with other mysterious deaths in his wake. Coincidentally, the other candidates vying for the position have either disappeared, suffered fatal injuries or been consumed by some sudden shocking scandal.

"Most of the scandals were either clear set ups or pure innuendo, but in such a serious election even the hint of scandal knocks the opponent right out of the running. So far, Mandrake has managed to sidestep any real suspicion of wrong doing.

"He hires others to do his dirty work so nothing can be traced back to him. If they are caught, they themselves inexplicably die or disappear before they can be interrogated."

Járon paused and studied Keyleigh to see what she was thinking of the entire affair.

Her brows were daggered down as she listened and worked to comprehend what he was telling her. Surprise, confusion, and anger all stitched across her lovely face.

He said, "I had no plans one way or the other to waste the guy unless I had to, but now," he shook his head eyes simmering in the red haze of vengeance.

The fucker had kidnapped Keyleigh and was going to keep her, assault her. Járon felt his skin heat with guilt, pretty much the same as what he had done. He found the parallels between himself and Mandrake disturbing.

"No, please, Járon, don't go after him because of me, please," her blues rounded in sudden fear.

"Keyleigh, there is-"

"He could kill you if you try! Oh my gosh, now I've made it a bigger more horrible thing. I shouldn't have told you," she lowered her head and covered her eyes with her hands to staunch the tears.

"*Na*, Keyleigh-"

"I should just," she shook her head resigned to her fate. "I will return to him, it's the only way."

"Ah, *na*, sweet, *na* damned way, baby. None of this is your fault. It was pure coincidence that led you to my land. Now that I know the truth of that bastard I would never let you go back to him. You aren't leaving this house. I will keep you safe, I promise. As far as Mandrake is concerned, I will do what I have to do. C'mere."

He rolled an arm around her and pulled her against his chest. "Thank God you are not in a relationship with that fucker, uh, sorry, scumbag."

Tipping her head up so their eyes could connect, his fingertips touched lightly under her chin. With a casual hope, he said, "Circumstances have brought us together. Now that we know each other's truths, what then, Keyleigh, what are our chances of...a relationship? I mean you and me together?"

Letting down her guard, now that she had her secret burden off her chest, Járon distracted her with his question. She snuggled into his strong, protective warmth, asked with a small yawn, "What do you mean by relationship?"

Tightening his arms around her, he stroked his hand from her shoulder down her back. "Well, this was my dilemma..." his hand curled under her jaw turning her face up.

His fingers gently stretching around her throat and neck, now that she said she wasn't any part of Mandrake, he could drink his fill of looking at her, allow his feelings and desire seep through his body without slamming a lid on them. He hoped.

"I, ah, had thought, planned, that when my mission was over, ah," feeling the unique burn of a blush on his cheeks, his voice roughened.

"I wasn't going to take you to Mandrake. Well, if he survives, he'll be in custody. But, ah, before I let you go, I was going to try to win you over. I want you with me, Keyleigh, permanently, forever. What do you think?"

The minute he'd found the beauty clinging to the horse in his woods, Járon had plotted in the back of his mind how to keep her by his side. Even thinking she was Mandrake's whore, Járon could not deny his overwhelming desire for her.

As time went on and they spent days together, he no longer cared that Mandrake had had her first. The physical craving he'd felt for Keyleigh had morphed into a keen feeling for the woman herself.

Fiery brows shot up. Stunned, she had not expected that. "I- I-" she had no idea what to say.

Both arms around her, he said gently, "Tis okay, *nenita,* no pressure."

His deep masculine voice low, he made a leisurely swipe at her lips with his. "But, I will ask you, can we work on it? I mean, you and me, together? Hell, tis as much a shock to me as to you. Okay, maybe more for you, I've had time to wrap my head around it."

Eyes wide as blue pancakes, her lips parted, yes, she was in shock.

His mouth twitched. After the kisses they'd shared, the meals, the camaraderie, the gifts he's bought her, really, she should have at least a clue.

But then, he reminded himself of her youth, her clear inexperience with men. He felt some guilt over his even suggesting a relationship with him.

"You're so sweet and tender, fresh; I'm a cold murdering bastard, Keyleigh. I can understand you saying *na.* Hell, I've kept you here against your will, for fuck's sake. Hurt you, called you foul names, and forced myself on you. It was all right what I did, for my job and my safety, but it was all wrong too."

He forked furrows of frustration through the top of his hair with unnerved fingers. He wanted to convince her and all he was doing was telling her why she shouldn't give him a chance.

Járon didn't dare bring up the spanking incident, she'd be out the door so fast, no woman wants to be punished, abused, bullied.

Keyleigh remained silent. Wariness and confusion were in the indentation in her forehead, insecurity in the clear vivacity of her eyes.

Járon said, "I'll take it as slow as you need, I just," he drew a long breath. "I've never been in this situation before, wanting a woman by my side, forever."

There were plenty of women who had offered that to him over his lifetime, but this one, she was going to be a challenge.

Although at the back of his mind, he had been planning all along how to keep her, still, he even surprised himself when he asked the question out loud.

Yet, just the thought of her leaving him had thrust the words right out of his mouth.

Seeing her downcast eyes, his words came out laced with irony, "It figures, I have to choose the one woman in the world who doesn't want me. But," his sigh deep, he said, "I understand, Keyleigh." However, he didn't say it with resignation. He had no intentions of giving her up.

"No, Járon, that's not true. I…" Her smile shy, she said softly, "I like you. A lot. Like you said about me, it's…unexpected. You are a tough…mercenary or whatever you are, and it scares the heck out of me. But," her shoulder lifted in a small shrug.

"I enjoy your company, and I see how kind and caring you are with the animals. You have risked your life to save mine. Even though you have treated me…pretty uh, boorishly," at his gloomy nod she patted his hand.

Keyleigh continued, "I do understand that your kind of life, the way you were brought up. I heard bits and pieces of you and your brothers' conversation about your," she paused at his grim expression, "uh, childhood. You didn't learn how to treat women respectfully, but I see you changing, or trying to anyway, and I see your remorse for the coarseness you exhibited with me."

Her sigh drowsy and happy as he drifted one finger down her arm, she said, "Now I feel safe, protected when I'm with you."

His brows slanted down in a slight frown. "*Da*, that's all lovely," he said somewhat dismissively. Then he said matter-of-fact, "You should feel safe with me. I would never let anything, anyone hurt you. I am trained to take out an army."

And he had exhibited that swift, skilled, violent ruthlessness when he easily and quickly, with very little motion, took out those men in the woods.

"But what about me as…a man? Those things you said aren't personal things between you and me. I mean like physical attraction."

The blush that pinked her cheeks emboldened him to go on.

"Like, baby, since the day I pulled you off that horse, tis all I can do to keep my hands off you, and I mean all the time, every second of every day. How do you feel, um, in that respect, about me?"

His stomach twisted in anxiety. Hell, he'd never felt anxiety in his whole life since witnessing his parents' gruesome murders. But, she just gazed at him with those big blues, as if taking toll of him.

Járon couldn't believe this gorgeous, tiny little woman, the most feminine, graceful creature he'd ever met, turned his stomach inside out.

She was smart and witty and funny, for once he really enjoyed conversing with a woman, spending time with her. So much so that he dreaded the thought of her not being with him. He wanted her in his bed at night, and be able to gaze upon her sweet face every morning.

Normally, he'd take one look at a delicate little thing like her and fear he was too tough of a man, too rough for her, that he'd break her like a china doll in Godzilla's hands. Too crass, too crude, she deserved a gentleman, a nice guy, and that he certainly was not.

But, he sighed while he waited for her response, he was so drawn to her it was like he was the tide and she was the shore, and the moon was out and full and beckoning.

"Keyleigh," he grew uncomfortable at her not answering, "be straight with me, I don't ever want falseness between us, ever, even if tis painful."

He ducked his head. "And I'm thinking what you're going to say is going to be…painful." His lips pulled in, his gut sinking further the longer she was quiet.

What could he do if she chose to leave him? Would he have the temerity to still hold her against her will while he upped his seduction game?

Just because Keyleigh was young and inexperienced, Járon knew he could bring her around. A more worldly woman would not be so easily led. And, she was so responsive to his touch, he knew if he had the time he could make her his. But will he have that time? What will he do if she fights him to leave?

Keyleigh crossed her arms and rubbed her upper arms with her hands, lips crooked with shy disconcertment. "Um, I," cheeks already stained pink darkened. "I find you very handsome, Járon."

She smiled at his short bashful grin. "You're big, intimidating, formidable, and yes, tough as nails, but," her gaze fell with embarrassment. "I like being with you, touching you, and when you touch me-" she broke off and looked away.

"When I touch you," he prodded her to continue.

157

"It feels, good. Your touch makes me feel, good. And," cheeks turned from pink to crimson, she said, "uh, kind of sizzly, you know, down there." Her lips pulled in and she stared down at her feet not seeing his huge grin.

He found her embarrassment, and lack of sophisticated sexuality compelling, wholly alluring. And adorable. Now there's a word Járon never knew was even in his vocabulary.

"But," her eyes rose to his, she said, "I just, don't know. How can I stay with…a man who held me captive, kept me chained? How can I reconcile being kidnapped and held prisoner by Mr. Mandrake, then you basically did the same thing?"

"*Da*, I know." His eyes reflected his ambiguity over his actions. He had solid reasons why he took her from the woods and kept her, she could have been a part of, or a danger to his mission.

Járon sighed. He had fought it every way he could, mostly by being an asshole to her, but he'd known deep down, he'd wanted her the second he'd pulled her off the horse and into his arms.

"You're right, but, Keyleigh, Mandrake was going to keep you as his sex slave, I…" he broke off knowing he was on the edge of doing the same thing if she said no to him. He wasn't a nice man either, he should send her away, from him, except, he knew he couldn't.

Listening to him, watching the marbling of emotions that passed over his normally implacable face, she said, "The work you do, Járon… it's just, crazy, I don't know if I can give my heart and soul to a- an assassin."

Nodding ruefully, he told her, "Honey, tis true that is what I was bred and trained for. However, most of the jobs my brothers and I do are like this current one. We are sent to protect someone, or extricate someone in danger in a foreign country, we do a lot of rescue work.

"We don't run around willy-nilly slaughtering people, and certainly never innocent people, or women or children. We mostly rescue, that's why I will see to it that you will never have to fear anything, or anyone ever again in your life.

"Instead of going out on the front lines for every mission, I can spend more of my time doing the research and investigating if that's what you would want. Just give me the chance to win you over. A shot is all I ask."

Keyleigh studied his face, demeanor, timber of his low voice. This icy killing machine was willing to tone down his life's work, for her. She didn't know what to say.

She was drawn to him; there was no doubt about that, and the thought now of leaving him made her stomach pitch. But what if all it was on her part was that she desired him like a Stockholm kind of thing, or now, as her hero for rescuing her from those men?

How could she sort out her feelings if she was with him, she needed to be apart to figure it out.

She looked up at his hard face, rugged with strength and harshness, yet his lips and eyes were soft and earnest, waiting for her response. The thought of not being with him made her feel empty inside.

He stood up. "Let's give it time, give you time, sweetheart. Let's go to bed and take each day one at a time, okay?" Then he bent and scooped her up in his arms.

Not until he was traipsing down the hall did she say, "Where are we going? The sofa-"

159

"I'm putting you where you should have been from the start, my *neníta.*" He carried her to his bedroom and set her down to sit on the edge of the bed.

Keyleigh looked up at him, trembles of uncertainty in her voice, she asked, "Are we…you know, going to have, uh…sex?"

Her shy nervousness was so fucking endearing he couldn't stand it. Shaking his head, he said, "*Na*, sweetheart, you aren't ready. You will sleep here, the other bedrooms aren't furnished. I will be on the couch."

"No, don't be ridiculous, Járon," she insisted and went to get up. "You won't be comfortable on the couch, you're too big. I'm just fine there."

He put his hand on her shoulder to hold her down. "*Na*, as you just saw a few minutes ago, I can fit just fine on that big couch, and quite nicely too with you under me." His mouth turned up at the sweet blush that brushed across her high cheekbones.

"Wait, Járon," her voice even shyer. "I want you here, with me. Maybe not making love…yet," her blushing smile increased. "But can't you sleep with me here, in your bed? Please?"

His head was already shaking. "*Na*, I can't lie beside you like that and not," she was looking up at him so pretty, so appealing, he rubbed his eyes.

She said, "Járon, I'm scared. It was, I mean," her arms around her body didn't hold in the shiver. "I'm afraid they're going to come back and- finish the job."

"Oh, Keyleigh, honey, those men are dead. Trust me, they won't be coming back."

"I know, but that one got away. I don't want to be alone."

His exhale did not take away any of the tension of what she was asking him to do. Damn, who was he kidding? He could refuse her nothing.

"Okay. But, seriously, you want us to sleep together and not fuck, sorry, make love, we need to stay dressed or there's no way I won't be all over that hot little body."

Her grin big and contagious, she said, "Okay." She pulled back the sheet and climbed in. After settling, she waited for him to follow.

Standing still, he contemplated how strong his control was. It was steel with everything else, but not with this petite little fox.

"Ahh," Járon groaned as he sat down on the mattress. He looked at Keyleigh.

She was smiling that shy little smile up at him. Like she had zero reservations that she could trust him.

His sigh laborious, he slid in to lie down beside her. Then pulled the blankets over them both.

There was silence for a minute as they both lay awkward, but oddly comfortable.

Járon said, "I can't lie here and have you so close and not touch you. I need to hold you, sweetheart, c'mere."

He looped his arm around her and pulled her back into his chest, his knees curved behind hers, his hand tucked over her waist.

It felt perfect to him. He wanted this for the rest of his life. He needed to convince her she wanted it too.

Without letting her loose first to her family. No doubt seeing the differences in the couple, her parents would try hard to keep them apart, horrified that their innocent little girl was in the clutches of a hardcore, paid assassin.

They would be right, but, he sighed again, pulling her closer. Tucking his nose in her hair, he'd tried to fight it and couldn't. It was all up to her now.

The only good thing about all his sexual experience, cold and rough though it was, after their episode on the couch earlier, he knew he could seduce her.

Maybe that was wrong, but, he yawned, all is fair in love and war. Right

Chapter Sixteen

"Uh, Boss," Warren shuffled his muscled bulk through the open door of the den.

Several men sprawled around the lavish room on luxurious divans and cushioned chairs, smoking cigars, each held a drink in his hand. The conversation halted, they all looked to Warren.

Except for the boss-man. As usual, Maximillion Mandrake was staring at his reflection in the gold-framed mirror.

Most of the fixtures in the lavish room were edged with gold. The paintings, lamp sconces, glass cabinets, the bar set off to the side of the room, the round antique doorknobs, even the ornate furniture was embossed with gold studs.

Facing the baroque mirror, Mandrake's eyes flicked to Warren then down to the crystal glass filled with rich cognac he cradled in his hand.

One hand tucked in his trouser pocket with the suit jacket draped behind his wrist, Mandrake lifted the snifter and took a genteel sip before lowering the glass to his side.

Holding the snifter with his fingertips, he tilted it back and forth, watching the amber liquid slightly slosh in the glass.

Warren watched him anxiously. He'd only needed one warning to learn not to speak to the boss unless he asked you a question or directly gave you permission to talk. Warren's head still ached when it rained from the crack in the skull he'd earned when speaking out of turn.

Mandrake said, "You have word of her?"

The thick head nodded. Warren scratched the light brown buzz-cut with a couple of wide fingers topped with dirty nails. He didn't say anything else.

Mandrake snapped, "Well? What did you find out?"

Blinking thick lids, Warren answered, "Yuh. Chester and Sasha just happened to be in the right place at the right time and heard someone give a description of her. She has that uh, what d'ya call it, eunuch looks?"

"Huh," Mandrake snorted. Lips rising at the corners exposing abnormally sharp canines, he said, "Unique, Warren. The word is unique. And, yes, the girl is the epitome of unique.

Mandrake's head tilted back as he drained the glass. Eyes closed in elation, the deviant smile broadened. He asked, "Where?"

A slick smile lifted Warren's dull face. Suddenly he was important to the boss. He replied smugly, "Tucked away, hidden the little bitch is, but closer than you would think." He scratched under an armpit, then seeing Mandrake's look of disgust, he stuck his hand inside the top of his pants.

Pockmarks pitted his ruddy skin. Unfortunately, Warren was one of those big beefy men that turned even uglier when he smiled.

Probably because it wasn't a nice smile, not a smile of friendliness or mirth. No, it was usually a mean smile because he was either watching someone get hurt, or he was hurting someone. Or anticipating hurting someone.

"I done good, eh, Boss?" he asked eagerly. Now on the boss' good side, forgetting Mandrake's repugnance, he resumed scratching his armpit.

Mandrake finally turned and appraised his repulsive henchman with an ominously pleased visage. "About goddamned time you earned your coin."

Turning back to the mirror, his handsome grin wide, he ordered, "Get a team together and go get her. Kill anyone who gets in your way."

Now those were words that made Warren smile. And he did. Broadly and eagerly. Which only made the ugly man look nastier when he exposed broken and rotting teeth that had large separations between them. At least those that he still retained.

"Yessir!" Warren crowed gleefully. He waited for some sort of praise for bringing the news the boss wanted to hear. But Mandrake had moved his gaze from the mirror to stare ponderously out the window.

Finally, Mandrake gloated to himself. That little bitch would soon be back in his grasp. In his bed. And she would learn a very long, very painful lesson about trying to escape from him.

He'd planned a gilded cage for her. But now? After humiliating him, and running away before he got a taste of her? Keyleigh St. James' cage would be made up of cold steel, lashing whips, and a lot of anguished tears. That woman was going to pay for her actions with her torn and bleeding flesh.

Perhaps even a broken bone or two as a reminder of who owns her.

165

Oh yeah, he was going to enjoy teaching her a lesson. Make that many, torturous lessons.

And while he was doling out her punishments, he would be sating his appetite on her lily-white young skin.

Oh, yeah.

Chapter Seventeen

"**M**mm," Keyleigh felt so delicious she purred in her sleep. Under her was soft, cushiony, and what was partially on the top of her, was hard, heavy, but felt so good, smelled, manly.

She couldn't help squirming; she just had to get more of that feel good stuff. Strangely, her breasts felt clamped, clutched, molded and massaged. Her sensitive nipples pinched, plucked, making her yearn for more.

Moaning, "*Uhh*," her back arched, pushing her body into whatever was on her, caressing her.

Still in the obscure world between sleep and awake, she felt something coarse touch her face, her lips, when she moaned, his tongue slipped in to claim hers.

His night's beard rasping her face, he unlatched his kneading hands from her breasts, and pushed the covers down to cup the tenderness suddenly burning between her legs.

"Open your legs for me, my sweet Keyleigh," Járon whispered against her mouth. He had undone her pants as she slept and pushed them down a little, enough he could get his big hand inside them and trickle his fingers over her panties. He nudged her thighs apart with his knee.

They had each gotten up at different times in the late night to use the bathroom and brush their teeth, thank God, his breath was warm and minty.

Her lashes fluttered, lids split, a glimmer of topaz flickered out. Her sultry smile so intoxicating it clenched both his heart and his groin.

Járon moved his face back a few inches so she would know it was him and not be frightened waking in a strange bed with a man climbing all over her.

Her legs squiggled and her arms rose over her head in a luxurious stretch.

"Ah, *nenita,* here I was working so hard on my restraint, and you curl back like a sinful kitten, hell woman."

His growl rattled into her throat as his mouth came back down on hers harder than before, his hunger on the prowl, already unbridling was magnifying exponentially in all directions.

Shifting lower in the bed, he pushed her blouse up, unhooked her bra, pushed it up and sucked in a nipple like he'd been hot and thirsty and it was an ice cube floating in sweet iced tea.

Bracing on one elbow, he gripped a breast and suckled, harder than he meant to, but, she tasted so decadent groans roiled from his chest, deep and ravenous.

Awakening slowly, inch by sumptuous inch, sprawling in the soft sheets, still hazy, Keyleigh murmured, "Járon? What, uhh…"

His teeth nipped harder, her body lifted to his mouth that was doing glorious things to her swelling breasts and throbbing nipples.

"*Da*," he chuckled. "Were you expecting someone else in *my* bed?" He left her breast to kiss her, and reached back down between her legs. Her heat burned right through the silk panties making him groan with desire.

Keyleigh's mouth opened to his, she accepted his tongue with a roused whimper. Her hips snaking up to get more of his fingers into action, "More," she groaned, surprising both of them.

"Sweetheart," Járon murmured, thrilled at her response he obliged her.

He pulled her jeans down and tugged them and her socks off. When her knees came up in instinctive protection, he pushed them back down and slid his calloused hand over her panties.

Stroking her slit through the silk with his big fingers, he was rewarded with her soft cry and undulating hips.

"Keyleigh, baby," he said quietly as he rubbed circles over her clit with his thumb and thrilled at her slender hips reaching, rotating to get more.

Delicious hums effervesced delightfully from her parted lips. Her palms splayed on his chest, fingers closing, gripping his shirt.

Her body splayed and writhed on the mattress so wantonly, Járon's groin begged him to finish the deed, and finish it now, fast, hard, unrelenting.

Voice husky with desire, he warned her, "If you want me to stop, you need to say so right now. I'm afraid I've allowed myself to go too far, and in a short, *very* short time, I will be unable to cease even if you ask."

Only sighing moans of pleasure and short cutting gasps at his fingers' manipulating her woman's flesh reached his ears.

Lying beside her on his side, Keyleigh on her back, Járon pushed her thighs further apart, settled his lips on hers. Reaching down inside her panties, he stroked his fingers down her slit, and slowly dipped his finger just slightly inside her.

A groan dragged out of his throat and his shaft went from iron to steel when her silk poured into his palm.

He said thickly, "Keyleigh? Do you want to make love, with me...right now?"

His penis strained like a hawk trapped in a cage wanting out at the fluttering finch, needing release, screaming to be inside Keyleigh.

"Yes, Járon," she said and suddenly rolled onto her knees.

"Huh?" He sat up slowly, puzzled at her movement. "Yes what?"

She announced, "I'm ready. What about our clothes, aren't we supposed to," her gaze fell to the hard bulge in his jeans, "um, take them off? Are you going to just...put it in?"

His lip quirking at her naiveté, he followed her, climbing to his knees. Drawing his rough hand down the side of her soft face, he whispered in awe, "God, Keyleigh, you are so sweet, so beautiful, I can't remember my life before you."

Her eyes lowered reticently. "That's...nice of you to say, Járon." She cocked her head and said shyly, "I- I'm not sure how to do this."

Smiling, he said, "*Da*, we take our clothes off, but, not yet, for me. I'm too, on the brink. We need to get you there, make you ready. Don't worry, I will take care of everything, of you. You only need to relax, trust me, and enjoy."

She sat back on her heels, confusion on her face. "The brink? Of what?"

His laugh burst out. "Keyleigh, you are so, green. I can't wait to make you mine."

White flames of scorching desire flickered in his dark eyes dipping to her full breasts swelling half exposed under her raised shirt. His gaze strolled down to the tiny swath of pink silk that barely covered her lady parts that he knew were hot and wet.

Her brows pulled down in a frown. "I told you that I was extremely sheltered. I was seldom allowed to be around other people. My parents feared so much someone would harm or kidnap one of us.

"Our tutor taught us, math, science, reading, all regular stuff, but that was all, we had no," her cheeks pinked, "you know, sex education. And our books and television time were severely limited and monitored."

"Baby," he crooned, his hand on the side of her face, he nipped at her lips. "I wasn't making fun of you. I was thinking how much I can't wait to teach you, make you mine. Only mine. Let's start your first lesson."

He caught the hem of her blouse and lifted it. She raised her arms and he pulled it off her and tossed it to the floor, then drew her bra off and it joined the blouse.

Groans of euphoria rustled deep in his thick chest, the flames in his eyes spiked as he beheld her beauty.

"Damn, Keyleigh," he said with appreciation, "you have the most spectacular tits I've ever seen, and I have to add, tasted and felt." If his eyes were lasers her chest would be burnt to a crisp.

"I'd rather not hear about other breasts you've seen," she said with a frown, then pinched one of his nipples over his shirt as a rebuke.

"Hey," he squawked with a laugh, his hand went to cover his nipple.

Járon offered her a tender smile. "Baby, trust me, I have no thoughts of anyone ever before you, and never will again. I just want to gobble you up, then put you on a pedestal and honor you the rest of my life. Except when I take you down to gobble you some more." His lips curved up in a wolfish grin.

"Gee, how…interesting. You would take me down to-gobble me?"

Grinning at her, he said, "Of course I would have to take you down from your pedestal to fuck you, then I would put you back up every time."

He laughed at her brow braided, not sure how to take his teasing.

Járon said with snicker, "You'd get dizzy going up and down that pedestal all day, and night, long."

Her eyes popped in speculation.

He said quickly, "First lesson, my sweet," his gaze went from her trusting blues to her bare breasts. His tongue circled his lips he explained, "Tis that men are generally instantly ready, women need more," he palmed her breasts and moaned at the sheer soft, suppleness of them in his big hard hands.

Keyleigh's back arched, pressing her full flesh tighter into his grip, "More what?" she whispered.

"More of this," he fondled her breasts, tweaked at her nipples until they were hard peaks and her body swooned.

"Stay just like that," he ordered sliding off the bed. Standing beside the bed, he stared at Keyleigh like she was melting ice cream he needed to slurp up quickly.

On her knees, sitting back on her heels, her legs spread slightly, she was wearing only a tiny pair of pink silk panties.

Her hands set on her thighs, hair a fiery curl down her back, her beautiful plump breasts, high and firm, and round and tipped with the most suckable nipples. A bewildered look covered her lovely soft face.

Reaching back over his shoulder, Járon grabbed his shirt, dragged it over his head and let it fall. Then he quickly removed his socks, belt, and undid the top button of his jeans.

He went to his dresser, opened it, took out a condom and returned to the bed, setting the condom on the table beside the bed.

"Járon," her eyes wide at his bared chest, her mouth dropped. She said with fascination, "You are so, strong, muscular, with big wide shoulders and such a powerful chest. Can I touch the hair on your chest?" she asked shyly.

"Ah, Keyleigh, baby, you can touch anything you want, anytime you want."

He moved to get back on the bed with her. The thick mattress barely shifted from his weight.

When her dainty hands buried into the dark matting on his chest, he about went over the cliff.

Hell, he'd had more than his share of women touching his chest, but this, her, so soft and shy. Her small hands exploring his rocky pecs, little feminine fingers sifting through his hair, fingertips grazing his nipples. Her pretty eyes intent on discovering everything about his body, damn he loved this girl.

That thought should have been like a bucket of ice water over his head, but, it wasn't. He decided he would shelve that errant thought to contemplate later when his loins weren't broiling and he could string a full sentence together.

His timbre low, he murmured, "I said women need more, tis true, but, we males never get enough of looking and touching, licking and sucking the female body, and yours, my sweet, is the best of the best."

Brows down between her eyes, Keyleigh reminded him, "Járon, no more talk of other women, remember?"

His lips ticked up. "Honey, there is not a shred of any other woman in my mind. There is no room for anyone else in there, you fill it completely."

Járon's smile wry, he clarified, "Tis just, I'm trying to tell you how I feel about you." He shrugged. "You know what an unromantic crude bastard I am, I keep saying the wrong thing."

Blue eyes twinkled at him, her smile soft and warm, Keyleigh responded, "You are very romantic, Járon, just in different ways. You bring me things I barely even mention, every time I turn around there's something new in the kitchen, on the coffee table.

"You help me rescue the injured animals because you know it's what I want. And," she petted his rugged face, "there is nothing more romantic in the whole wide world than a man that throws his life on the line to rescue me."

He ducked his head at the praise. Járon wasn't used to hearing compliments, especially from women. And, the word romantic had never been used in relation to him. He would have shoved his fist in anyone's jaw that tried it.

Her eyes twinkling with mischief, Keyleigh said with a saucy note, "Now, I want to see how spectacular *your* body is." Using his words, she said with a grin, "Already what I see it's the best of the best."

She was still sitting back on her heels and studying his body.

While she was feeling the differences between him and her, caressing his shoulders, his biceps, he tugged her panties down and took thcm off hcr.

Nudging her knees further apart, he cupped her woman's mound and felt its warmth, her heat, the silk of her desire spreading over his palm. With a yielding moan, her hips thrust into his hand.

Járon grasped a breast, clutching it harder as his lust built to raging desire, then he lifted her up to her knees.

Sighing with aroused sensation, "Ahh, Járon," Keyleigh dug her fingers into his hair, scraped across his scalp to grip inky black locks in her hands.

When his fingers stroked her sex, scissored her soft folds, and pressed her tender swelling bud with the pad of his thumb, a sweet gasp hitched up her chest. She flattened her bosom against his hard chest.

Carefully, he pushed a finger up, slowly inside her. Letting her silk cover his finger, then he paused.

"Baby," his voice held a hint of worry.

"Hmm?" Her hips pushed back at his finger urging him to go deeper.

"You, ah, you're too tight, too small…" A brow arched in surprised question, he asked, "Are you a virgin?"

Nodding, she rubbed their chests together and moved her mouth to his neck, sucking his flesh like he'd done to her. Licking to behind his ear, she bit him, giggling when he jumped with a groan.

She mumbled as she licked him, "Of course. I just told you how sheltered I was. No sex education or contact with males, means no sex."

He had spent so much time thinking she was Mandrake's woman that he had taken her words of being raised in somewhat isolation with a grain of salt.

Sure, he could tell she was quite green, inexperienced, yet, she was too beautiful, too sexy, too plush for a man not to have put his hands on her.

Járon leaned back from her, dropped his hands.

"Keyleigh, listen," he started, his dick pounded in his jeans yelling at him to shut up and give it what it wanted.

Ignoring it, he said, "I didn't know, didn't understand." Shaking his head with alarming misgiving, he told her, "Sweetheart, I can't do that."

Honey brows furrowed in confusion. "Do what?" Her palms slid over his chest.

Sucking in a deep breath, he said reluctantly, "I can't take your virginity. It wouldn't be right. I'm a fucking soldier, a vicious killer with years of blood and violence on my hands, and you, you're so…young, and sweet, so pure, *na*."

He shook his head with more determination and moved from her. "I can't do that to you. You deserve a better guy, a decent guy, a younger more tamed man, not a damned crude warrior like me."

Chapter Eighteen

Disbelief colored her skin, hurt filled her eyes. "You don't want me? You're turned off because I don't have the experience of your- your regular women? That's so," she moved to scramble off the bed, look for her clothes.

"*Na neníta*, wait." On his knees on the bed, he caught her around the waist and pulled her back. Cradling her face, he made her look at him.

"Tis not that, Keyleigh. I want nothing more in the world, in this fucking galaxy than to make love with you. I'm dying to be inside you, so much I could explode right now with the need of you. But, I'm not good enough for you, sweetheart, you deserve a lot better than a cold, hard cynical man with blood, harsh death on his hands."

His head lowered, he could no longer look at her, his fingers around the back of her neck dug in her hair. He needed to let her go but he couldn't make his fingers release her.

"I don't know how to treat a woman right, you know that. I'm a foulmouthed, brutal son of a bitch. I can't stand that I'll hurt you. I won't mean to, but-"

Her mouth opened in incredulity then anger. "How dare you say that, Járon Rameau, how dare you take this from us." She slammed her hands on her hips making her bare breasts bounce, catching his attention.

"I want you to teach me, I want you to be the one I lose my virginity to. I don't want some fumbling young frat boy to do it," she sidled to him, curled her hands around his lean hips.

Chin down, looking up at him through long curly lashes, she said gently, "I want you, only you Járon, please, don't deny us for some misplaced stupid honor."

Járon stared at her, all pretty and pink from her lips to her nipples to her sex that glistened from her moisture, that was for him.

His gaze rose to her gleaming eyes looking at him like he was…wanted. Desired. By her. Fuck. It dug in his craw how much he feared hurting her, physically, mentally, by being the ruthless asshole that he knew he was.

But, he sighed, he also knew, as much as he protested, there was no way he was walking away from her and letting her go into another man's arms. Letting some other guy make her a woman, be her first, her only. *Na.* Honor just bit the dust.

He put a hand at her back, the other under her knees, lifted her and laid her on her back.

Bending to her, he kissed her, licked and sucked from her lips, down her neck, over her breasts. When he bit her nipples her body quivered, a happy sound sighed from her parted lips.

Kissing down her body, on his knees, Járon pushed her legs wide apart and settled his open mouth on her core like he was going to bite it whole like she was a sweet fresh peach.

Her gasp was sharp with surprise, but her pelvis reached up to him, he smiled against her tender pussy.

"Járon, what are you doing, you- *ahh,* oh God, that's…"

His tongue was magic, slicking up her and in her, he grazed his teeth, his tongue back and forth on her clit and gently slid his finger just a bit inside her.

"Já- *rone,*" she cried. "You're making me sizzle, like heat and electricity together, *God,*" her hips lifted to meet his foraging mouth.

Pulling back slightly, he said, "Sweetheart, you have to know, there's a part that will hurt, wait, tell me, you use tampons, right?"

Blinking at the ceiling she spouted, "Járon! You're embarrassing me, why are you asking me something like that now?" Embarrassed, she tried to close and curl her legs up away from him.

Pushing her legs back down he said, "Just answer me baby, do you?"

"I uh, yes, why-"

"Never mind, I'll explain later." She would have basically broken her own virginity. Thank God, he wasn't going to have to suffer through hurting her by tearing through her hymen.

He tucked his face back down, trilled his fingers up the inside of her thigh, her legs quivered from his touch but then stiffened from the unfamiliar sensations.

Rubbing his thumb over her sex, he said softly, "Relax, honey, trust me to take care of you, okay?"

Sucking her nether lips, he moved his finger inside, deeper, slowly, then faster. Her hips bucked up and whimpers floated from her parted lips. She clutched fistfuls of his hair, her head whipped back and forth.

When her hips were thrashing so much he had to hold her down, and her cries grew gusty and hitching, and little wheezing squeals caught in her throat, a flush spread over her chest, Járon pushed a second finger inside her.

Stretching her, stroking her hot spots, he pumped until he felt her body soaring up to the top of the moon about to sail over it.

"Járon, God, help me," she begged, chest heaving, hips frantically rushing at his hands, at his mouth. "Help me, Járon," whimpers squeezed out as she started to slide deliriously over the big golden moon.

Járon instructed, "Go baby, let go, you know I have you, let it go." He thrust his fingers and rolled her bud then pinched it hard and she bolted up and let out a harsh rasping scream.

Gasping his name, her legs widened as her body rippled in uncontrollable quakes.

Járon felt her orgasm jolt and grind against his mouth, her sheath squeezing his fingers. Before the tremors stopped and her breathing still rapid as if she'd run a marathon race, Járon removed his fingers, spun off the bed and quickly shucked his jeans, socks, grabbed the condom and rolled it on.

Trembling and huffing, her body still squirming, Járon moved so she wouldn't see his penis.

As inexperienced as she was, he didn't want her yet to see his length and thickness, it would likely freak her out. Time later to introduce her hands, and hopefully that lush little mouth, to his manhood.

Back on the bed, he moved between her knees, he could see her flat belly still sucking in and out, legs quivering on the sheets, her breasts rosy with orgasmic flush.

She raised her slender arms to him, wanting him, her smile wobbly and dazed.

Járon couldn't believe it. His gaze fell to her swollen clit, tender and shimmering and up to her equally radiant eyes. He had fantasized and prayed for this day, this moment, claiming her, making her his.

He lowered his body down until he was on his elbows on either side of her, then bent his head, kissed her gently.

Her eyes had closed, now they opened with a happy blurry smile.

Stroking his fingers down her face, he murmured, "I love you, Keyleigh."

Her lashes flew up, lips parted in dismay.

Covering her mouth with his, he plunged his tongue in to taste her. His fist wrapped around his throbbing phallus, he carefully nudged it to her opening, slowly pushing inside.

Seeing her face strained, lids scrunched down tight, Járon held his breath, pausing so her body could adapt to him. His exhale released none of his sexual tension.

Murmuring roughly with the effort to hold back from slamming into her, he said, "This will be, uncomfortable at first baby; you're so small, so tight, it'll get easier." He pushed, inching inside her, pausing every little bit for her to adjust, expand to him.

"Járon," she gasped, "you're, big, like, really big, hard as, *uhh*," she grunted as he wormed in and in. Deeper and deeper, until he finally pushed to the end of her and stopped.

"It, hurts, you fill me too- too-"

"Just breathe, relax your legs baby, feel me inside you, can you feel me throbbing against your satin walls?" Her sheath suddenly squeezed him, he jerked inside her, she squeaked.

He growled, "Shit, Keyleigh, I almost lost it."

"Mmm." She flexed her vagina again and giggled at his curse.

"Yes, I can feel you, Járon, throbbing inside me, it's, uh," she groaned as he pulled out almost all the way, then moved carefully back inside, gathering her silk to smooth the way. Each time he slowly pulled out then rocked back inside her it was easier.

On his elbows, Járon leaned over her, black hair flopping in his eyes, his temples damp with sweat. "You okay now, my precious *nenita?*"

Her head brushed the mattress with her nod. The prettiest smile in the world graced her gentle face as she looked up at him.

As he kissed her, he sank deeper into her with each thrust, then his momentum increased.

His head bowed, hair brushed Keyleigh's face, she giggled. Lifting his head, he smiled at her.

"Ah, I have not pounded you into dazed incomprehension yet? I need to fix that," and he thrust hard, fast, going deeper every time.

He plunged into her so hard, he wrapped his arm around her shoulder to hold her from getting pushed from him, and put his hand under her bottom to lift her to him.

His thrusts now propelled little grunts from her. Keyleigh's lashes fluttered, lips parted with rapid breaths.

When an almost inaudible, pulsating wail came nonstop from rasping throat, he cupped her breast, kneaded it roughly, and turned slightly so he rubbed her clit with each plunge.

His shaft swelled impossibly bigger, growing even harder with every drive inside. Their mixed breaths husky, heavy, his chest sliding over hers with his thrusts, the hair scrubbing over her tender skin.

Groaning, his ragged voice tight, he muttered in his language then said, "I can't hold back any longer. Look at me now, *nenita,* you are on the tip of the spire about to blast off. Baby, I want you looking at me, seeing, knowing the man who is claiming you."

"Járon," her hoarse cry, body writhing under him, she dug her nails into his shoulders, which made him smile and grow even impossibly hotter.

Pushing up her lids heavy with misted passion, Keyleigh moaned, "I feel-" she broke off when he slammed a grunt from her and dragged back over her clit making her entire body shudder with her wail.

The strain of holding back was in his furrowed forehead, clenching jaw, the sweat now across his hairline, he held on needing to wait for her.

His eyes lowered to her full breasts that bobbed and shook with his rough rugged thrusts. The crimson flush was spreading across her chest, her breathing was so shallow and rapid she was more gulping than breathing.

Other women did filter into his head, he recalled how mostly he just wanted to get his rocks off as fast as possible and move on, but with Keyleigh, he never wanted this to end, he wanted to stay inside her, hearing her purrs of delight and cries of euphoria forever. But he couldn't hold back any longer.

"Now baby, now," he commanded, and drove into her until wailing cries rose up from her chest and her eyes rolled back in her head.

"Look at me, Keyleigh," he gasped his demand.

She forced her wobbling eyes to spool back to him, her spine arched bucking her at him, her hips slamming against his equaling his deep plunges.

The wails inched to a scream scraping through her hoarse throat until she was no longer in reality.

Keyleigh was flying, soaring above the clouds to the heavens as stars burst inside her, burning through her soul and exploding out of her banging body.

Járon clutched her hair in his fist, arching her neck, pulling her head back so he could watch her as she came hard and fierce, and totally abandoned with his name on her lips.

Her face clenched with the exquisite piercing pain of it. Keyleigh's body shook and shuddered and rippled, heaving crazily under him, against him.

Her sheath seized him, spasms grinding, wringing, milking his thick shaft buried deep inside her.

Groaning, "*God, Keyleigh,*" he let go with a growl, driving into her with deep mad thrusts. Pinioning faster and faster so hard he thought he'd break her, but he was gone, out of control.

Wild, unrestrained thrusts hammering until he felt the tight fist of heat in his balls cramp and dynamite up and out him. Járon dove into orbit, mind a blank blazing sun of lights, flashes, blood roaring in his head, nothing but sheer sensation.

He had never before experienced this extreme explosion. Like a ship hurtled by a hurricane crashing against the shore breaking, splintering into a million brilliant pieces. His ejaculation undulated from him, bursting his seeds for what seemed like forever.

His growl grated, harshly guttural, the sound of a beast claiming his female. Taking her, pulsating like a wild thing inside Keyleigh, throbbing with the profound agony of it.

With a shout of her name, Járon plunged a few more times, then held taut, feeling his life's essence pumping out of him, then he collapsed, shifting at the last second to not crush Keyleigh.

His big hand still on her butt, he pulled her to lie on her side facing him, her head in the cradle of his arm.

They lay, breaths still ragged and heavy, then he rolled onto his back bringing her to sprawl over him.

Keyleigh threw her arm over his chest, sifted her fingers into the manly fur and nestled into him.

Her breasts settled on his chest, she murmured with a deep breath-calming sigh, "I can feel your heat right through the hair on your chest. Your heart pounding against my ear, Járon, like a berserk bass drum," her head rose and dipped with his heaving breaths.

Járon couldn't talk. Still trying to catch his breath, spiraling through the blinding daze still beating in his head, his body, coming down to earth. His arm rolled around her pressing her against him, he breathed deeply, exhaled slowly.

Hissed, "Damn, Keyleigh," then he took another heavy breath, heaved her tighter.

"Nothing like that ever," gasping, he kissed the top of her head, "never felt that before." His hand slightly shaky, he netted her head tipping it back so he could look at her.

He saw passion-hazed, glowing topazes under thick half-mast lids peering up at him, swollen lips in a dreamy smile. "You all right, babe?" he asked with his own elated smile.

Her lids lowered, then rose halfway up as if they weighed a ton. Her nod brushed her face over his chest. She giggled at the tiny shiver that rippled over his chest at her movement.

She said softly, "I'll admit," a small yawn slipped out, "I was sort of…scared. You're so strong, huge, and it hurt some, but," the yawn crept through happy lips. "Gosh, Járon," sigh, she rubbed her cheek against his matting of hair. "It was the most…amazing, kinda mind blowing, how soon can we do it again?"

His lips in her hair, he smiled against the fragrant locks damp with their sweat. Stroking her hair, her back, he said, "Ah, we will wait a bit, see how tender," he hugged her tight, "sore you are. As soon as you are fine-"

He lifted her head, licked her swollen lips then pushed them open in a gentle, indulgent kiss. "And honey," his growl rumbled deep, "you are damned fine." His mouth sealed over hers, he felt his shaft already hardening, the burn building in his testicles.

"Mmm," he hummed, pulling away. "Need to stop that for now."

"Oh, you've had your fill of kissing me?" Keyleigh nestled into his hard warmth.

"Ha!" his laugh barked laugh. "Never, sweetheart, trust me, never going to get enough." Snuggling her, Járon sighed, "Never."

They lay cuddled, half-dozing.

Then Járon shook himself. "Gotta get rid of this." He rolled off the bed and stumbled to the bathroom.

Returning, he grabbed a handful of condoms then scooped her up.

Laughing at her sleepy squeal, he carried her to the bathroom where they spent time soaping each other and showering.

When they were squeaky clean, Járon pushed her up against the wall, staked her hands above her head on the tile, and took her again.

They napped.

He woke her, both hands clutching her bottom, he slid into her, this was the quickest yet.

Járon was astounded, the shine wasn't wearing off. He only wanted her more, harder, faster, more desperately again and again.

Chapter Nineteen

Much later, they rose, ate, and stared at each other across the table.

"Keyleigh," Járon said. Sipping his coffee, he reached for her hand and asked, "You okay, baby? Any regrets?"

The house was dark, still time before dawn broke, but it felt cozier just the two of them in the dim illumination from the small light over the stove.

Half her face was shadowed, but her smile was clear as a bell, a delicate crystal bell. "Yes," she replied with a serious expression.

His heart dropped. "You do?"

Nodding, she said, "Yeah, I wish I'd met your sooner."

The side of his mouth tugged up in a grin. "You are a little minx. As soon as we're done eating I'm going to show you what your punishment is for trying to upset me," the grin turned to a leer.

"Hmm," she murmured. Her gaze strolled down the front of him and flipped back up. "Does my punishment entail us getting naked and back into bed?"

His lids hooded, the grin deepened. "*Na*. I'm thinking about bending you over this table, shoving your feet wide apart, and with your tits in my hands taking you from behind. What do you think about that?"

"Yikes!" A blush rolled up her neck to her cheeks, but she said coyly, "I'm thinking I need to be naughtier."

His laugh woofed sharp and dirty. "Oh yeah, that remark deserves its own punishment, c'mere-" he leaned over the table then stopped moving. His head cocked.

"What is it?"

"I can hear the hens, they only make noise this early if there's something out there." He stood up, snagged his phone off the counter, went to the door and shoved his boots on.

"Something?" Her voice tightened with puzzled concern.

"*Da*, like an animal looking for breakfast. I need to go check it out. You stay here."

Lowering his head, he glared at her and ordered, "And I mean that, Keyleigh, do not leave the house, I don't know what's out there."

"Járon-"

He held a hand up stopping her. His head cocked again as he stood in the threshold of the kitchen door. He whispered, "Shh."

"What?" she whispered back.

"I saw a shadow, tis not an animal, tis a human." He started for the living room.

"Is it your brothers?"

"*Na*," he said quietly. "They wouldn't fool around like that, they know I'll shoot first and ask questions later. Stay here."

Not wanting to waste time getting a key, he jerked a locked drawer open, breaking it, and grabbed the gun that was inside and several mags.

But, she had gotten up and followed behind him.

Járon moved alongside the wall and held his arm out to keep her flush against the wall.

When he reached the window, he carefully peered out, said to her, "You do not leave this house Keyleigh, if you do I swear to God I will paddle your-"

A barrage of bullets broke through high up in the window, spewing shards of glass across the room.

Járon grabbed Keyleigh and shoved her into a slight alcove. Putting his hand on her shoulder he pushed her down to the floor.

"Crawl to the closet, get inside, close the door and then do not fucking move from there until I come for you," he commanded then crouched back to the window.

Peering out, he could see shadows of men, at least three, maneuvering around the house.

A voice rang loud and clear, "Just send the girl out, cowboy, we'll take her and leave, let you live. You got thirty seconds to think about it, then we're comin' in."

Keyleigh hadn't moved. "Járon?" she whispered, her voice shaky, "are you going to- to- send me out?"

He didn't look at her, he was busy scanning outside what he could see from the side of the window. He barked, "Get in the fucking closet, Keyleigh, now!" Digging out his phone he sent a text.

"Járon, you should, I mean, I'll go, there's no point in both of us-"

"Motherfucker," he ground out. Turning, he grabbed her and dragged her to the closet, opened it, thrust her inside.

"I can't do what I need to if I'm standing here arguing with you. Stay the fuck inside, no matter what, until I come for you," he slammed the door.

At that moment a hail of bullets burst through the rest of the window shattering most of it, bullets crashed into the front door.

A man outside shouted, "Send her out, boy, and you'll live, don't make us come in there and get her! There'll be nuthin' left of you for your dear mama to bury!"

Járon swiftly crept to the window. Leaning to it, he stuck his hand through the cut glass and fired his gun. He wished he had time to get his shotgun, he really needed it. He reached through and fired several more shots.

"Oh yeah?" the man outside yelled. "That's how you want to play it? You got twenty seconds to throw that broad out or you're a dead man!"

A volley of bullets slammed against the door.

Járon fired a few more rounds, then tucked the gun into the back of his belt and ran to the alcove he'd pushed Keyleigh in.

Jumping up a few times, he punched at the ceiling until a trap door opened, then he jumped again, grabbed the edges of the door and pulled himself up into the attic.

Running silently across the wood slats, he made his way to another trap door, pushed it up, climbed out, and was on the roof.

That part of the roof was relatively flat so walking on it wasn't difficult.

Keeping low, he crept to the side, got down on his belly and peered over the edge of the shingles.

It wasn't yet daybreak, but the horizon was lightening just enough he could make out three, four, then several more men hiding behind trees.

Two of the men were furtively creeping in the shadows towards the house with shotguns raised.

Járon wriggled his head and shoulders over the edge.

When the two men were almost under him, he reached his hand over the roof and rapid-fired twice into the tops of both their heads, they dropped like sacks of dirt.

He heard cursing then a hail of gunfire shot all around showing him they didn't know exactly where he was.

Járon prayed to God Keyleigh had obeyed him and stayed in the closet. The fucking attackers must have assumed he'd tuck her safely out of the way otherwise they wouldn't be taking the chance of a bullet hitting her.

On his hands and feet, he crawled to the back of the house and got down on his belly.

Peering carefully over the edge, he saw two more men sneaking up on the house. They were not yet aware he was shooting from the roof. When they got close enough, he killed them both with one shot each to their heads.

More boisterous cursing came from the woods along with gunfire. Bullets sprayed the front of the house. Fragments of wood flew, the gutter burst into pieces, the shards ejected up in the air.

Járon needed to capture one of the men alive to find out if they were the transients that had attacked Keyleigh before, or they were Mandrake's people coming for her. He stopped shooting and lay still, and waited.

The men thinking they might have killed him, slipped out from the cover of the trees and ran towards the house with guns up and shooting just in case.

Járon crept to the very edge of the roof. When the men were upon the house, one had his hand on the front door knob, Járon dropped over the side and landed on top of him.

One punch and he knocked him out then turned to the others.

Járon moved like a tornado taking them out before they could shoot him. Kicked one in the face, slammed his boot into the knee of another shoving the bone out the back of his leg, both collapsed to the grass.

He stomped on the neck of the one with the broken knee who was screaming at the top of his lungs, crushing his windpipe, he died instantly.

Jumping on the other guy, Járon twisted his head breaking his neck.

Still more emerged from the woods, one ran straight at him. Járon stepped to the side, caught the man by his collar and hair and slammed his head into another one right behind him.

Bending quickly, Járon snatched a knife off one of the dead men and slashed at a man that had his gun aimed at Járon's head, and ducked.

The man dodged the knife but his shot went wild and Járon jumped him.

The guy was a huge bruiser, cordons of muscles wound over his shoulders and down his massive arms. Járon pummeled his face so fast with punches the man staggered backwards then Járon jumped on him knocking him on his back.

He jabbed his knee into his crotch, the heavyweight howled in pain, and Járon stabbed the knife directly into his heart. The thug started, eyes wide, gagged, sputtered, his legs jerked then grew still.

"That's enough, asshole," a voice a dozen yards away coming out of the trees called out.

Still leaning over the big guy, Járon cranked his head in the dim twilight to look at the man by the trees.

Then he hopped behind the dead man, lifted his back and positioned himself in a crouch using the huge man as a shield, so the man aiming down on him couldn't get a clean shot.

Stepping out of the cover of dark forest, the man yelled, "Get up, fucker, get on your feet!" He slowly stalked towards him.

Járon's eyes darted around the yard looking for somewhere to run, something to use as cover or a weapon, his gun was empty, extra mags gone, and the knife he had was still in the big guy.

He yanked it out, but it wouldn't do him any good at this distance, the gun would get him first. He stayed crouched to be a smaller target, but the man kept coming, shotgun raised and aimed.

"You are one dead motherfucker," the man snarled. "All we wanted was the fucking girl. All you had to do was send the bitch out, and you would live out the day. But no, you had to be some kind of hero."

He kept stalking until he was close enough to hit Járon easily, and Járon had nowhere to hide from the bullet. The man was still too far away for him to throw the knife.

"I gotta say, you are some kind of a fighting machine, bro, the likes I've never seen." Waving the gun with his praise, he shrugged.

"I can't believe you singlehandedly took out the entire team. Too bad, we coulda used a soldier like you. Say your prayers, boy," the gun up, finger pulling on the trigger-

Járon dove as he heard the gunshot, and another and another. Landing on the grass, he twisted and rolled, he didn't feel any bullets strike. His head tucked in, he looked back.

The thug, was swaying, eyes hard and cold, turned colder by the second, then he fell flat on his face.

On his knees, Járon looked to the woods and called out, "You took your damned sweet time you bastard!"

He got to his feet as his brother Khol appeared from the thicket of trees with a shit-eating grin on his face.

The brothers walked to each other, gave a quick one-armed hug then stood back.

"*Yah*, well, I drove like a bat outta hell when I got your text. I scoured the area on my way in, I didn't see any others lurking. Where's Keyleigh? I heard the guy say he was after her."

"*Da*," Járon nodded, and the brothers headed to the house.

"Nice," Khol grinned at the shot out window and front of the house peppered with bullets.

"Huh," Járon grunted. He bent and grabbed the front of the shirt of the man he had dropped down on and merely knocked out.

Jerking him to his feet, he slapped him to wake him.

"Wha- wha-" The thug opened his bleary eyes as Khol moved behind him and tied his wrists behind his back.

Járon shoved him against the house and got in his face.

"You have one chance to tell me the truth then my brother here starts shooting off body parts, one at a time until you either spill or die from blood loss. Dying from exsanguination is a fucking slow, painful way to go. He's going to start with your tool-"

Khol shot him in the foot. The man screamed, lifting his knee he hopped on one leg, his hands tied behind his back.

"Khol, bro, what the fuck? I said his dick."

"Let's be fair, J, you hadn't asked your question yet. I was just giving him a little pop to show we're serious."

While the brothers argued, the man cried like a baby leaning against the house. He would have fallen except Jároon kept his big hand on his chest holding him up against the wall.

"Oh, shit, *da*, you're right, sorry, okay." Jároon turned to the man who cowered, shrinking against the wall.

"Who sent you for the girl? You have one chance to answer, you don't answer you lose your dick. No more playing with the women for you, shithead."

"'Tis probably tiny anyway, might have to shoot twice to hit it," Khol chuckled, taunting the man.

But the hood was too scared and in too much pain to express any anger.

"Okay, okay," he cried, standing on one foot. Bending his knee, he held the injured foot off the ground.

His voice shaking with tears, he told them, "Maximillion Mandrake, he sent us. The bitch was his prize or something and she escaped, ran from him," a sob choked out. Wincing in agony, he groaned, "He wants her back."

Jároon leaned his muscled forearm into the man's neck and asked, "How did you know she was here?"

The thug gulped, sniffed hard, blinked back the flood of tears pouring down his face.

His voice croaked out from under the pressure of Jároon's choking arm, "A- a vagrant, some dude was in a bar shooting off his mouth about him and his friends stealing horses and looking to poach. They, uh," he groaned in pain, "snatched this girl, took her to the woods to rape her when they were fucked up by some one-man killing machine."

His gaze sprung briefly up at Jároon, corners of his lips jacked in as he realized Jároon was the killing machine that slaughtered the vagrant's friends.

"The dude," the man gasped, cried, sniffed hard then spit. "He went on about how beautiful the girl was, long, golden tawny hair with fire in it, rocking bod, bitchin' tits-oof!"

Járon punched him in the stomach, then put his hands on his head and twisted it once, hard, and let the dead man drop to the ground.

The front door creaked open a hair.

"Goddammit, Keyleigh," Járon cursed. He pulled the door and grabbed her arm yanking her out.

"I fucking told you to stay in the closet. Will you never listen to me?" Last thing he needed was for her to see him kill in cold blood, he hoped she hadn't seen him dispatch the blabber.

Her skin ivory white with fear, she mumbled, "The gunshots stopped, and I didn't hear anything. I was so afraid they'd killed you, I had to come out and see if you were okay-"

He slammed her to his chest and wrapped both arms around her, hugging her tight, his face in her hair. His hand cradled her head against his chest as she wetted his shirt with tears of relief.

"Tis okay, baby, everything is okay." His accent thickened with emotion, he peered over her head at his brother.

Khol crossed his arms over his chest and grinned at his brother.

No one ever thought Járon even had a heart, much less would lose it to a woman. And such a petite, dainty, gorgeous thing. If anything, they would have expected Járon to choose a bitch that was as big, tough, hard and cold as Járon himself was.

He said to Járon, "What next? We going after Mandrake now, or waiting for Porth to arrive?"

Járon frowned at his brother and shook his head. The less Keyleigh knew the better off he'd be. She would nag him, try to talk him out of going after Mandrake.

Keyleigh pulled from him. "No, Járon, you can't still be thinking of doing anything! You see how dangerous, how ruthless, how rich he is that he can hire gangs of men to come after me. Let that Porth man take care of himself, please, don't go after him-"

"Ah," Járon groaned. Rolling his eyes at his brother's snicker he drew Keyleigh back inside the house.

Chapter Twenty

Járon and Keyleigh sat on the couch.

Pulling her close, Járon wrapped his arm around her. He knew his brother would give him a hard time about it later, but he had to kiss her.

The entire time he was outside fighting, he was thinking about her stashed inside. Was she injured? What if he didn't take out all of the hoods and they were able to get to her? He'd killed the rat quickly so he could hurry to her.

Sitting on the thick arm of an easy chair with a longneck dangling between thumb and fingers, Khol smirked at the couple.

It was hilarious, his little brother, his vicious, ice-in-his-veins brother, had fallen hard for the delicate woman cradled against him.

Even as obnoxious as Járon had been towards Keyleigh that night of the dinner, it was clear he was head over heels for her. Like the boy on the playground that tugged the girl's pigtails to show he didn't care, it was obvious he wanted her.

Khol's smile softened, and if Keyleigh didn't have feelings for his brother, she wouldn't have cared enough to go the trouble to show him what a big jerk he was, by strutting around like the whore he kept calling her.

His smile filled with admiration for the woman, she was a nervy little thing all right, locking horns with his brute of a brother. And she had bravely disobeyed Jàron's order to stay inside to see if he was okay.

Khol could see who would be wearing the pants in their family, he snorted, and it sure as hell wasn't gonna be Jàron.

In the middle of sucking her face off, Jàron clasped Keyleigh to his chest, his hand webbing the back of her head. He wondered how quickly he could get rid of his brother and take Keyleigh back to bed when she pushed him back.

Ducking her head, embarrassed at Khol obviously enjoying the show, Keyleigh said, "Jàron, we need to talk about Mr. Mandrake. You have to see that he is invincible, you will get yourself and your brothers killed. You must listen to me-" Jàron kissed her to shut her up.

His hand cupping her jaw, he smiled at her. "Honey, you obviously don't know the Rameau brothers. We have a job to do, and we're going to do it."

He squeezed her jaw when she started to protest. "*Na*, you can't talk me out of it. Even if we weren't doing a job we were hired to do, I would take the motherfucker out because of you.

"I won't allow some madman roaming free out there that kidnapped you, he would die for that alone, but he is determined to come after you. I will not let that danger live to harm you. And that's it, you and I are not talking about this again. *Na*," he shook his head and covered her mouth with his fingers to halt her continuing objections.

"We're done, honey. I don't want to hear you talk about something you can't change."

She flattened her hands on his chest and angrily pushed at him, but he didn't move an inch.

"Don't you dare tell me what I can and can't say, Járon Rameau, you try and you will find yourself talking to empty air. You have bullied me enough. I am done with being held captive and pushed around. I mean it."

Muttering, "Keyleigh," he tried to kiss her, but she turned her head. Following her dodges, his mouth chased after hers.

"Hey," Khol cut in, "what's this? Is this that silk crap you're producing?" He held up a length of material.

Keyleigh turned her head to face Khol. "Yes," she replied, her cheeks blushing pink from Járon attentions. She put a hand up to his face to hold him back. "It's a vest. I knitted Járon a vest out of the silk."

Járon looked at her, his jaw dropped. He said incredulous, "For me? You made that for me?" His big hands settled on her shoulders and he kissed her, long, gentle, hungry.

When they parted, she combed her fingers through a thick lock of black hair that tumbled over one of his brows.

Forgetting Khol was there, Keyleigh set her hands on either side of Járon's face, held him while pressing her lips on his. Licking his lips like he'd done to her before slipping her tongue inside his welcoming mouth.

The cell at his belt vibrated, Khol unhooked it and answered, "*Yah*, Vic?"

Járon and Keyleigh stopped kissing and looked at him.

Khol nodded. "*Da*, all right." He nodded again with a grin at Járon and said, "*Da*, he is fine, *yah*, and the little one is too," he winked at Keyleigh. "We'll fill you in when we see you. Ciao," he clicked off and re-hooked his phone.

He said to his brother, "Porth is here. Remi is on him. Victoro is with Mandra-" he broke off at Járon's brief shake of his head. But it was too late.

"No, Járon, please, please don't go there, let someone else do it," Keyleigh begged him.

He squeezed her shoulders and insisted, "*Na*, enough, *neníta,* stop." His fingers like steel pegs wound over her slender shoulders.

"J," Khol said quietly. "The event is tomorrow evening. What are you going to do with," his eyes shifted to Keyleigh.

"I'll take her to the secure haven in the city. She'll be safe there, tis impenetrable, we're the only ones who know about it. Gastron will be with her, no one can get past him."

"She is sitting right here, stop talking about me like I'm slow or a child," Keyleigh said crossly then quickly stood up before he could grab her.

"I can stay here. I will be perfectly fine, someone needs to see to the animals." She folded her arms over her breasts, chin raised in a mutinous preemption.

"Okay, time for me to go. I'll meet you at-" Khol glanced at Járon then rolled his eyes. "Ah, you know where. I already called the boys to come repair this damage and clear up the…yard. Later bro. See ya, beautiful, glad you're all right."

Khol stepped to her, bent and kissed her on the cheek. Járon walked him to the door where they spoke quietly.

With a huff Keyleigh strode to the bathroom.

When she returned, Khol was gone. She opened her mouth, but Járon spoke over her.

"Don't," he held a palm up to her. "Are you going to waste our night on useless chatter about something you can't change, or," he wriggled his brows at her, "do you want some more lessons?"

"Járon," she started, trailed off.

Járon's hard face was unyielding. Lids hooded, jaw set, there was not going to be any arguing with him. Like a stalwart mountain, she could push and prod and badger until the cows came home, or rather goats, he would not be moved.

"You are so bull-headed," she scolded him.

"*Da*, back at ya, baby. Now, which lesson do you want next, you bent over the table with your ass in the air and I show you what it feels like being plundered by my big cock from behind, or," damn he loved the way she blushed. "I can show you a different way to…pleasure me."

Perplexed, Keyleigh couldn't figure out how she could do that. Her gaze slipped down to the bulge that was expanding and hardening in his jeans. Her cheeks darkened further.

"Oh, wow." She thought about his mouth on her most private parts. "You mean, you want me to- to put my mouth on," eyes bright on his groin with anticipation, her tongue traced her lips.

"*Da*, okay, you catch on quick. Come here and let me get those clothes off you, I want to play with your body while I teach you-"

A knock at the door interrupted him. "Aw, shit, must be the guys to fix the window. They fucking got here fast. You go get in the bedroom just in case."

Járon started for the door, then barked at her, "Keyleigh, please do as I tell you. I can't take care of us if I have to worry about your safety, okay?"

Face scrunched in irritation, Keyleigh marched off to the bedroom.

When Járon heard the door close, shaking his head, he went to answer whomever was knocking like the energizer bunny.

He paused by the broken window and peered out, he wasn't taking any chances. "Ah fuck," he groaned out a string of invectives. What the hell was she doing here?

He swung the door sprayed with bullets open with a disgruntled, "*Yah*? How can I help you Miss O'Shea?"

"Holy shit, cowboy, what the hell happened here? Shoot-out at the OK Corral?" Shannon O'Shea waggled her head in incredulity.

Substantial lips hanging open, she took in the broken window and door stippled with bullets, as she pushed past him forcing her way into his house.

"Uh, Miss O'Shea, what are you doing here?" Járon tried to block her way, but short of socking her one, or shoving her, she just bulldozed past him barging her way into the living room.

He slapped his forehead with his palm then dragged his hand down over his eyes. How was he going to get rid of her before she saw Keyleigh, or vice versa?

She swiveled to face him. "Hell, cowboy, that accent is so seductive, your deep husky voice, makes me tingle all over."

He couldn't believe the blowsy woman came out to a goat farm dressed in a miniscule skirt, blouse open to her navel, and six-inch heels. The sides of her shoulder-length blonde hair were pinned up, leaving the back curling up across her shoulder blades.

Thickly feathered false lashes batted at him. Her gaze heating as it scrolled down the length of him, pausing at his crotch that was still semi-hard from being with Keyleigh.

She licked her lips. Somehow it didn't enflame Járon like it did when Keyleigh did it, it just grossed him out. "Miss-"

Shannon simpered to him, put her hands on his chest and cooed, "Dang, hon, but you are a big one, all over it seems." She inclined her head with a giggle eyeing his groin.

"Miss O'Shea," Járon said firmly while grasping her wrists trying to pull them off him without hurting her. "I'm, uh busy, I've got animals to feed, why don't you mosey on out of here, hop in that little BMW of yours, and head back to town? You're going to get your pretty outfit all dirty, you know?"

Setting his palm on her back, he tried to nudge her to the door but she stood fast.

"Oh, come on, handsome, you gotta be wanting some female company hanging way out here with nothing but donkeys and hens." Shoving her breasts flush against his chest, she moaned as she wrapped her arms around his neck and rubbed over him.

"Hot damn, cowboy, you have the hardest chest. You hard like that, down there? For me?" She reached down to cup his manhood with a large boxy hand, nails red and long like claws clinched his man's package.

"Oh yeah," she gushed, squeezing, "you are fucking hung."

Járon twisted to the side out of her grip with a grunt. "Goats, not donkeys, you need to go, Miss, now. I don't have time for this shit. I told you before I'm not interested."

He clasped her wrists, holding the one away from his dick and forcefully turned her around with the other. "You touch me again and I'll snap every fucking finger in half."

Thick ruby lips pushed out in a pout. "Oh, come on, baby, I gave you my number, waited for you to call. Go on, sugar, go try to tell me you don't want me as much as I want you!" She grabbed at his manhood again.

"Yes, Járon, tell us how much you want her?"

Járon groaned at Keyleigh's voice from the doorway.

Swinging around and seeing Keyleigh, Shannon's blonde brows hacked between her hazel eyes. "Who is this, cowboy? You didn't tell me I had competition." Her gaze swept Keyleigh's jean-clad slender figure and plopped a hand on her ample hip.

Snorting, "Huh," she dismissed Keyleigh as inconsequential and turned back to Járon. "Honey, please, tell me, there's no way you could prefer that skinny, bratty little slut to me."

She traced her palms over her body from her big breasts, down her waist and over broad, round hips. Her sneer at Keyleigh told her she didn't think more of the younger girl than she would a pesky fly.

Stepping from Shannon, Járon moved to Keyleigh. "Keyleigh, baby, don't even think about it. This whore, I don't-"

Shannon threw herself at him and latched her wide lips over his before he could stop her.

Keyleigh's gasp sharp, and pained expression struck Járon like a punch.

When he wrestled Shannon off him and turned, Keyleigh was gone.

"You bitch," he blasted Shannon giving her a shove. He ran to the door shouting, "Keyleigh, come back here!" As soon as he stepped outside he came to an abrupt halt.

A troop of men were lined up a dozen feet away.

In the middle of the group, a man had his arm around Keyleigh and was holding a gun to her neck, the smile of a viper about to strike curved like a scythe up his angular face.

"Maximillion Mandrake," Járon stated, his eyes on Keyleigh.

She struggled in vain to get loose from the abductor she'd escaped from before falling into Járon's arms. A cluster of humiliation, anger, and fear knit across her brow, crimping her beautiful face red with her struggles.

"Ah, you have me at a disadvantage, son. I don't know your name, but I've heard a lot about you. Some kind of killing machine the shitbag said." He glanced pointedly at the bodies that still littered the ground.

"Apparently what he said was true judging by my men there."

Járon turned his head slightly to say to Shannon standing behind him, "This was a set up, you bitch, you distracted us so they could get here undetected."

Now that the octopus squall called Shannon had stalled, he noticed the chickens putting up more of a ruckus.

"Oh, Cowboy, it doesn't mean I don't want you, but he paid a lot of money, put the word out he was looking for her."

The sneer in place she tipped a haughty chin at Keyleigh and said, "I figure he takes her," a hefty shoulder shrugged, "and that leaves you, for me." Her hands pawed down his back. Járon ignored her.

"Do shut up woman, damn but that broad can talk, huh, *Cowboy*?" Mandrake smirked at Járon.

"Let her go, Mandrake, you take her and kill me, there are others that will come after you, you're fucked."

Thick shoulders bunched, his fists clenched. Seeing Keyleigh held by the bastard that had kidnapped her to keep as his own personal sex slave, remembering she said he'd had her drugged, hit, starved, fury poured off Járon in violent waves of loathing.

Dark brows glowered low over empty eyes that contained nothing. No light, no warmth, no humanity. Mandrake's smile slithered into a harsh slash. "From what I've heard, *Cowboy*, ain't nothing goin' to keep you from coming after her, so," he suddenly fired his pistol numerous times at Járon.

The impact of the bullets striking Járon in the chest jolted shocked grunts from him. He looked at Keyleigh before his eyes glazed, and he dropped, crumpled to the ground.

"*Noooo!*" Keyleigh screamed.

"Shut up you fucking bitch." Mandrake backhanded her so hard he almost knocked her out. She crashed dazed to the ground.

He crouched, and stood up with her in his arms. Shooting a look of disgust at Járon lying still on the ground, he sneered, "Some hero," spat at him and carried Keyleigh to a car that was pulling into the drive.

"Hey, what about me? Where's my money? You were just supposed to take her, you weren't supposed to kill him," Shannon whined, tripping in her high heels after the men that were piling into cars.

Mandrake carried Keyleigh to his vehicle. Setting her inside the backseat, he glanced at a few of his soldiers and nodded. "They'll take care of you," he said to Shannon then climbed in beside Keyleigh.

One of his men closed the door, and the huge SUV sped down the road.

Four men approached Shannon. One said with a leer, "We got your reward in here, sweetheart, come with us," he gestured to a car.

"Oh! Oh great, and I get all your hunky company on the way home too?" Shannon giggled and skittered with little tripping steps to the car, gushing when the four men helped her inside.

They climbed in after her, closing the doors as her lustful laughter turned to excruciating screams.

Chapter Twenty~One

Throwing the door open, it hit the wall and bounced back, Maximillion Mandrake blocked it with his arm as he entered the room.

At the window, Keyleigh didn't turn around, didn't flinch, didn't move.

He said to her, "Keyleigh, let me see how you look."

Her image reflected back at her in the glass. Anguish permeated every fiber of her being, but the topaz windows to her soul glowed huge and empty.

"Keyleigh," Mandrake said again, his shoes hitting the floor hard in his stride to her. His voice like a throaty dark hiss, he demanded, "You will look at me when I'm speaking to you." He stopped a few feet from her.

She slowly turned to face him. Her gaze direct, straight, unwavering, the blue eyes blank. The long lashes rolled down slowly, once, then stayed up.

"Ah, you look incredible, honey." Mandrake reached for her arm.

Now she did flinch, lips tightened. A scowl scrunched his long, aquiline fortyish face. His voice a snarly gnarl, he told her, "You will get over this attitude, my little escapee, but for now, only until tomorrow will I tolerate it."

His deep-set dark brown eyes rose to the top of her golden tawny hair. The maid had styled it almost wild in big fat curls, with her natural sparking fiery filaments waving around her head and down her back.

She'd done Keyleigh's makeup masking her normal childlike face with the huge round blue eyes, small nose and tiny plump lips. Over those, she painted striking highlights accentuating Keyleigh's beauty.

The makeup, and the haunted pain dazing her eyes, enhanced her breathtaking beauty with sorrowful, exotic mystery.

The shimmering red dress sleeked over the curve of her breasts. The bodice scooped low, revealing the swells of her pale mounds. Barely there, lace shimmers of tiny sleeves covered a few inches of her arms below her shoulders.

The dress hugged the tiny waist, and flared slightly at her slender but rounded hips flowing down to pool on the floor. A long slit up the front exposed a golden stiletto, a lithe leg, and almost, but not quite, her ribbon of black silk panties.

Mandrake knew everything she wore, including her lingerie, he had ordered it.

"God, but I want you so insanely I can taste it," Mandrake growled leaning into her. He lifted her hair and breathed across the back of her neck, inhaling deeply with a hungry sigh. His cock swelled with the agony of delayed desire.

Keyleigh stood like a figurine. Glacial marble, smooth, cold, hard, and allowed him to paw her. For, she had learned, to rebuff him, he retaliated. With brute force.

He kissed her cheek, setting his hand on the top swells of her breasts. Licking inside her ear, he slid his tongue to the soft skin on her neck, and sucked, hard.

Realizing he was deliberately trying to mark her, Keyleigh instinctively pushed at him with a sound of dissent.

He pressed his fingers into her cleavage, and dug them into her flesh. With his other hand, he clutched the back of her neck and squeezed, holding her in place as he sucked harder.

Regardless of his possible retribution, Keyleigh struggled, twisting, wrenching, slapping at his arms until he released her. She would endure a few nasty slaps to prevent him from leaving his brand on her. He may hold her captive, but she refused to allow him to think he owned her.

Well, he may own her body, she knew it was futile to fight him, but he would never own her soul, her heart, her mind.

He leaned back panting, his hand slid down to her waist. Eyes fogged with lusty desire, wetting his mouth with his rough tongue, he dragged his hand over the top of his long dark hair lightly slivered with grey at the temples. It hung straight down just past his collar.

Lids lowered, hooded to eclipse his lust for her, cruelly etched lips curved up in a smirk.

Maximillion Mandrake was a tall, broad shouldered male. He'd spent years in combat in his country, his muscles were strongly hewn. He was a big, powerful, debonair warrior in a tuxedo.

He was here to eliminate his rival for dictator, Anastas Porth. He couldn't get near him in their country, but here, Porth couldn't bring his full entourage of soldiers, all of his security.

Mandrake lifted a few of her curls, letting them drift through his fingers. "I will leave you alone, as I told you, until after the ball tonight. I don't dare jump you now, not yet. Once I begin, I fear I would be unable to tear myself away from between your lily white thighs for some time."

He suddenly reached down and curled his hard fingers over her sex before she could back away from him. "This is mine now," he sneered, gripping harder.

A thunderclap of laughter at the disgust on her face echoed in the room as she slapped at his hand.

Mandrake moved his face close to hers and said, "I could take you quickly right now against the wall," his gaze trolled down her, tongue pushing through his lips like the flicking of a serpent's forked tongue.

Keyleigh tried to turn her head, but he curled his hand around her jaw, holding her taut.

His eyes shifting back and forth across her face, he grinned obscenely at her disgust, and leered at the fear radiating from her wide blues.

"But I want to take my time, I want to go all night long the first time. Besides, I need my wits about me tonight."

He moved his hand from between her legs to the top of her breast, then stroked his fingers up further and into her hair that flowed over her shoulder.

Murmuring against the side of her lips, he said, "After Porth is dead, you and I," he lowered his mouth and licked her neck, "will celebrate. I am saving you with anticipation to relish as my reward."

His male scent and rich cologne irritating her nostrils, Keyleigh stood and let him slobber on her, knowing it only added to his thrill when she fought him.

Besides, what did she care anyway, Járon was dead. She'd seen him shot, four, five times, she didn't know. He'd crumpled to the ground, and lay so terribly still. A tear evolved and rolled down her cheek, it fell on Mandrake's hand.

He pulled back and frowned at it. Then he gripped her chin, jerked her face to his and ground out with jealous possessiveness, "He is dead, best you learn quickly to forget him. I'd hate to have to beat his memory out of you."

Gripping a handful of her hair, he bent and kissed her violently, so hard she cried out.

He let her go so suddenly she stumbled.

Declaring, "I will be the only man that occupies your mind from now on. He took what was mine," he clenched his hand into a fist, jerked and twisted it. "And I took his life. We're even I think."

Jealousy flowed over the malice in his eyes as he saw she still pined for the cowboy. Well, he'll fuck the man right out of her memory.

"Come, it's time, my sweet, let's go." A sly curl to the side of his lip dented seeing her wipe his slobber off her lips with revulsion. He leaned in with a threat, "That will be the last time you do that, darling. Next time you will feel my fist in your gut, your kidney, your breast, anywhere that it will cause hidden pain."

Taking her hand, he tucked it into his arm and said quietly, "Just remember, my dear, you do as I say, you be compliant, and I won't butcher your family."

The words spoken with such menacing frost, chills ran up the back of Keyleigh's spine,

"I told you when I brought you here that we have your brother. His life is in my hands. You understand?" This time he cinched her chin with a few fingers, lifting her face up to his.

He actually felt a spike of pride the way her eyes flashed furiously at him, lips firmed with defiance. Her small hand on his arm was stiff and cold.

"Damn, you are so sweet, I can't wait to take you. All that fire and sugar, hot, syrupy heat, I can't wait to taste that inferno down below, chomp the living fuck out of you." He kissed her hard again.

"Now, go, repair your lipstick." He smacked her on her butt to get her to move.

When she'd fixed the damage he'd wrought to her makeup, Mandrake drew her out of the room.

He ushered her to the top of the stairs where they paused to overlook the crowd gathered below.

The majestic hall was all glimmering white marble and gold. Chandeliers blinding with crystals shining and twinkling filled the ceiling. Crowds of guests in elegant, colorful ball attire teemed the grand foyer into the main room.

People danced to a band, drank and ate, laughed, and took pictures from shadowed corners.

A small stage was set with a microphone for Anastas Porth to give his acceptance speech. Mandrake's sniper was on his way.

"Come, darling, I have people to introduce to you to, and we must dance." His hands on her waist, Mandrake lowered his head to touch his forehead against hers.

"A precursor to later when I get you naked, feeling those sumptuous tits wedged against my bare chest. See the fair mounds calling to me, to my lips, my hands, feel your ass under my palms. While soaking up your juices coating me as I drill hard inside you. Ah," he stuck a finger under his collar and black satin bow tie, stretching them with a clearing of his throat.

He chuckled. "I need to stop doing that, dear. I get a fucking boner every time I think about you, and me, together."

Observing her biting her lip to keep the revulsion from showing on her face, he warned, "Be careful, my sweet. You know you will pay dearly later for exhibiting any blatant distaste for me."

He dropped his hand to twine their fingers and drew her down the staircase.

Pausing on a step, he bent his head to her and whispered, "That is why I have forgone taking you yet. My mind gets so fucked up, I can't think straight. Tonight I have to be acutely aware, say the right things at the precise right time."

Eyes staring blankly straight ahead, lips a tight line, Keyleigh made no response.

Squeezing her hand, he scowled down at her. "I've had enough of the silent treatment, Keyleigh. You'd better lighten up, talk to me. I want everyone to know you belong to me. I will rule Československa with you at my side.

"So, get cozier with me, woman, or your family will suffer. Don't forget that I have your brother. You got that?" He crushed her hand hard enough to eke tears out of the corners of her eyes.

"Yes," she murmured faintly. Keyleigh told herself to buck up. Járon would have been disappointed in her for acting like a mouse, so drowned in her sorrow for his loss she had no energy, no spirit, no desire to live.

She had to comply or he would harm Daniel. But, that didn't mean she had to give into Mandrake without a fight. He was going to take her later tonight. Well, if she couldn't get away, escape the building, then by God, she would ensure she did some damage to him.

She refused to be the meek little lamb led to slaughter, even though her heart was so broken, the pieces lay scraping at the bottom of her aching stomach.

For the rest of the evening, Keyleigh held her head high, nodded graciously when introduced to people, danced elegantly when Mandrake forced her into his arms, and fought off his hand that kept creeping up the slit on her thigh.

Other men came to them requesting a dance with her.

Mandrake's arm tightened possessively around her waist, warning them off with a snarl and narrowed eyes.

He growled under a coarse breath, "Not unless you want to die." He looked so morbidly malevolent, the men all quickly shuffled away.

But, Mandrake had to dance with various women for political tendering. When he did, he left Keyleigh near a wall semi-encircled by his men until he returned to pull her back into his arms.

Right now, he barely moved when dancing with her, he really just wanted to feel her body pressed up against his and his hands on her. His palms were as low down her back as he could get away with decently in public without actually grabbing her ass.

Nabbing a flute off a passing tray and handing it to her, Mandrake said for what seemed like the thousandth time forcing another glass of champagne in her hands, "Drink up." He figured if he got her liquored up she would be more malleable, not fight him so much, or at least less intensely.

"I've really never drank much, Mr. Mandrake, I don't care for any more." Keyleigh subtly wriggled out of his embrace.

His voice low and mean, he gripped her arm. Winding his fingers tightly around it, he squeezed hard pulling her up close. "Knock it off with the mister shit, Keyleigh. I've told you to stop."

Pinching her arm, he breathed booze into her face. "We are about to become engaged, how does it look you being so formal with me? Don't make me tell you again, I have warned you to do as I say. Your brother is sequestered and every time you piss me off I signal one of my men to go give him a visit. You understand what I mean?"

Daggers of blue glared angrily at him. Keyleigh jerked her arm, but he held her and pinched harder. "I have to use the ladies room," she said through grit teeth.

He held her for a moment, seething eye to seething eye. Then he glanced from her with a nod to one of his men. "Brant will take you."

"Mist- uh, Maximillion, I am quite capable of going to the ladies room on my own." She tried again to break from him, but he just ground his fingers into her skin.

"Yeah, sure, it's the return you aren't so capable of. Brant will take you and bring you right back to my side." His gaze swept the busy, boisterous room, women in colorful luxuriant ball gowns, men in tuxedoes, mingling or twirling on the dance floor.

"I see Premier Golthrup, he will be an ally of mine once Porth is disposed of. I will speak with him while you are away."

Mandrake pulled her in hard and forced his fierce kiss on her. Knowing he hurt her, a tiny thrill of electric shock sizzled in his groin at the awareness. It was titillating that he held her captive and she would be forced to do what he willed, anything, everything.

He couldn't wait to get her alone and show her how mindlessly enraged he had been to find she had escaped. He wanted to hurt her. He couldn't wait to hurt her. The thought brought explicit joy, and a jolting current of lust hardened his dick.

The sick, sadistic hungriness on his face clearly indicated to Keyleigh what he was thinking.

When he let her go, it took effort for Keyleigh not to wipe his saliva off her mouth.

Holding up the side of her long shimmering skirt, she hurried as gracefully as possible through the crowded room attempting to elude Brant, her escort.

Behind her, the hulking behemoth bodyguard, with short choppy dark hair and a lurching face, big and square with tiny eyes that peered out from piggy lids, just rudely elbowed past people to follow her.

Crude with his ugly mug, the boorish bully ignored the gasps of affront at being shoved aside as he moved them out of his way.

Briefly out of Brant's view, Keyleigh ducked into a hallway. Quickly trying door after door until one of them opened and she slipped inside.

Clutching her skirt, she hurried across the carpeted den to the window and thrust aside the drapes.

She put her face up to the glass, and her shoulders drooped. There were more than three stories up on a sheer wall of slate stone, she couldn't jump or climb down.

"Darn," she exclaimed with disappointment.

Tossing the curtain, she turned to look around the room for maybe a phone. She could call her father; he could gather troops to come find her brother and tell the police about the planned assassination.

Keyleigh feared Mandrake's promise of retribution on her family if she didn't cooperate with him, but since there was such a huge political thing, a planned murder of a diplomat and all, then tons of policemen would be involved.

They would go after Mandrake en masse, and Keyleigh and her family could hide until the smoke settled and Mandrake was in custody.

But, the room was filled with only books and a few tables and easy chairs. There was no landline, no way to contact the outside world.

Footsteps and low shouts pounded down the hall.

Goose bumps raced up her spine, they were looking for her. Mandrake would never let her go. He was obsessed with her, and now that she knew his plans to assassinate Porth, she would be a witness, he definitely would never let her go.

She must get to someone, warn them of the imminent murder, and try to save her brother. The desperate thing of it though, was that she didn't know where Mandrake had stashed Daniel.

Even if she contacted the police and told them everything, Mandrake might still possibly be able to harm Daniel before he was found.

Keyleigh crept to the door and put her ear to it.

When she finally heard the footsteps and voices disappear, she carefully opened the door and peered out.

The hall was empty. She needed to find a stairwell.

She ran the opposite way of the men hunting her, if you could call stumbling and tripping, clicking down the hall in the sky high heels, catching on the rug fibers with every other step, running.

Reaching another hall, Keyleigh started thinking she'd stumbled her way into a labyrinth. There was no way out, one corridor led to another then another until- she saw an exit sign over a door that looked different from the others.

She raced to it, flung it open, aha, it was a stairwell!

Her skirt bunched in one hand, the other on the handrail so she didn't fall and break her neck, Keyleigh went as fast as she was able to down the stairs.

Her heels clacking so loud on the cement steps she feared the echoes could be heard a block away.

Hammering heart, her palms sweaty on the cold metal railing, Keyleigh was so anxious she could barely draw a breath.

One more set of stairs and she'd be on the bottom floor. She could just push the door open and run outside, find a policeman to warn of the impending murder.

Pushing the door open, she rushed out- and slammed full body into Maximillion Mandrake.

She collided into him with a bone-shocking bang, so hard she bounced back and he deliberately let her stagger off balance backwards. She would have fallen if she hadn't slammed into the slate wall.

He stood there, 6' 4" of solid strength. Long dark hair combed straight back, like an eagle, Keyleigh thought.

The predatory fowl swooping down to catch his prey in his talons, and soar off with her to his nest where he could take his time devouring her.

Ripping off piece after piece of her skin with his razor sharp beak, slashing her flesh with claws like slicing spikes. Then picking at the last of her corpse until even her blood and bones were screaming.

Stunned, she pushed from the wall and frantically scanned the small area for an escape.

"Keyleigh," he called. Sinister peaks drew the corners of his mouth up in a ghastly smile. Foreboding eyes gleamed his anticipating tearing her apart.

His nasty voice like the deep dark core of the earth where hell resides, ground out with livid repercussion, "You dared flee from me? Again?" He flung his hand out and viciously slapped her, bashing her back into the wall.

Brain jarred, Keyleigh's palms hit the wall to hold herself up.

Before she could clear her head, he dug his fingers painfully into her arm, jerked her back inside and forced her back up the stairs.

Keyleigh's heart stopped with rigid fear. Hope snatched out of her hands, she struggled to swallow her tears and panic. Trapped, caught in the talons of the preying eagle.

"You will pay for this, sweetheart," he hissed, dragging her roughly, uncaring that she tripped and stumbled.

"You will pay with your hide and your brother's hide. Only a few minutes before Porth is to die and you make me waste my time hunting for you? Hell, if I didn't crave you so goddamned badly I'd fucking kill you right now. Beat you until there was nothing left but a gory pulp for the janitor to mop up."

Keyleigh begged, "Then let me go, Mr. Mandrake. I swear I won't talk, I just want to go home," she worked to keep the despair from shaking her voice.

So strange, he killed Járon never knowing that Járon was secreted in the country on a mission to stop Mandrake from murdering his rival.

The coincidence was that Keyleigh had bumbled onto Járon's property, and that signed his death warrant. It will be because of her that the poor dictator will also die without Járon to stop Mandrake.

She had fled from Mandrake, then landed on Járon 's doorstep leading to his death and soon to be the man, Porth. One domino led to the next. Keyleigh was the lead domino tile.

It was her fault the others would topple. And, her heart clenched, how many others would suffer when the corrupt and immoral Mandrake was elected in place of Porth?

Mandrake viciously swung her around and brutally slammed her against the wall. Face red and unforgiving, with sociopathic ire he snarled, "Never. You will be the mother of my progeny, so shut the fuck up and do as I tell you. Now, come, I don't want to hear your sniveling."

He grabbed her again and pushed her with rough brusqueness up the stairs.

As soon as they emerged from the stairwell, Mandrake's men circled them. He was taking no more chances with her. He looked pointedly at one of the men.

The man nodded sharply. "Aye, Johannsen is in place. As soon as Porth gets on the podium."

"Good." Mandrake nodded back.

Rolling his arm around Keyleigh, he ushered her to the back of the room, away from the site of the impending assassination. Distancing himself from the catastrophic scene about to take place.

Several of his men gathered in front of him and Keyleigh like a human wall of muscle. His guards were all unarmed; everyone had to pass through metal detectors to enter the building.

Only Porth's security was allowed weapons. Even the building had been swept with a detection device to ensure no one came ahead of time to stow a weapon inside.

However, Mandrake's sniper had smuggled in such odd, small pieces of his rifle all week, nothing on its own registered as lethal under the device. The main components and ammo he had buried under a block of cement in the cellar.

Mandrake laid his hand on Keyleigh's shoulder by her neck.

Next to her ear he whispered cruelly, "If you even look like your mouth is opening to utter a warning, a scream, I will slap my hand over it and cut off your air until to suffocate. Hear me?"

When she didn't answer, his fingers strung around her neck showing her he would do as he threatened.

No worries, Keyleigh had never doubted Mandrake would not ruthlessly murder anyone for any imperial or trivial reason.

The crowd suddenly got louder, people cheering and clapping.

Anastas Porth climbed the short steps to the podium. A league of guards surrounded him.

Grinning amiably, he nodded and waved.

The crowd clamored louder

Chapter Twenty-Two

His Bluetooth in his ear, Remi Rameau whispered, "Porth is on the podium. Tis the only time he won't be completely covered by security, it will happen now."

Blending in with Porth's security soldiers, Remi wore the same tan and olive trimmed uniform. They were working with the guards so they were able to bring in guns.

"That fuck Mandrake has Keyleigh plastered against the wall, has his bloody hands all over her. The poor girl looks horrified and miserable. He would hurt her, likely kill her if we tried to get through his barricade of soldiers to get to her."

Across the room, with an imperceptible nod, Khol murmured, "Too bad we weren't able to get to her before the asshole did when she ditched the hulk."

Near the stage, Khol was in the same plain clothes. A suit and tie, that the security team surrounding Porth more closely, wore.

Replying, "*Da*," Remi smoothly moved through the room, his gaze going everywhere, seeking out where the sniper could be hidden. "But we must stop the assassination and couldn't show our hand. We will go for her afterwards."

His eyes shifted to where Mandrake stood reeking in pomposity inside his circle of muscle, his burly arm holding Keyleigh like glue to his side.

"Vic," Khol whispered, "any sign of him?"

All he heard was a crackle of static. Khol asked again, "Vic, come in," he waited but only heard static. "Shit," he muttered under his breath.

Khol strolled the room doing the same as Remi, searching for the hidey-holes they'd discovered on their prior recon that had a direct unobstructed view of the podium.

There was only one that had an invisible escape, which would make sense for the sniper to use. But there was a piece of carpeted square column that went almost to the ceiling blocking any view of the stage. It was a support pillar.

The brothers had checked it out several times in the past few days, there was no way the shot could be fired from there.

"Thank you, thank you all," Anastas Porth bellowed with cheerful confidence, his arms out in an effusive welcome with the stance of a winner.

The vote had come in yesterday. He had beaten Maximillion Mandrake as expected, by a landslide.

The only thing that could prevent Porth from taking dictatorship of their country, Československa, and making it a democracy, would be Porth's death.

Fully aware Mandrake had gone after Porth the past year with deadly pursuit, but Porth was a noble, selfless man who never harbored ill will, he still nodded generously through the crowd to the defeated Maximillion.

Mandrake lifted a hand in salute with a warm smile, the gracious loser. Behind the faux smile, his lids tapered in bedeviling glee.

In mere minutes Porth's blood would be splattered all over the stage, and Mandrake would shout out his denunciation of the atrocious act.

His expression would be of stunned disbelief, even as he made his way arrogantly through the crowd to take over from the deceased dictator who lasted only a day as the Prima Dictaorus.

His heart oscillated like a paddle-fan on high speed in exhilaration, blood strummed and prickled in his veins. Mandrake couldn't wait for the sound of the shot ringing through the room. The hole exploding in Porth's head between his eyes bleeding like a river, people screaming, the chaotic hysteria.

Then he, the Honorable Maximillion Antonio Mandrake, would boldly march up the stage steps, calm and confident. He would ease the chaos, take charge, smoothly take over the job of dictator.

He glanced down at Keyleigh and frowned. The little bitch didn't even try to hide her anger and her revulsion of him.

Nodding with a biting smile, he thought, she'd soon learn who her master was, and after he *trained* her, with his fists and severe discipline, when she healed she would stand obediently by his side as his bride.

Oh yes, he gave her a harsh squeeze, smiling wider at her gasp of pain, life was good, and about to get better.

Remi and Khol with unnoticeable movement, progressed ever so slowly towards Mandrake's posse.

The crowd's cheer was deafening at the beginning of Porth's speech.

The Prime Dictator's wide toothy smile spread over the people as he waved at them, asking them to settle down. But they kept roaring with good will.

Porth just laughed and grinned, dipped his head with happy acknowledgment and waved.

Near the wall, Mandrake was practically dancing on his toes, itching with expectation. The suspense was killing him.

The shot had to be soon or he'd crush Keyleigh with his exuberant excitement.

He craned his head over the crowd; he wanted to see the second the bullet slammed into Porth's head, should happen any second-

Bang!

The gunshot reverberated, instantly silencing the room.

Mandrake tugged his suit coat down, then his sleeves. He palmed one hand over his lacquered hair and gave his shoulders a little calming shuffle.

It took extreme effort for him to keep the ebullience off his face. He schooled his expression into one of shocked dismay, and grief.

Then, he drew Keyleigh's hand in his arm as he began his march to the podium to claim his rightful position.

Instant mayhem exploded, people dashed about screaming in terror, just as Mandrake had imagined in all his dreams, but, he abruptly halted.

Seeing his eyes rounded and his mouth falling open in confusion, Keyleigh looked up at the stage.

Anastas Porth was standing shocked, bewildered, but alive and uninjured.

Then his security swiftly gathered around him, shoving him to the stage floor.

At that moment, Remi and Khol attacked Mandrake's team- fists flying, howls of pain screamed out as the brothers wailed on the men.

Suddenly, Victoro was there too. He grinned at his brothers with a sharp nod, and joined them, taking out hired merc after merc.

But, in the pandemonium, Mandrake grabbed Keyleigh's hand, and before the Rameau brothers could fight their way to her, he ran with her behind his team of falling men to the nearest exit.

On the stage, pushing his men aside, Porth climbed to his feet and was calling for calm.

The security team that wasn't surrounding him, immediately fanned through the crowd searching for who had fired the gunshot.

Within a few short moments, standing amidst the pile of unconscious soldiers, the crowd steering widely clear of them, the three Rameau brothers grinned at each other. They had successfully subverted the planned assassination.

"How'd you do it?" Remi asked Vic with a pat on his back. "There's no bullet damage in the wall behind Porth, where did it go?"

Victoro shrugged. "It was nothing. The sniper was, as we expected, in that alcove. That spot with the wide carpeted column blocking the view. I gave it another check before the guests were allowed in, and discovered he'd sawed a piece out of the pillar."

"Ah, clever man," Khol noted.

"*Yah*, smart assassin." Vic replied. "He stowed the shotgun inside and replaced the piece of carpet over the post."

"Should have worked like a charm," Remi said.

Khol grinned at him. "*Da*, except he met his match when he ran up against the Rameau brothers, aye?"

Victoro told them, "There was a design pattern in the carpet so the cutting wasn't noticeable. I set up down the aisle from him. In the dark, he was so intent on Porth, he never saw me. I could have easily shot him but," he sighed.

"But?" Remi said with a grin.

Vic replied, "Československa needs the sniper to testify against Mandrake. Unfortunately, he turned just as I reached him. I got my chokehold in, jerked him off his feet and shoved his arm up, but the gun went off anyway. The bullet is in the ceiling. If he hadn't moved at the last split second the gun would never have fired."

"*Yah*, well," Remi drawled, "the event needed a little action. Think about the headlines, 'Brazen assassination attempted failed.' All the extra publicity will only enhance the entire affair. Besides, Porth's security will take all of the credit."

Khol agreed, "True that. We are invisible. That's why the government pays us the big bucks. Complete the mission with 100% stealth. No one will know our part in the aborted assassination."

"We don't do it for the glory, bros," Vic reminded them.

Khol shook his head, concurring "*Na*, we do it to make things right. Take out the bad guys, rescue the good ones."

"Right," Remi granted, and said with a chuckle, "and the large cake they pay us don't hurt."

The brothers laughed, bumped fists.

"Let's get this shit cleaned up," Khol said as the other security was coming towards them. "We got some 'splaining to do.

Chapter Twenty-Three

Maximillion Mandrake dashed down the staircase with a vice grip on Keyleigh's hand, dragging her with him.

His threat of, "You don't come with me without fighting, I will drag you by your hair down these stairs, and your brother will die," spurred her to keep up with him.

All he had to do was get to his car parked in the back, and they were out of there. He'd race to his private plane and hightail it to another country where he had a safe place hidden away.

He would have to wait and see if anyone figured out it was him that put the hit out on Porth. Right now, he had every right as everyone else that was fleeing the terrible shooting scene.

If no one pointed the finger at him, Mandrake would then return to his mansion in Československa. Damn, but he wanted that dictatorship. He'd have to revert back to his gun-running and human sex-trades for income. The underground dealings always came with their own danger, and he'd wanted out for a while.

Yes, he wanted the high income they generated, but he didn't want to keep having to watch over his shoulder for some young and greedy fool to want to kill him and take over his business. With being the country's leader, he'd have all the money, power and prestige without the peril.

"*Uh-*" Keyleigh banged against the wall all the way down the stairs. The jagged cement scraping her arm, her elbow bumping on the rough wall every few feet.

She hardly felt the pain. Hopped up with the adrenalin of the entire escapade, the shocking blast of gunfire, sudden bedlam, everyone running, screaming, Porth calling for calm, and Mandrake tearing down the stairs cursing a blue streak hauling her with him was dulling any pain from injuries she was incurring.

Their clapping footsteps, his heavy huffs, her short shallow breaths and sporadic grunts from smashing against the walls resounded unnaturally loud and frantic in the tightly enclosed cement stairwell.

At the bottom of the stairs, Mandrake shoved the exit door open and dragged Keyleigh out.

He couldn't think about what happened now, what the fuckup was, he had to get the hell out of there before people started pointing the finger at him and seeking him out.

Now, once all the smoke had cleared and he ensured no one was looking at him for the shooting, he'd have to go after the new dictator in his own country. It'll be so much more difficult, but still possible to assassinate him there.

The shit-assed sniper must have missed; how the hell had that happened? But Mandrake didn't need to worry about him, he would have been long gone out of that hidden staircase at the back of the-

"Maximillion Mandrake," a deep accented voice with a deadly edge of mirth came from the shadows. "Fancy meeting you here."

Chills ran up the back of Keyleigh's neck, she cried, "Járon!"

His strapping body moved towards them. He might sound amused, but there was pure lethality glittering in his obsidian eyes.

He shifted those fatality promising, vengeful eyes from Mandrake to Keyleigh where a warm love glowed through the flint like gilded moons straight to her heart.

He said softly, "Hi baby, my *neníta*, you okay?"

Eyes popping wide, her mouth dropped open. Her voice incredulous in awe, she spouted, "Me? How did you- I saw you die, he shot you, right in the chest, Járon, how-"

With a grin, he unbuttoned his shirt, pulled the sides apart and revealed the vest she had knit him with the goat silk. Several burn marks puckered over the front.

"It worked, baby. I put it on while you were in the bathroom before this asshole," he gestured with his head to Mandrake, "showed up. Miraculously, I only wanted to show you how it fit," he grinned.

"It turned out to be a blessing in disguise. The bullets were strong enough to knock me out, and one did hit me in the side of my chest," he held a hand up as her lips parted in distress. "I'm fine, sweetheart, but tis why it took me so long to get to you. I had to recover."

She stood gawking, eyes wide like she must be dreaming. "Járon," Keyleigh's voice grew husky as tears sprung, "I've been so devastated, so aggrieved."

His lips bunched at the anguish in her pretty eyes and voice filled with grief.

"I'm sorry, baby, I had to stand in the shadows watching this prick maul you all night, but we had to wait until his sniper made his move. Now, I can dispose of him, pay him back for what he's done to you."

The love left Járon's dark vindictive eyes as they flit to Mandrake. Lids lowered over the malice in his gaze, his brow mercilessly hard, revealing the rage that burned through him.

"Who in the hell *are* you?" Mandrake railed. Aware Járon was the man his people kept telling him about that took out his entire team as well as the vagrants in the woods, he yanked Keyleigh in front of him.

Járon's voice deadly quiet, he said, "They call me, *ná což však.*"

The color drained from Mandrake's face. A bit of tremor in his frightened voice, he murmured, "The Silent Death?"

Járon's grin was like the last thing a duck saw before the crocodile snapped his teeth over it.

Panic raced across Mandrake's face sweating with alarm. He snarled, "Get the hell out of my way you big fucker or I'll snap her neck."

His hands were on the sides of her head, ready to twist it if Járon came any closer. Mandrake declared with fright and anger, "I swear, I will kill her," he started pushing her towards his car.

Keyleigh suddenly screamed, "Baby chick!" and kicked Mandrake in the shin.

He yelped and moved his hands from her head, and she dropped to the ground.

Just as she hoped, Járon understood her meaning. The time when they were in the coop and she had bent to pick up the chicken, Járon would know she was dropping down.

He leaped at Mandrake- ramming him into the stone wall of the building and immediately started wailing ruthlessly on him- every powerful blow savage and vengeful and pitiless.

Only a few howls burst from Mandrake, he could merely try to block Járon's vicious blows. Járon was striking so hard and fast Mandrake couldn't get a hit in.

The brothers jogged up. Vic and Khol grabbed Járon's arms pulling him off the would-be dictator.

"Yo, bro," Vic laughed, "you can't kill him, living in prison will be a better punishment."

Remi hurried over to Keyleigh and helped her get to her feet. "You all right honey?" he asked her while she tugged her skirt back down, now that everyone got a quick glimpse of her black panties.

"I am now," she cried and hurried to Járon. His arms wide to receive her, he grabbed her up in the air, twirled her around, then hugged her against him.

His arm around her waist, his other hand cupped the back of her head while they kissed, deep, wrapped up in their own world for the moment. Love swirling in their mouths, tongues combing each other's with relief, and gratitude.

When they didn't come up for air, Khol went right up to Járon's ear and cleared his throat, loud.

"Ahem. As soon as we clean up, bro," Khol's sarcasm grating in Járon's ear, "you two can get a room."

Járon set Keyleigh on her feet, stuffed his large hands under her hair and lifted the big, inflated curls. "Nice," he grinned with a lopsided slant, "but I like you natural. Now that dress, glory be," his gaze flowing down her figure swathed in the gown.

He whistled. Then leaned in and whispered in her ear, "I can't wait to peel that baby right off you, *neníta,* very slowly, kissing and licking every-"

Keyleigh slapped her hand over his mouth and said, "Hush!" Her cheeks bright pink, head lowered, she peeped at his brothers. They were all standing with ear-to-ear grins, hearing every word Járon said.

The four brothers laughed at her embarrassment.

Khol said, "J, take her home, we'll take care of cleanup and the police business here."

They glanced down at the bloody mess that was Mandrake, then away as if he was nothing but dirt on the ground.

His arm around her shoulders, Járon fist-bumped with his brothers, then walked Keyleigh to the truck he had parked around to the side of the building.

Keyleigh rested against the back of the seat waiting for him to go around and climb in behind the wheel.

When he was seated, her head turned towards him, a happy smile lighting her pale face.

He reached for her hand and twined their fingers. "Ready to go home, my *neníta?*"

"Home," she repeated, letting out a tight breath feeling it loosen every bit of anxiety and sorrow that had nested inside her when she thought he had been killed. "I like the sound of that."

Squeezing her fingers, Járon agreed warmly, "*Da,* me too. Anywhere with you, Keyleigh, is home for me. As long as you are there, the place doesn't matter. I don't need anything else."

Leaning over, Keyleigh brushed his lips with a kiss, "Me too, Járon. My home is you."

Grinning at her, Járon started the vehicle and pulled out of the lot, slipping down side streets to avoid the hullaballoo that now surrounded the building.

He wanted to get clear away from the police, media, security, civilians rushing like bees in and out and around the frenetic hive of hubbub.

Járon said, "From now on, our home is wherever we are together, *neníta.*"

He lifted her hand and kissed it, then faced the road with a contented satisfied smile softening the harsh edges of his rugged face.

Epilogue

"Oh, Mother, please," Keyleigh wailed. "He is an honorable man."

"Humph," her mother, Jaclyn, grunted. "He abducted you, sweetheart, kept you against your will. And, I'm sure he," her cheeks turned red, "forced himself on you. You can tell he's not a man that accepts no. Your father says he's no better than an outlaw, Keyleigh."

Trying to keep her patience, Keyleigh sighed and explained for the tenth, no, the hundredth time, "Járon saved my life, risking his own, Mother, more than once. He is brave and loyal and-"

"And a mercenary, honey. He- he kills for money. Honey, do you hear me? He kills people. You want to- to sleep beside a murderer? Have the father of your children with hands saturated in blood?" Her voice filled with dreaded awe, Jaclyn's shoulders shivered.

"Listen to me, Keyleigh," Jaclyn tried to persuade her daughter to understand the true weight of the situation. She pinched her lips indicating for her daughter to hear her out.

"He's much too brawny and tough. I'm afraid he will physically hurt you. We don't even know yet what country he's from. Seriously, what if he's a- a communist?"

"Mother, really, you're being-"

"And that unusual accent is pretty heavy. I mean, he sounds like he could be in the Russian mob or something." Her hands landed on her hips, slender like Keyleigh's but a little fuller from bearing children and middle age.

When Keyleigh started her objections again, Jaclyn went on quickly, "And, he's too old for you, at least in years of experience and living in the world. Keyleigh, honey, you are so...innocent." Her lids narrowed at her daughter. Sighing as if disheartened, she said with antipathy, "At least you were."

"Mother-"

Her mother spoke right over her, "Plus, he is somewhat coarse. Yes, he's careful in front of you and me, but I've heard the vulgar language he uses when with your father or brother."

With a short nod, Keyleigh said, "Exactly. In front of us ladies, he will curb his language. He and I came to an understanding regarding that. He is well aware that if he calls me any kind of names or is...abusive in any way, I will be gone."

Keyleigh recalled their conversation the day after they got home. Járon asked her to stay with him. Permanently.

She had replied to him, "Before I give you my answer, I want to be clear. If you ever call me any kind of name, or are...abusive, a bully to me, I will leave you. You will never find me. You understand me?"

To which he had responded with a smug smile, big arms crossed over his powerful chest, "I will always find you, *nenita.*"

With a crooked grin, she squinted a blue eye and advised him, "That's called stalking, Járon."

The huge shoulders shrugged. "Whatever. You think I care?" He had taken her hands in his, and said solemnly, "Keyleigh, if you leave me because you no longer care for me, I would let you go. Above all else I want your happiness."

He squeezed her hands gently and said, "But, if you leave me because I was stupid, then *da*, I would stalk you. And sweetheart, trust me, I would find you and bring you home."

His hand had slid around the back of her head, pulling her to him. His lips almost on hers, he murmured, "Then I would spend eternity making it up to you, my beautiful *nenita*."

Turning her head from his persistent lips, she insisted, "And the spanking, Járon, there will be none of that. I mean it."

"Mmm." Their lips meeting, he murmured, "I will show you when spanking can be erotic fun. You have much to learn," he licked her lips, "and I can't wait to teach you."

They had bussed lips for a few moments. Then he said with a serious grin, "And, if you violate your safety, you will be punished. You can hate me all you want, but there is nothing more important in this world than your safety. I refuse to let even you jeopardize it."

He gave her a hard kiss and went on, "If I have to smack it into your behind to make you understand this, then, so be it."

Keyleigh responded ruefully, "Now Járon," she had frowned, lips pushed out in a moue. "You can't-"

"Uh huh, I can." He sucked on her lips then her tongue hushing her.

After a luscious kiss, Járon had swung her up in his arms and was headed to the bedroom when they heard the motion detectors go off, which was a coop full of squawking hens.

They looked out the front window and Keyleigh had groaned.

A car was pulling up the driveway. A rental agency name was imprinted on the side of the vehicle.

She declared with irritation, "My parents." Her eyes rolling, she had said, "How on earth did they find me? I called them and told them that when we were settled that I, *we*," she smiled up at him, "would go see them."

Stifling his groan, Járon said, "I'm thinking one of my brothers felt the need to make our lives miserable for a while for their own entertainment. I can hear Remi and Vic giggling like schoolboys right now."

That was yesterday. Her parents and brother bunked on blankets and pillows on the floor of two of the unfurnished bedrooms.

Járon had slept on the couch, and Keyleigh in his bedroom, alone, to appease her parents. She offered the bedroom to her parents, but Járon wouldn't hear of it. He said she'd already suffered enough, and never again would he allow her to endure any discomfort at all.

Then her folks had harangued her ever since about Járon not being suitable for her, and they didn't even know about the spanking incident.

It was enough when they'd learned he had abducted her for heaven's sake, and held her against her will, kept her a prisoner!

Keyleigh had explained why, and about the mission and the entire exploit.

But it didn't matter. They said they liked him well enough, even with the vague description of his job, that to them sounded a bit secretively shady. Just the fact that he admitted to committing assassinations albeit legally for the good of the government, still…

But he was just too ruggedly tough, too harsh looking, and she was their dainty little daughter.

Jaclyn claimed that the violence virtually emanated from his strapping brawn, and dark hooded eyes. She shivered with apprehension when he was near.

No, they were insisting she go home with them. Some time away from the scary guy, and their daughter would see reason.

They decided that Keyleigh would eventually realize that she was only thinking she has feelings for him because he had brainwashed her. And, since he had rescued her, he was her white knight and all that bollocks.

Her parents figured maybe she was so terrified of him, she was afraid to tell him she wanted to go home.

As soon as they got her back to her normal life, she would understand, and be relieved she was out of his dangerous clutches.

It was like fighting a brick wall. They weren't going to give up.

Blowing out a gush of air in frustration, Keyleigh grumbled, "I need to go see Járon."

As she started out of the kitchen, she mumbled in exasperation, "I don't even know where he is."

Her brother Daniel entered with a huge grin. He liked Járon, a lot.

Of course he did. Járon carried weapons and was an admitted hired assassin, if only for the government, but still, he had blood on his hands, and he could kill with those bare hands.

Jaclyn cringed every time she looked at his huge hard paws.

"He's out by the barns, Keybee," Daniel offered, grabbing an apple out of a basket on the counter. He took a big crunching bite out of it.

Talking while chomping, ignoring his mother's frown at speaking with his mouth full, as well as telling his sister where to find the outlaw, he said, "Járon had to get away from Dad." Eyes the same blue as Keyleigh's skewed to her.

"Dad wouldn't stop with his questions. He wanted to know all about the work Járon did. What kinds of weapons does he use, how many bodies does he think he has under his belt, what countries has he fought in. How he learned his hand-to-hand combat, on and freakin' on. Geesh." Daniel took another bite of the apple.

Crunch, crunch, he swallowed and said, "The poor guy had to go hide." He winked at his sister. "But hey, the cool dude does have some great stories. He's seen so much action that he says-"

"Daniel," Jaclyn broke in, "enough!"

Daniel smirked at her, bit the apple, then grinned at his sister. "Like I said, check out the barns."

"Thanks, Daniel, you're the best brother ever!" Keyleigh kissed him on his cheek and headed for the door.

"I know!" he called out after with a rascally grin as the door closed.

Then he turned to his mother, his smile lessened at her frowning reproach.

With his own rebuke, he said, "Listen Ma, the man saved my life, and Keyleigh's. His toughness and occupation mean nothing compared to that. If he hadn't had the training he'd had, we both would have been toast."

Taking another bite, he continued, speaking over his mother's protests, "Járon would never harm a hair on my sister's head. You've seen the way he looks at her. That big tough guy would die if she ever left him. He'd fight the entire world to protect her. Really, Ma, you can't ask for a better guardian than him."

"But Daniel-"

"And," he said, taking another huge bite, "my sis is deeply in love with him. Leave them alone."

Outside, Keyleigh strode over the winter grass.

It was a balmy day. The sun heated the land and made the day bright and blue.

She hurried across the pastures to the weathered brown barns. Off to the corner near the stables, led by the recalcitrant Jocky, the goats were busy trying to chew their way through the fence. The grass was greener they had decided, on the other side.

When she reached the barns, she saw Járon. He was swinging an ax, chopping blocks of wood.

"Hey," she called out, shyly approaching him.

He looked strong and gorgeous. Dark eyes gleaming with vitality, robust broad shoulders stretched the shirt across his thick back. Lean hips, huge biceps that bulged with every swing of the ax, the man was serious eye-candy.

And, a beautiful smile that he had seldom revealed before meeting Keyleigh, expanded now seeing her.

He set the ax down and pulled off his work gloves. Dropping them on the wood, he pronged his fingers through his tousled black waves in an effort to neaten them.

"Hey yourself." He moved to join her.

They walked over to a wooden fence and leaned against one of the horizontal logs.

He asked, "What are you doing out here?"

Keyleigh raised her hand and set it lovingly on the side of his face. "I came to rescue you from my father, but I see he's finally left you alone."

Járon leaned into her palm, soaking up the warmth and affection.

"*Da*. Listen, Keyleigh," his tone serious, disturbed. "I know they're telling you I'm *na* good for you, tis what I've always known. I will understand if you leave with them, take some time to-"

On tiptoe, Keyleigh plunked her mouth over his, and wound her arms around his neck.

Instantly distracted, Járon heated like a struck match just kissing her.

Putting his hands on her waist, he lifted her, setting her on the top log of the fence then moved between her jean-clad legs while keeping their mouths joined.

Keyleigh's fingers dragged through his thick hair, mussing what he'd just neatened.

When his hands stroked down her back, over her waist, and then onto her thighs, her groan descended into his mouth and down his throat.

He spread her legs wider so he could get closer, nestling his growing erection against her corc. He moved his hands under her blouse, then paused.

She could feel his grin on her mouth.

Járon murmured, "Damn, *neníta*, you don't have a bra on," his palms slid up to cup her bare breasts. "Did you do that on purpose?"

His big strong hands, warm on her skin made her flesh quiver with desire. "Yes," she admitted, moaning as he kneaded her breasts, pinched her nipples, then cupped the full globes again.

Her breaths turning gaspy, she responded, "Since my parents came we haven't been…alone…you know."

"Ah," he groaned, his long fingers tightened over her plump breasts with a low growl of pleasure. "So you thought you would tease the fuck out of me and drive me crazy when we can't do anything about it while they're here?"

He pushed her blouse up and lowered his head. His hair brushed her sensitive skin. The cool air drafted over her naked flesh, springing goose bumps down her arms, and a fabulous shiver that wrung through her entire body.

He licked one nipple then bit the other.

At her body rippling deliciously in his hands, he whispered, "I bet if I shoved my hand down those jeans I'd find you wet, I'd find," he hesitated, narrowed his eyes at her, "are you wearing panties?"

She ducked her head and peered up through the curl of her lashes with a sheepish smile, and brief coquettish shake of her head.

"Oh, lord, Keyleigh, you're going to be the death of me." He sucked all over her breasts, his hard fingers clenching them while he suckled, then he reached for her belt.

"Uh, Járon, um, my parents might come out any second, my brother," her neck arched as he moved his lips to her neck and licked behind her ear before sucking her soft fair flesh.

Apologizing, "Sorry babe," he tugged at her belt. Her shirt scrunched up and his hungry eyes latched onto her creamy breasts, the pink nipples wet from his tongue.

"I can't wait for the honeymoon, and those people are not going to leave us alone until then, I can tell that now."

"Wait, honeymoon?"

He nodded his head, black hair flopping over his brow. His hands cupping her soft plump pillows, he informed her, "You are going to marry me, right?"

Squeezing her breasts then teasing her nipples, he looked up through the lock of hair at her with that hint of boyishness in his smile.

Her hands stroked around his neck. "Yes, Járon, I am going to marry you. The sooner the better."

Still fondling her soft flesh, he'd never get enough of touching her, he said, "We will have to talk about where we're going to live. I have a house in my country, but you may want to be near your family. Maybe we can have two homes."

He lifted her off the fence, holding her so her legs could swing around his waist and he started walking.

An arm under her bottom, the other tucked around the back of her head, he smiled, and said while licking her lips, "Tell me you love me, my *nenita.*"

"Where are we going?" Her eyes popped around the meadow fearing she'd see her parents running hell for leather towards them.

Her blouse was up, her bare breasts bouncing against his chest. His eyes were more on them and her mouth than where he was heading, he'd managed to unbuckle her belt.

He repeated, "Tell me you love me, *nenita.*"

Her sigh soft and sweet, she nuzzled her head into the corner of his shoulder and neck, fingers twining in his hair,

Rolling her eyes, "Ai," Keyleigh teasingly complained. "You are such a bully." She kissed his chin, his cheek, his lips and giggled. "I love you, Járon. Where are we going?"

His grin the size of all outdoors, he told her, "There's a spot in the back of the barn. I made sure it was clean and warm with pillows and fresh blankets, and," he sucked on her lips, both hands tucked under her butt. "No one but me knows tis there. I thought you'd never come out looking for me. We need to practice for the honeymoon."

As he entered the barn with her, Jàron demanded with a pleased smile, "Tell me again, Keyleigh, tell me you love me."

Her giggles tickled in his ear as they slipped into the dimness of the barn out of sight.

Voice soft with adoration, Keyleigh replied, "I love you, Jàron. I love you."

His smile huge, he said, "And I love you, my beautiful *nenita*."

The End

Dear Reader, thank you for purchasing Jezábel and the Assassin! *I know you could have picked any number of books to read, but you picked this book and for that I am extremely grateful.*

I hope you enjoyed this novel, and if you did, please leave a review where you purchased it, and look for other exciting titles in my name!

Now, I've included the first chapters of my novel, Wrath of Wolf. A Romance/Suspense with murder, intrigue, and sexual situations. If you find it enticing and want to see what thrilling things happen with Ketherine DeMar and Wolfgang Valdimar, please purchase the book!

And, of course, if you love it, please don't forget to leave a review!

A warning though, there may be triggers for some people sensitive to nonconsensual events.

Wrath of Wolf

Chapter One

"*F*or cripe's sake, Ollie," Annabella groused from the passenger seat, "slow down. We have an hour before we have to be at dinner with your stupid family. I wanna stop for a drink. I need fortification to spend even a minute with your pompous father and his imbecilic friends."

Her bulbous bosom rounding over the seatbelt jostled like mad from the swerves and bumps as the car cruised the uneven road.

The Lincoln SUV easily hugged the ancient winding road as it coiled down and around the mountain like a thin black snake. The last of the dropped autumn leaves whooshed behind the vehicle like a confetti tail.

The night pitch black, there was nothing to illuminate the shrouded asphalt except the beaming headlights. Even the bordering trees were just dark craggy phantoms looming along both sides of the narrow two-lane road.

Ollie Duncan let out a loud, beleaguered sigh. Thumping a thumb irritably on the steering wheel, he grumbled, "Will you shut it for just one damned second? Nag, nag, nag, I'm tired of your incessant complaining. And FYI, my brothers aren't coming until Christmas."

Her double chin wobbling, Annabella retorted nastily, "Screw you, Ollie, and your father, and Talon DeMar that insists on having their special retreats at the lodge. Just because all of your father's frat brothers grew up together doesn't mean we have to spend every blasted minute of our time with them. I'm bored out of my tree with the McShanes, Ansberrys and the Burtons and the others."

Ollie nodded, peering into the dark night ensuring he kept the car on his side of the twisting road. "Yeah, the king himself, Talon DeMar and his clan will already be there, and of course Talon's right-hand knight, Stone Cash will be present as well."

"Oh just great." Annabella tipped her head back with a scowl. "That bitch Ketherine will be hanging about then, won't she? When Caralina passed, Talon dragged her daughter from her schooling in Italy to run the company with him per Caralina's will. From archeology to building bridges, I bet Ketherine hates every second of it." The scowl turned into a gloating smile.

Ollie shot her a quick frown. "Keti is not a bitch, she's just…kind of…cold."

"Uh huh," Annabella grunted. "Glacier kitten the men call her, Glitty for short." Her coarse laugh a piggish sound, she said, "Glitty Kitty. Even though so much older than Keti, as soon as her little tits sprouted you boys were on her like barbeque sauce on ribs."

Her pudgy lips twisted in antipathy. "They say she's beautiful like a soft icy statue. Michael McShane says a goddess statue. Huh. I think she's butt ugly and too- too-"

"Dainty?" Ollie smiled.

Her eyes narrowed at him, she spat, "No. I was thinking brittle, too slender for most men's tastes. Stick thin as if she's still in her teens for Pete's sake. Those green eyes unattractively too big for her fragile face."

A small chuckle, Ollie remarked, "I think you mean delicate. Or even ethereal."

Annabella snorted. "Come on, that is so over-used, so cliché. She's hardly a wraith. Unfortunately her damned curves have filled out since she suddenly left home at 13. She's nothing but ignorant trailer trash from her mother's side of the family. Talon, her stepfather put the kibosh on her archeological studies, and rightly so.

"Honestly, rooting around in the dirt like a sow. I heard he's planning an arranged marriage for her. Good thing. Keep her away from all you horndogs." A jealous sneer pinched Annabella's melon round face.

She prattled on, "I hear Talon wants her to marry Rein van Baer. That old perv was sniffing after the girl when she was barely out of diapers."

His shoulders hunched, Ollie tugged the wheel tightly to the right to keep on the serpentine roadway. He agreed, "I know. Poor Keti did not want to come home to Talon…her bastard of a father, rather stepfather, and be forced to work with him. Her mother left her half of the business to Keti. But they each have 50-50 of the company and all documents have to be signed by both."

Annabella snickered. "Yeah. Remember that time Talon tried to forge Keti's signature and he got caught? He was lucky, he only got a slap on the wrist. But he learned his lesson, I'll say."

Ollie leaned over the wheel squinting into the dark. "And Rein van Baer is not that old. Like my dad, he's in his fifties." He shrugged one shoulder. "But compared to young Keti, yeah, he's old."

4

There was silence in the car for a few minutes. Annabella rummaged in her huge purse for her cigarettes.

At the sound Ollie made, she huffed and slammed the pack back in the bag and tossed the purse on the floor with an annoyed sigh.

"Second hand smoke is just a stupid myth, Ollie, for people to put guilt complexes on smokers." She pulled out a package of Twinkies instead.

His head swiveling as he struggled to follow the dark road, Ollie tried to cajole his wife. "It won't be as crowded this year though. Most of the other siblings won't be there. They have work and other shit to attend to. It'll just be the older generation, the basic fathers, their wives and one or two of their children, the younger generation like me at the lodge."

"Yeah, I hear as usual the guys are bringing a plus one." After a minute of unsuccessfully trying to open the package of Twinkies, Annabella used her teeth to tear the wrapping apart.

Ollie nodded. Speaking over the loud crinkling of wrapping as Annabella fought with it, he said, "Yes, a wife, fiancée and a girlfriend or two."

"God," his wife groaned. "I hate this mountain we have to get around to get to the mansion. It's damp and chilling this far north of Oregon. Listen," her whining voice turned to a fake, but gentle coaxing. "There's that bar just past the exit off this ghastly hill. O'Shareef's, we can get a cocktail there."

Rolling his eyes, her husband sniped, "Oh sure. We want to join the party reeking of booze. Leave it to you to know where every watering hole in the Northwest is. Of course everyone is used to you and your all-consuming love of food and alcohol. You just-"

"Look out!" Annabella screeched.

A truck suddenly emerged from the gloaming darkness and was barreling straight at them right in their lane.

"Omigod! Omigod!" Ollie yelled as he wrenched the wheel to the right to avoid the truck. But the truck clipped the front bumper and the Duncans' SUV veered sharply off the road.

Annabella's screams were so loud they almost drowned out Ollie's frightened wails as the SUV went flying out of control and crashed through the wooden fence.

Pieces of wood shot out in all directions like brown fireworks. Their screams mingled as the car careened wildly for several yards before it flew off the side of the mountain.

The car rolled and bashed over rocks and grass as it tore down the mountain then it suddenly smashed into a tree and that stopped it dead.

Metal clanking against the stalwart tree proved Mother Nature was stronger than mankind as the car wrapped around the redwood's thick trunk like a paperclip.

The mangled Lincoln wheezed and rattled then whistling steam plumed from under the crushed hood.

****

He pulled off to the side of the road and carefully parked the stolen tow-truck far over on the shoulder.

Climbing out, he closed the door then trod across the grass. "Boy," he muttered, "what a bitch stopping the truck and getting turned around in that skinny driveway. Now, let's see how I did."

Stepping over the pieces of broken fence, he sauntered to the rim of the grassy area and looked down.

"Yowzer," he let out a whistle. "I didn't mean to smash 'em up so much. I thought the fence would stop the car. Shit, I hope they're still breathing or this won't be any fun at all. Now," he put a finger to his chin and pondered.

Mumbling to himself, he said, "Gonna be rough getting them and the car up. Especially that Porky Pig Annabella. Thank God the car's descent was halted so near from the road. Tree ain't looking too happy though," he grinned.

"I guess I can tie a rope around ol' Ollie and the pig and to my truck and drag 'em up the side of the mountain. Okay then, off to work!" He spun around to grab the rope from his vehicle.

****

Ollie's head was pounding, and Annabella's screams weren't helping any. *What the hell is the matter with her now?*

He didn't move for a minute trying to get his bearings. "Ahh," the groan scraped out as pain hit, everywhere. Dizziness flooded his brain making him slightly nauseous.

"What the-" He was lying in a funny position. On his stomach but his hips were pushed up over a pillow, oddly shoving his ass up in the air.

He moved an arm, then started when he realized he couldn't budge it. His arms were splayed out to the side, and they were bound to a bed frame. He tugged at his legs only to find they were spread apart and also immobilized.

Blinking rapidly, he took in the closest wall. The room had a cabin feel to it with the rough wood walls, and the cowboy lamp on the nightstand beside the bed, he didn't recognize where he was.

On the table Ollie saw a box. Squinting at it, he read the title on the lid, it said 'wood burning kit.'

Annabella's screaming went on and on. Only his wife could shriek that piercingly, sound goes right through a man's head. How can he think with her caterwauling?

"Annabella, for crying out loud, shut the hell up!" He cranked his head so he could see more than the mattress he was lying on. "What kind of game are you playing tying me up like-" His eyes widened in confusion.

On the floor beside the bed, Annabella was on her back, it appeared that her hands were bound behind her. Naked as a beached whale, she was writhing and squirming, and peeling paint with her screams.

Covered with scrapes and bruises, her hair was matted with dirt and dead leaves, and a man was on top of her, banging her. Hard.

Seeing red, the wooziness clearing, Ollie shouted, "Hey! Annabella you slut, what's the matter with you?" His own yelling made his head hurt worse. "You're so freakin' obnoxious to be screwing him while I'm right here! I want no part of your sick fantasy."

He could now feel his entire body ached. The SUV crashing through the fence flashed in his mind. Remembering the car going over a cliff, the last thing he recalled was the Lincoln rolling over and over and-

Annabella stopped screaming, but now she was making gagging, gurgling sounds.

"What-"

The man screwing his wife turned his head and grinned at Ollie. "Oh, took you long enough to come around, Ol." His hands were wrapped around Annabella's throat, and he was squeezing the very life out of her, even as his hips pounded between her sausage fat kicking legs.

"Hey! Stop that!" Ollie could see Annabella's face turning scarlet, her eyes bulging out of her head. "Shit, man, you're killing her! Stop!" Ollie jerked at his binds, struggling to get free and get the freak off his wife.

It was too late. Annabella made no more sounds, no more movements. Her now bone-white face was frozen with the terrified eyes bulging, her tongue lolled out the side of her open mouth.

Ollie's brain fizzled and went blank as confusion and horror took his breath. He stared blankly as the man ejaculated into his wife with a moan.

Grunting as he pulled from her, the man carefully peeled the condom off, tied it and then bustled to his feet doing his pants up.

Ollie couldn't form a sentence, he stammered, "Wha, wha, wha…"

The man's head fell back honking out a laugh. He grinned at Ollie with dark mirth. "Aren't you the lucky ones I came upon first?" His grin widened at the bound Ollie's bewilderment. "Ah, you're curious to know what's gonna happen next?"

With gloved hands, he pulled a plastic baggie from his pocket. He dropped the condom in the bag, sealed it and tucked it in his pocket.

Ollie blinked at him, his mouth opening and closing like a gasping fish.

"Well," the man said, rolling down the long sleeves of his white shirt and smoothed the cuffs. He chuckled. "I won't keep you in suspense, Ol. I'm going to do the same thing to you as I did to Annabella," he jerked his head at Ollie's dead wife lying like a trussed hog on the floor.

Frowning at her, he remarked, "I don't care much for the fat ones, but," he shrugged, "a man's gotta do what a man's gotta do for the cause, you know what I mean?"

If possible, Ollie's eyes rounded even wider at the man. His gaze lowered to the man's zipper and he gulped. "Y-you're going to- to rape me?"

The man turned to him and nodded gleefully. "Yep. And kill you." He frowned at the dead woman, his lips pulled in.

He looked back to Ollie and smiled. "Oh, don't worry, I'm not going to rape you with my dick, ew, no," he grimaced and shook his head. "I am not a homosexual. You know very well I like the ladies. No, I'll be using that," he looked pointedly towards a wall.

Painfully, Ollie angled his head to see what the man was talking about, and he blanched. His stomach revolted at the sight of the iron rod leaning against the wall. "Wha-" he choked.

His eyes twitched back to the male who had just killed his wife. He said, "Bro," swallowing trying to wet his dry throat, "we- we're practically family! Why?" His voice an anguished cry, tears poured down his cheeks wetting the sheet beneath him.

The man deliberately stepped over Annabella as if she was just a crumpled piece of trash left on the floor and ambled over to the wall and picked up the iron bar.

Tapping the bar against his palm, his eyes gleaming with tormenting delight he moved to where Ollie lay trembling.

That was when Ollie fully comprehended that he was buck-naked, his bound legs spread, with his butt pushed up in the air.

"Since you asked so nicely, Ol, I'm gonna tell you why I'm doing this." The man's eyes darkened as the torturous doom of hell stalked into them. He lifted the iron rod and placed it near Ollie's rear end.

Ollie started screaming.

Shaking his head, the man said blithely, "Now Ol, my bro, how can I tell you my story over all that yowling? You need to hush now. So," he began, pushing the bar, speaking like he was telling a fairytale, "a long, long time ago, there was this little boy," he pushed harder.

Ollie screamed so loud the windows rattled.

"Quiet now, Ol, I can't think with all that noise."

Chapter Two

"*He*'s calling for you," hanging up the landline, Griselda Borda, Talon DeMar's administrative assistant told Ketherine as the young woman snagged her coat off a hook by the door.

Watching Ketherine, Griselda crossed her arms, and said, "Nigel, his snooty majordomo said everyone else except for the younger Duncans have been there for several days and you'd best get your behind on the way tout de suite."

Slipping the coat on, Ketherine tugged her long hair out from under the collar and picked her purse up off the desk. With a stressed sigh, she replied, "I know. He commanded me to be there to help serve cocktails as the others arrived."

Griselda shook her head with a, "Tsk tsk." The fortyish woman with short curly dark hair said kindly, "Honey, I shouldn't say this against your dad, but it's terrible how he treats you. Like you're a servant, not his daughter, and certainly not as his partner. I don't understand why you put up with it? You're what, 22, 23 now?"

Ketherine buttoned the cashmere coat so dark blue it looked black, a gift from her late mother. Her smile dim, she replied, "He made sure the Santatini University cancelled my scholarships forcing me to leave the dorms as well as the school. I worked for the school and therefore I had no income or home. I had to return to Blackslade, Father's estate. My mom…"

She swallowed the lump of sadness the thought of her mother always brought. "She made sure I was her beneficiary because Father was always pulling dirty deals that hurt innocent people, and my mother hoped I could counteract them like she always had. It's a tough job, he's such a sly bully."

The older woman agreed with a sad frown. She asked, "But why do you stay with him? Why do you do his bidding? Like going to the lodge for the holiday season? He expects everyone to continue their work from there. Why don't you refuse and stay here?"

Slipping a blue and red silk scarf under the collar of the coat, Ketherine smoothed the scarf tails making sure both sides were even.

The averseness evident in her voice, she explained, "It was a codicil of the will that my stepfather insisted my mother add. He wanted to be able to keep his…thumb, make that fist, over me. He deliberately ruined my credit and made false accusations of embezzlement against me to keep me in his clutches.

"He's made it so I can't work anywhere else but at the company. Not even a burger joint will hire me. He thinks if he holds these things over my head I'll do everything he dictates."

Her faced wreathed in commiseration, Griselda said, "But, honey, why don't you fight him? Tell the law what happened, tell them what's going on?"

13

Ketherine's expression turned dour, plush lips curved down with devastating remembrance of when she was a child under Talon DeMar's care.

Her mother had married Talon when Ketherine was less than two, and Caralina had been grateful that Talon adopted her baby. Keti had gained two much older stepbrothers in the blended marriage.

A shiver of horror rolled through Ketherine's body. She pushed out of her brain the reason why at thirteen she had begged her mother to send her out of the country to a boarding school.

Somewhere where she would be safe from the shattering horror that made her forever shut herself off from people. Out of reach of Satan's claws.

Ever since then she'd kept herself walled up in self-protection, she learned the hard way that she couldn't trust anyone.

"Honey?" Griselda brought her out of her painful musings.

Ketherine gave the secretary a vague smile that didn't reach her eyes. "Father has Constable Carmichael on his payroll. He only says the word and I'm tossed into prison for…forever."

Before Griselda could respond, Ketherine forced a cheerful, "Have a good evening, Gris, I'll see you I'm sure at some point at the lodge."

She turned quickly and strode out the door. She didn't need pity, or false hope, she needed strength, everything she had to keep herself together to face the demons that were waiting for her.

****

14

About the Author

Louise Furley loves writing romance with a huge helping of suspense. She finds it exciting to study new lands and learn everything she can about the area and the natives that call it home.

Her idea of fun is researching ideas, studying enigmatic modes of science, archeology, and different ways to kill someone. Her Significant Other, Bob, finds the last to be particularly notable. He remains wary yet gives Louise his full support with her writing adventures.

Sunny Florida is home where Louise is a graduate of St. Thomas University with a master's degree in Mental Health. This degree is essential for exploring the deviant soul, and understanding the mind of a killer, while finding it exhilarating, frightening and sad all at the same time. With artistic license, Louise can be judge, jury, and sometimes executioner!

Louise is the author of numerous published novels. When not researching or writing, she is dreaming of unique plots, and discovering fresh ventures she hasn't yet experienced in the world.

Ride along with her as she travels new and thrilling journeys!

Louise Furley